G000054561

James

So he *can* write after all!

Many thanks for all your work this year.

Happy Christmas 1983

Tyler

THE DECEMBER ULTIMATUM

Other books by Michael Nicholson

THE PARTRIDGE KITE

RED JOKER

THE DECEMBER ULTIMATUM

Michael Nicholson

For Denis and Edith Slater,
with gratitude and affection.

FIRST PUBLISHED IN GREAT BRITAIN IN 1983 BY ROBSON BOOKS LTD., BOLSOVER HOUSE, 5-6 CLIPSTONE STREET, LONDON W1P 7EP.

British Library Cataloguing in Publication Data

Nicholson, Michael, *1937*-
December ultimatum.
I. Title
823'.914 [F] PR6064.I/

ISBN 0-86051-228-2

Printed in Great Britain by Biddles Ltd., Guildford

December 20th

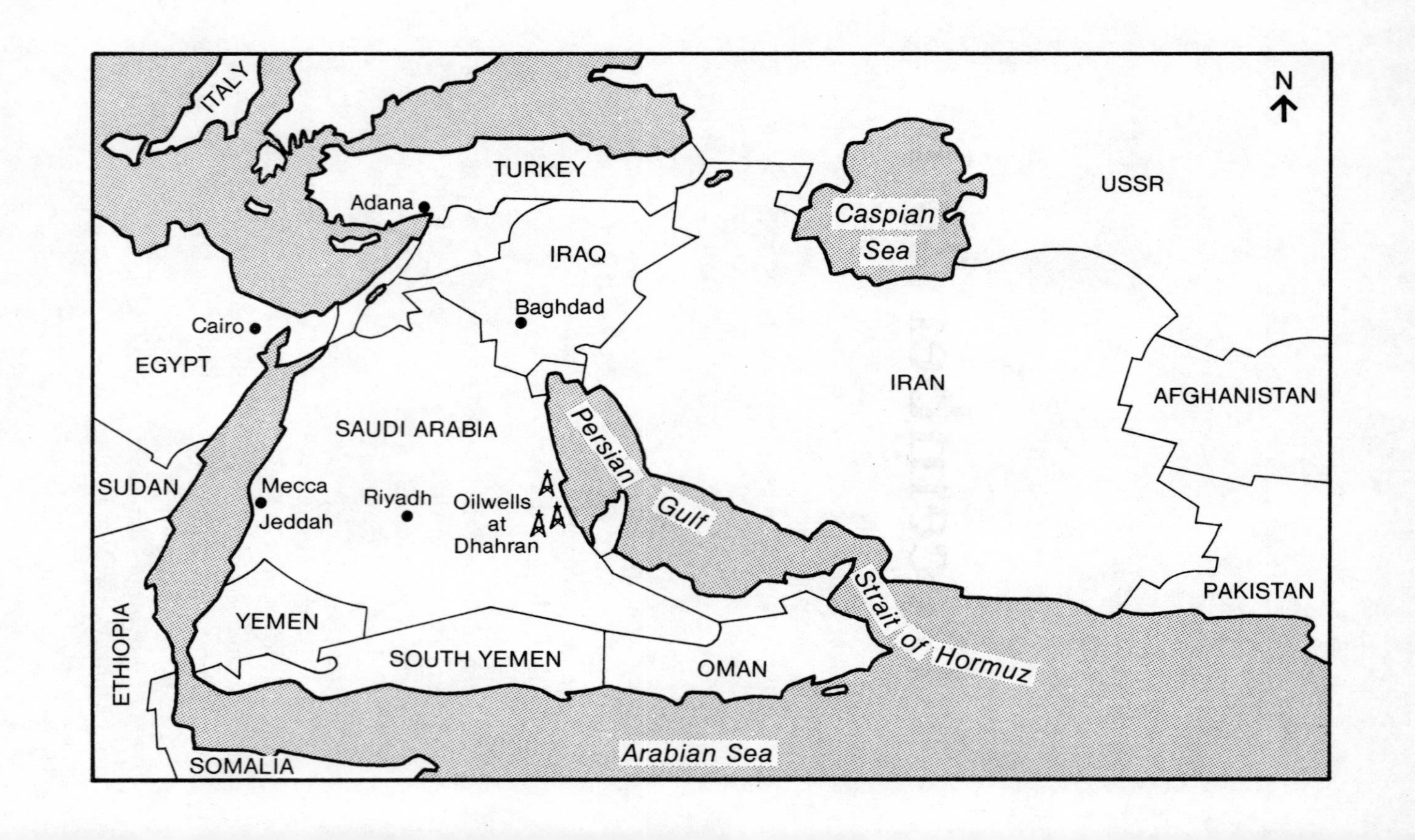
N
ITALY
TURKEY
Adana
USSR
Caspian Sea
IRAQ
Baghdad
Cairo
EGYPT
IRAN
AFGHANISTAN
SAUDI ARABIA
Persian Gulf
SUDAN
Mecca
Jeddah
Riyadh
Oilwells at Dhahran
PAKISTAN
Strait of Hormuz
YEMEN
SOUTH YEMEN
OMAN
ETHIOPIA
Arabian Sea
SOMALIA

Radio Riyadh

'This is the Islamic People's Democratic Republic broadcasting to the world from Riyadh.

'The House of Ibn Saud has been deposed. The leadership of the new Saudi Arabian Republic has been accepted by Rahbar, the supreme leader.

'After a day and night of heroic fighting, commandos of the Islamic People's Revolutionary Forces are victorious and have occupied the Palace of King Fahd, his government offices and his military bases.

'In his first proclamation, Rahbar has dedicated his life to return the nation to Islamic purity under the eyes of God and the guidance on earth of Mohammed.

'Rahbar pledges that the Islamic People's Democratic Republic will be cleared of the evils and contamination of Western influence. By decree, all non-Islamics will leave the country, all non-Islamic institutions will be destroyed. After the deportation of foreigners, seaports and airports will be closed. The oilfields will be shut down for one year from this day.

'The Islamic People of Saudi Arabia reaffirm their eternal love of God, their everlasting guardianship of Mecca and the devotion and obedience to the Koran as written by the prophet Mohammed.

'Long live Rahbar!

'Long live the Islamic People's Democratic Republic!

'Allah Akbar!'

'The oil has stopped flowing'

'There are riots in Riyadh, sir. Seem to be connected with the Jeddah disaster.'

Rain clattered on the window-pane. A small square travelling-clock made of black plastic by Krups was pushed to one side to make way for the tea tray. It was one minute past six in the evening and as Simmonds waited for an answer, he watched the dribbles of rain run down the long sash windows.

'That stupid fire gives absolutely no heat out, Simmonds. None at all.'

He pulled it closer to the desk by its cord.

'Sir, the signals say there have also been attacks—in Jeddah and Medina, and American cars—that is cars belonging to Americans—have been set on fire.'

He leaned forward and poured tea from the china pot covered in a patchworked tea-cosy.

'Our people have already signalled their evacuation plans, sir. Very quick off the mark in the circumstances.' He waited again.

'Now it's burning my ankles.' Simmonds pulled the fire a foot away. 'And draw the curtains while you're about it.'

He walked behind the desk and pulled the heavy green velvets together, closing out a cold and wet December Whitehall.

'Evacuation seems a little hasty, Simmonds. Not the first time, is it? Trouble there?'

The bone-china teacup tinkled as the silver spoon swirled a sugar lump.

'No, sir. But nothing like this before. They've warned us of a special Saudi flight coming in tonight. Landing at RAF Brize Norton.'

'If the Saudis are still flying, Simmonds, I can't imagine they think there's much in it.'

'Not a scheduled flight, sir. And our people used a Beta code just to tell us.'

'Stupid asses! Into code to tell us of a flight departure. Do they intend coding every time a Saudi aircraft takes off?'

'No, sir. I wouldn't think so. Not after this one.'

The Foreign Secretary sipped his milkless tea and looked over the rim of the cup to the empty Victorian fireplace and its brass filigreed fender bordering the Persian rug. He was cold and the collar of his shirt felt damp. He looked at the obsolete brass fire-tongs and poker hanging from their brass gibbet with its immense claw feet.

'D'you know, Simmonds,' he said, 'when I first came here as a Parliamentary Under-Secretary during the war we had the most enormous coal fires. The grate-irons were regularly white-hot. Coming into this room then was like entering an oven. The typists used to toast muffins for us at elevenses and tea-time. I can't remember ever being cold then. Never.'

'The signal says, sir, they've attacked the airfield at Riyadh. Eleven planes set alight. Blown up two—both DC-10s. Their entire airline fleet destroyed.'

'Really? But you said a moment ago, Simmonds, one had taken off. Pour me another cup, and add some water from the flask. It's too strong. I hate strong tea.'

Simmonds did as he was told.

'A deal's been arranged, sir. To get the King and his family away in case things got out of hand.'

'The King, Simmonds?'

'Out, sir.'
'Good Lord!'
'A plane load of princes.'
'The hell there is. Our people know?'
'They told us, sir. In the signal.'
'What are they doing?'
'I'm afraid they've already done it. All British women and children are on board the King's flight. Plus two male sick. Sixty-seven Brits altogether. It seems our men are under virtual siege inside the Consulate. Quite a lot of non-service Brits in there too. It looks as if we'll have to depend on the Americans to get them out. Unless you're willing to risk a Hercules.'
'This has happened while I've been in Cabinet?'
'Yes, sir.' He took the china cup carefully from the Foreign Secretary's hand and put it back on its china saucer.
'But Cabinet only lasted an hour.'
'This signal has only just arrived, sir. I telephoned the PM's office but you were already on your way back.'
The Foreign Secretary slowly stood up, and winced at the sharp pain of a sprained ankle—casualty of a polo accident a week before. He turned to the window and pulled one of the velvet drapes aside.
'This is extraordinary,' he said. 'The most stable country in the entire Middle East. And Fahd? Always cast-iron safe for us. Always.'
He pulled a handkerchief from the cuff of his jacket sleeve and wiped away the moisture on the window pane. The winter rain was falling fast. He could see nothing of the street below.
'The new leader?'
'Rahbar, sir.'
'What do we know of him?'
'He's the Crown Prince, sir.'
'The Crown Prince?'
'Abdullah.'
'The hell he is!'
'A new-born Muslim, sir. Founder of the New Islam.

One of the fundamentalists.'

'Oh, my God! Another one! The Embassy families are on the King's plane?'

'Arriving in about four hours. DC-10. Full security.'

'How did they do it?'

'They did a deal.'

'A deal?'

'Rahbar wanted the King and his family out. They were an embarrassment, divided loyalties and so on, but he couldn't risk their being seen leaving the international airport. Too many people. Anyway, there was wreckage on the runways. One of our people on the staff, someone called Muras, knew of an old RAF strip forty miles from the capital, one of ours during the war and forgotten about. Even the Saudis didn't know of it. So they did a deal. Muras would show them the strip if they would take our women and children out. And two male sick.'

'Where's the King going on to after Brize Norton?'

'He's not. He's staying, sir.'

'God! Why?'

'Our people say he will appeal for temporary asylum. He's got a large estate in the Lake District, somewhere on Ullswater. Remote and secure. They'll be after him now. Rahbar has sentenced him to death. Usual thing to do, now that he's out of the country.'

'Bad news, Simmonds. I'm going back to the PM. She'll call Washington.'

'There's worse, sir.'

'Shit!'

'They're closing the oilfields. Shutting them for a year. It's in the radio broadcast. Part of their return to Islamic purity. The text is here.' He held out a single sheet of paper.

Slowly the Foreign Secretary turned away from winter Whitehall back to the bleakness of his office. For a minute or more he said nothing. Simmonds held the piece of paper closer to him. He raised his long nose and looked through his bi-focals at the intricate patterns of the Persian rug beyond the desk. He took the paper. Simmonds felt the heat from the electric fire on the back of his trouser legs and he thought of the ghosts of typists past, white-hot coal fires, muffins and cocoa for elevenses.

When the Foreign Secretary spoke again, his voice seemed to come from the other end of a long tube.

'We shouldn't have got out when we did.'

'Out, sir?'

'Eden. We should have stayed in Suez. It was too soon. We shouldn't have let Eisenhower bully us the way he did.'

'Is that relevant, sir?'

'Relevant? Relevant?' He suddenly raised his voice, trembling. 'I'll tell you what's bloody relevant, Mr Simmonds! The biggest Arab oilfields are closing down. The oil has stopped flowing, to us, to the West, but most relevant of all to the USA. And, by God, it may take a bloody Great War to get it back again.'

His right hand hit the desk and the china teacup bounced in its saucer and turned on its side. Cold tea ran over the green leather desk-top and on to the fringe of the Persian rug.

'How much tighter?'

'You're telling me the Brits have got their people out with the King, and ours are still barricaded inside the compound?'

'Only their women and children, Mr President, and two male sick.'

'To hell with the male sick. Ours are going to be sick near death if we don't move them out fast. How come the Brits get out with the King and we don't even know he's leaving?'

'They did a deal, Mr President.'

'My ass they did! Doing a deal was something my father invented. So how come we didn't?'

'Someone on their staff knew of an airstrip, sir.'

'And someone on ours didn't?'

'Mr President, we have no one there who flew with the Royal Air Force.'

'That's part of our problem, Hartmann. We have people in all the wrong places.'

The young President stood up from his oak desk and walked to the centre of the Oval Office. Woven into the blue carpet beneath his feet were the golden words, '*E pluribus unum*': 'Out of many, one.'

Behind him, and draped each side of the desk, were the Stars and Stripes and corps colours of American regiments.

'So Rahbar is Abdullah—another freaking newborn Ayatollah, and Royalty this time.'

Jack Hartmann, Chief of the White House Staff, handed the President a single piece of paper. 'Not much to go on but we're working on it. We'll have more soon.'

'Anything since the broadcast?'

'Just religious music and occasional readings from the Koran. Random bits and pieces. Islamic Studies say it's not particularly relevant, and we can't read anything into them.'

The President read the paper.

'First Iran and now this. Another bastard Khomeini.'

'Or another Ghaddaffi, sir. He's not going to be easy.'

'Jack, you are master of the obvious and irritating understatement.'

The President unbuttoned his shirt collar and loosened the black silk knitted tie he had worn every day now since the death of his mother eleven months ago—the day before his Inauguration. He could not get over the timing of her death. It was unforgivable that she should have been denied that extra day when her youngest son made the ultimate office. She had waited so long.

He took off his jacket and threw it to Hartmann, ran his fingers through his thick black curly hair and tugged at his grey sideburns. Anxious habits, well known to those who lived and worked close to him.

'Get the others in, Jack. All of them, and fast, whatever they're doing. Tell them I want a contingency plan on the Rapid Deployment Force. I want Soviet dispersals in the Gulf area. I want the Agency here and tell Johns I want reasons why he missed out. Tell him his ass is on the line.'

'And the media, sir?'

'Christ! How do we move, Jack? Where's Peter, anyway? What's he saying?'

'He called from Miami, sir, a half hour ago. Flying straight up. Says the time will give him breathing space. They'll get him at the airport, this end. He says you go on air as soon as possible. He'll speak at the airport to hold them a while—but he's insistent we book Network time quickly.'

'He's right. Have him at the meeting. Get going, Jack.'

The Chief of the White House Staff, privy to all things Presidential, inclined his head as if to bow and walked quickly towards the side door to his own office. There he would begin the task of assembling the nation's Generals, the Director of the CIA, the President's Foreign Affairs Adviser who was in Washington, the Secretary of State who was not; send a White House car to meet Press Secretary Peter Schlesinger who would draft the first Presidential Press Release and prepare for the President's television and radio address to the nation. They were all men whose careers had been whelped and advanced on a succession of crises, large and small, personal and public.

'Jack!'

Hartmann, a yard from his office door, stopped and turned neatly on the ball of his right foot.

'Jack, I want two briefings before they get here. Get Grüber on oil. Tell him I want a rundown on supplies already en route to us out of the Gulf. Tell him I want exact figures on crude and refined stocks in the US, daily consumption, spot market prices and what we get if we want it. I want to know how much we've got left in the ground and how much we've got stored. And get one of your people to bring out Carter's plan on fuel rationing, November '79. As far as I know it is still mine to use without recourse to Congress.'

'Yes, sir.'

'Then get me General Volney Wagner, Readiness Command. Put him on the scrambler.'

'Wagner, sir? Before the Chiefs of Staff? Is that wise?'

'To hell with the wisdom, Jack. Wagner's in command of the Deployment Force and I want to know how available it is and how rapidly it can be mobilized.'

'You're considering using the Force, sir?'

'I've considered using intercontinental ballistic missiles, I've considered a rude phone call to the Kremlin, and ever since I got married I've considered divorce at the risk of excommunication. I doubt if I'll do any of those things, but I've considered them. Now you move, Jack. Get them here and have me briefed before they come.'

The door closed and the President went back to his desk and sat down. On the right of the red leather-bound blotter pad, something he had always regarded as quaintly antique, was the daily digest of the previous day's and overnight news published in the national and international press. There was also a short resumé of the three television Networks' nightly news bulletins as well as newspaper cuttings relating to anything the President had said or done, or what he was thought to be about to say or do. Only Hartmann and the President's wife knew he seldom read newspapers, and never this enormous pile. He read only what was necessary and pertinent to immediately impending decisions, discussions or statements, and Hartmann or Schlesinger could always be relied on to advise on those. Under the pile were news magazines which had been supplied to Reagan and had not been stopped when he left office. The President flipped through them quickly, glancing only at the story headlines, picture captions and cartoons. *Newsweek* was lamenting Bob Hope, *Time*'s front cover was on the newest silicon chip some wag had nicknamed the silicon wafer. It was the cover of the *Economist* that made him pull it across the desktop to fall into his lap. A cartoon caricature showed a man with Uncle Sam's traditional top hat and white beard dressed in John Bull's Union-Jack waistcoat, one leg was marked France and the other marked West Germany. The figure was stretched out on a mediaeval torture rack and Arabs were at each end turning the wheels. As the ropes tightened, sweat fell from the tortured man's brow into a barrel marked 'petro-dollars' and under the cartoon was the caption, 'How much tighter?'

In quick anger, the President thumped his fist down hard on the cover and winced with the sudden pain as his balls took the force of it. He looked at the grinning faces of the Arabs and cursed out loud. Would there still be an OPEC without the Saudis? What would they do with their oil now? With the Saudi fields, the major supply of oil exports, closed, the others—Libya, Iraq, Iran, Kuwait, Nigeria, Venezuela—would raise their prices sky-high, while everybody—especially the Japanese and French—scrambled for it, paying whatever was demanded.

'Right over the barrel. Every goddammed one of us.' He said it aloud to the portraits of past Presidents which lined the walls.

He looked down again at the crumpled *Economist* with the man on the rack now bent double with the force of the President's fist. What price today, what price tomorrow? Production deliberately depressed, tanker costs doubled, consumption insatiable, and now the biggest of them all capping their wells. They had been the only sensible influence in OPEC—the only ones in that collection of thieves and extortionists who had worked to keep prices to a reasonable level. But now Fahd had gone, and in his place was a newborn convert, a religious freak, a radical who was somewhat between Ghaddaffi and the preposterous megalomaniacs in Iran.

The white telephone buzzed quietly at his side. It would be Jack telling him Grüber had arrived to brief him. He put the magazine back into place on its pile, but as he did, he glimpsed Uncle Sam's face contorted on the glossy crumpled paper and for an instant he could feel pain and hear the drips of sweat and the clicks as the ratchet dropped into place on the wheel. How much tighter the rope, he thought, before the limbs were torn away?

He picked up the telephone, heard Hartmann's words and grunted. Seconds later the President's Special Adviser on Energy, Professor Nicholas Grüber, came into the room and closed the door ever so gently behind him. Without looking up from the cartoon, the President beckoned him to sit down in the easy chair opposite the desk.

'Professor Grüber.'

'Mr President?'

'What do you think happens to a man when you take his arms and legs away?'

Grüber coughed and cleared his throat. 'Well, sir. I suppose he experiences what you might call . . . sudden and permanent immobility.'

'You mean he's crippled.'

'That's right, sir.'

'So we've simply got to move before the rope tightens any further.'

'Sir?'

The President looked up. 'We've gotta move. And fast, Grüber. Before the next ratchet pin drops.'

'Rahbar–the new Messiah'

Franklin had been listening to the gunfire for a whole day and night, and slowly it had come nearer. He hadn't known it at the beginning, but the remnants of the army—men still loyal to King Fahd, still believing he was in the country—had fought their way out of their barracks through the narrow streets to the open spaces of the European suburbs where they thought the walled-off gardens of the big houses would give them mobility and protection. They had been wrong. Few of the peasant soldiers knew anything of Riyadh-suburbia, and they found out too late that the western boundary of the city, beyond the garden walls, was nothing but desert. Open, vulnerable, easy target desert. So they dug themselves in and fought their separate lonely battle from foxholes beneath the tamarisk trees.

Their enemy, commando-fedayeen of the new Islamic People's Democratic Republic, now surrounded them on three sides, the desert on the fourth. Artillery had been set up in the car park below Franklin's bedroom window—105 mm field-guns, 90 mm recoilless rifles, light and heavy mortars, light and heavy machine-guns and rocket-propelled grenades. By Franklin's reckoning, many thousands of rounds had been fired into those emplacements, but still there were men alive to fire back, men unable to run, refusing to surrender, unlikely to survive.

Just before dusk, from his shelter six floors up, Franklin had watched a family crossing the open square, walking quickly and in single file towards the hotel; a Swiss family. The father in front had held up the large red flag with the white cross high above his head. The mother with her two small blonde children clinging to her had waved white handkerchiefs. Another minute and they would have made it to the car park gates, just another fifty yards. But, with safety so near, the father panicked. A hundred yards down Al Madhar Road, he saw the guns of a halftrack pointing towards him and suddenly he ran, and screamed to his family to run after him. Then the young Islamic revolutionaries opened fire, and Franklin remembered the red tracers curving towards them and how the woman and her children seemed to explode. The father, unhurt, stopped and looked down at them, still waving his Swiss flag.

For half a minute or more they let him stand there. When he sank to his knees, as if to pray they shot him too. Later Franklin looked again, and saw that someone had covered the pile of gore with the red and white flag, draped it over them like colours on a military coffin. It was time for prayer and Arabs found the dead and bloody Christian gore offensive at such a time.

The silence for prayers was almost as shattering as the firefight. Standing sideways to the bedroom window, Franklin watched as the Saudis below paused in their killing to wipe their feet and touched their foreheads on the sand and offer thanks to their God and pray for salvation. He edged back around the perimeter of the room and opened his door. The corridor was full of people, guests, porters, room boys, cooks, all crouching in the dark. Mattresses had been lined along the walls to absorb the sound of the mortars and shells and the blast if it should come. He smelt blood. People wandered past, looking for greater safety or for a friend or a lost family, and in the light of their torches he could see glass splinters in their faces. Shirts were drenched in blood, bandages had been made from towels, arm slings from bed sheets. A boy was holding a hand-towel sopping red to his right eye, and when the boy noticed him he held the towel away and Franklin saw that the eye had been torn from its socket and only the pressure of the towel kept it in its place. Franklin backed into the bedroom and locked the door. Prayers would soon be over, the firefight would start again: he must forget what was outside his bedroom door and concentrate on his own survival.

He had never expected this. He had made a promise to himself three years earlier, standing on Brooklyn Bridge on New Year's Eve. No more wars, he had said, no more hassles, whatever the promise of glory and a bonus. Considering all he had done and all he had survived it was sensible and practical to draw a line through whatever ambitions were left. He had done and seen more than most in the trade; a long and reasonably successful career, with only casual injuries and a cholesterol level and blood pressure that hadn't upset the insurance company doctor. Anyway, he was tired of deception. Eighteen years was a long time to call yourself one thing when you were also something else. A long worrying time. He could never be certain somebody wouldn't finally expose him.

So, he had made a New Year's resolution. Life would henceforth be a great deal more comfortable and less of a worry. To this end he would gradually move away from the Agency, back into the paper, and find himself a chair there sans blood, sans guts, sans glory, sans bonus. And so, for the past three years, his by-line had appeared more frequently in the *New York Times*, and the Central Intelligency Agency, despite its protests and threatening innuendoes, had come to accept it had lost a good rover.

Less than a month ago he had celebrated his fiftieth birthday with his ex-wife on his small farm in New Hampshire in a further attempt at reconciliation. He had returned to New York to be told of his promotion to assistant editor—management status, with a rise—the prospect of rosy years and the occasional soft story abroad. Until two weeks ago it really did look as if the promise on Brooklyn Bridge was going to hold. Then Oberdorfer, the paper's financial editor, had got excited about the forthcoming OPEC meeting in Riyadh. Saudi contacts and Aramco friends had told him that the 1983 fiasco was about to be repeated, with the Iranians and Libyans trying again to destabilize the oil markets of the West both by raising the price of oil and by introducing mischievous variants on production levels. Oberdorfer sketched in the background: 'global petropolitics' had altered world opinions. While Western economic strategists in the late 1970s had wanted OPEC's demise, now the emphasis was on keeping it together.

'Keep the various mongrels in the same kennel,' Oberdorfer had said. 'That's the only way to stop one or other of them from using oil against us.'

The Saudis had held the cartel together, resisting other countries' desire to use oil as a weapon of pressure in international power politics. But now it seemed that Saudi oil had been chosen as just that weapon, with perfect timing because the Saudi royal family was so split they could not present a united front. They had, said Oberdorfer, other things on their minds. The trouble, as in all Royal dramas, was succession. When King Khalid died in 1982 his half-brother Fahd became King. That had been Khalid's wish and had long been known. It had made for continuity and stability and therefore made good Royal sense. Except that other half-brothers in succession, Crown Prince Abdullah and the younger Sultan, began plotting their own very separate ambitions.

It didn't help that there were two armies. Younger brother Sultan controlled the National Army on Kind Fahd's behalf whereas Abdullah was Commander of the National Guard, a thirty-thousand-strong force of Bedouin with tanks and modern artillery of their own. And the two commanders refused to speak to each other except at official functions. Sultan was aggressively reformist, well-read in British constitutional history and an advocate of constitutional monarchy. And Sultan began to go public.

There should be a Parliament, he said. There should be adult male suffrage. There is no Divine Right, he preached,

God did not choose my grandfather, Ibn Saud, nor my father Faisal nor my brother Khalid, nor my brother Fahd. The King should be elected by the people as a Constitutional Head of State; democracy, he decreed, is the cornerstone of national reform. And King Fahd said nothing to agree or condemn, which in many Saudis' eyes was tantamount to condoning Sultan's excesses.

Certainly Abdullah thought so. He was not for reform if it meant modernization and liberalization. He would be for it, however, if it meant a return to the old ways, the ways of Islam. In this he had the total support of the ULEMA, the stark, fiercely unyielding Muslim clergy. Very quickly Abdullah had become known and revered as a 'traditionalist'. And then, as the name and concept spread, as an Islamic 'fundamentalist'.

And Abdullah learnt other ways. He married a new Syrian wife from the Alawite sect, closing ties with the Syrian President Assad of the same sect. And through Assad, the Crown Prince began to make indirect contact with Moscow.

The family split came finally when King Fahd, unable to ignore the obvious any longer, went to the Americans for help. And for his own safety he secretly by-passed his own Embassy in Washington and dealt directly with the White House. Shortly afterwards, and on American advice, there followed widespread arrests and imprisonment of the militant 'fundamentalists'. King Fahd used Sultan's army to impose his law and order with one eye on Abdullah and his National Guard waiting by their tanks and Howitzers.

So the rift inside the great Saudi Royal House had been exposed, and, once exposed, the comforting sense of continuity could never again be reinstated. And the people shook their heads, kicked their goats and spat on the floor of their mud huts, angry at their slowness and dismal incomprehension.

Oberdorfer's briefing session had been concise but the predictions written into it had seemed distant. Franklin had asked him specifically how long before the fuse would blow.

Oberdorfer had answered, 'A year, rather than months. But one year rather than two. It's that soon.'

That was two weeks ago, and it had all seemed straightforward, even attractive. Away from New York, a big story, a touch of the old glory and a celebrated by-line, and a pause to think over the previous weekend's negotiations of remarriage.

But now suddenly Franklin was back to old routines, in the middle of a war as savage and as unexpected as any before.

There had been demonstrations and fighting in Jeddah in early October—but Franklin had not been concerned with events in the Gulf area then. And, two days ago, Jeddah had again seen fighting and death . . . The bedroom shook and the entire hotel felt as if it was shivering. The prayers were over, Allah was consoled, and the mortars had begun their bombardment again of the King's men across the Square. Franklin went down on his knees, crawled across the floor to the bathroom and dipped his head into the bath he had filled in the first hour of the coup, an old precaution. He sat on the stone-tiled floor and let the water run down over his shoulders and chest. When it reached his stomach it was as warm as his sweat.

He smelt his own excreta in the lavatory bowl and through the thin bathroom wall he could hear a woman crying and a man shouting obscenities in French. He crawled back towards the far wall, across the room lit up now by flame-throwers billowing across the car park. Someone was knocking on his door, and he heard his room-boy screaming to him that he had lost his towel and his eye had fallen out on to his cheek.

Franklin reached up to the desk by his bed, pulled his portable typewriter down and rested it on his lap. He steadied a torch on an open drawer and switched it on. It was still a long time to dawn, perhaps longer to the end of the fighting. He would write his story anyway, though it was a thousand to one chance it would ever reach New York, would be told long before he ever got out of Riyadh. Or would it? The story behind the story? Why it had happened?

The end of the House of Ibn Saud, all-powerful Saudi Kings fallen suddenly from Islamic grace in a coup engineered from the Kremlin—whose target was the Gulf and its oil.

It went far beyond what Oberdorfer had talked about, way beyond his understanding of Global petro-politics. As he had explained it the intrigue was OPEC's alone, an intrigue that was to serve the separate greedy members' own interests. He had said nothing about direct Soviet involvement.

But yesterday, only eighteen hours ago, Franklin had been summoned to the Palace for an audience with King Fahd. He had been given a minute to collect his notebook and pens; no camera, no tape recorder.

They had sat facing each other, Franklin on a cushion, the King flanked by six bodyguards. Another two stood by Franklin and so close he breathed in the sickly-sweet herb lotions they had rubbed into their bodies. The King was over-polite, ordering mocha coffee, thick and black and bitter, and served in English Doulton porcelain cups. During the first ten minutes of niceties, the King had offered ginger sticks and crystallized fruits and fresh dates stuffed with honeyed nuts. And then he had suddenly snapped his fingers and the coffee tray and bowls of fruits were quickly taken away and the bodyguards moved back to the edge of the carpet. He had spoken quietly but quickly, as if he had little time left.

'You are an American I can trust,' he said. 'You are CIA. I know you are a journalist but your loyalties must be the Agency's for me to talk as I wish and for you to carry my favour to Washington as I may need. Do I have your word?'

'Yes, your majesty,' said Franklin, 'you have it.'

The King wiped his lips with a silk handkerchief.

'You came to Riyadh to report the OPEC meeting. I fear you may leave with a story of much greater moment. I shall tell you why and I ask you to carry this information to your Government. I may not be able to.

'You will know from the briefing with your own people that certain OPEC members are planning to break up the Organization. Libya, Iran and Iraq. Others will follow.

What you will not know is that they will use this to destroy the House of Ibn Saud, to end the Kingdom for ever.'

He leaned back in his sofa and wiped the handkerchief across his forehead. A minute passed. Then he shifted himself forward and closer to Franklin. When he spoke it was little louder than a whisper.

'You know the problems within the family. It is no secret. Crown Prince Abdullah, Prince Sultan. They have ambitions, wide ones that encompass the Gulf, ambitions that move as opposites and so fiercely they will tear my Kingdom and the entire Gulf apart. And they have willing helpers who will use my brothers to suit themselves. The mischief-maker in Libya leads them. Crown Prince Abdullah thinks he is using them in his stupid endeavours to turn history backwards, to pull up a drawbridge and make the Kingdom an island where all progress, all civilization, is swept into the sea in the name of Islam. Abdullah is waiting for a mandate for his Islamic fundamentalism. He sees himself as the supreme leader, renouncing Western exchange for total power in the Islamic world. But he's a fool. He will gain nothing except his own death. Moscow alone will be the beneficiary.'

'Moscow?' repeated Franklin.

'Moscow. The collapse of OPEC, a market free-for-all, pricing fluctuations that would cripple the leading currencies, Ghaddaffi and the madmen in Iran using their oilwells against first one enemy and then another. Can you imgine the suicidal fighting that would begin right across Arabia? All this would delight Moscow. But the Politburo has grander ambitions than that. It would not be enough to deny the West the Gulf's oil. They want it for themselves. And they are in no hurry. They are championing Islamic reform because they know better than most the total chaos it would bring. They witnessed Iran. They watched the Ayatollah. They appreciate catastrophe.'

'Crown Prince Abdullah must know this?' asked Franklin.

'He is blind to it. He uses the simpleton's logic, the logic of all Third World revolutionaries from South America, Africa, Asia. If Moscow gives us guns we will take them. If

Moscow offers advisers we will take them. If Moscow teaches us propaganda we will listen. But we are nationalists first and when we have won our revolution we will send all things of Moscow back. Abdullah speaks that way and believes that way will work. He may well send the guns and advisers home when his new Islamic nation is founded, but he will not dig up the seeds the Russians leave behind.'

'And Prince Sultan?' asked Franklin.

'A visionary too. But increasingly a pragmatist who treads carefully and who treads with me in my direction. He is my Army Commander and he will fight for me. But first I must know my army. We have lost the National Guard to Abdullah. I must discover how much of his rot has infected my Army. And my Air Force.' For the next hour King Fahd briefed Franklin on the events that now made civil war inevitable, telling Franklin he thought he had another ten days to prepare.

But the countdown to the takeover was already under way. Even while preparations for the OPEC meeting were being finalized in the conference rooms of Riyadh, and final protocol was being discussed in the King's palace, bands of men were moving into the country from Iraq in the North and from Yemen in the South. They had come off ships in Jeddah and international airliners at Riyadh, men with a single purpose converging on the capital under a single banner. And the name they would shout in revolution was not Abdullah, Crown Prince of Saudi Arabia, but Rahbar, the saviour of Islam, the new Messiah sent as the prophet Mohammed had promised, to save Islam from evil, to purge Islam of all the impurities and contamination of the West. It was a plan of great religious fervour. It was a plan also helped along by Soviet-built AK-47 assault rifles, rocket-propelled grenades, mortars and machine-guns.

The propaganda had been borrowed from an earlier successful and equally-ambitious fanatic, the Ayatollah Khomeini of Iran. Like the Shah of Iran, King Fahd was represented as all that was evil, all that was threatening Islam, a man intoxicated by the petro-dollar, a charlatan won over by Western-American greed, who had taken the

Koran from his hand and substituted a chequebook, who had taken Islam from his heart and put there instead the harsh doctrine of American capitalism. The slogans would be scrawled across the roads and walls of Riyadh, Jeddah and Medina, and the graffiti was infectious: 'Fahd betrays Mohammed.' 'God has left us.' 'Build the Great Wall in Arabia.' 'Islam, Rise!' 'Rahbar, the New Messiah.' The aerosol cans had been distributed and the banners painted, waiting for Rahbar. And he, in turn, waited for the signal—not from people of Saudi Arabia, but from people who knew much better than he the strategy and timing for the coup.

Five years earlier few Saudi-watchers, academics, Pentagon emissaries, Aramco oilmen, political strategists, foreign relation specialists or Central Intelligence Agents would have considered a coup a remote possibility. The House of Ibn Saud, from Abd Al Aziz to King Fahd, had been the unquestioned rulers of the barren desert Kingdom with the biggest deposits of oil in the Middle East. Revolution was unthinkable. Unlike the Moslem Shi-ites in Iran, unlike Reza Pahlavi the Shah, the Saudi Kings had merged state and religious leadership into one. The political House of Ibn Saud had married into the religious House of Ibn Wahhabi, so that they were inseparable. Dissent against the King disputed the sanctity of Islam itself. So as religious leader, the King ruled by divine right, and his credentials were impeccable; he was ruler of the land of Mecca, birthplace of Mohammed and of Hadj, centre of pilgrimage for the world's eight hundred million Moslems.

Franklin stopped typing, put the typewriter on the floor and stretched his legs. The night outside was suddenly bright with flares. He turned the torch off as sweat ran into his eyes. The bathful of tepid water seemed a thousand yards away. He was beginning to feel helpless. He waited until the light of the flares had dimmed and began his typing again. The torch batteries were running low. He leaned closer to the paper.

The Shah of Iran had tampered with Islam, and Islam had won. But Islam and the King of the Saudis was the same—and who or what could pull them apart?

The answer was oil. And the things it could buy. Transistor radios, colour televisions, American cars, Japanese motor-cycles and the exciting new life-styles that came with them. Oil bought Western music and Western books, a Western culture full of new ideas that gave young men and women an appetite for more. Schools were built by Western contractors to Western designs with the Western curriculum in mind. Concrete arterial highways were beginning to stretch out from Riyadh to Mecca, Medina and Dhahran, increasing the speed of Saudi life, and spreading the invasion even quicker across the deserts. Seamen came off the merchant ships at Dhahran and Jeddah trading in alcohol, cigarettes and hashish. And Saudi women sold their bodies though the Koran forbad them even to show their faces.

There was a cancer in the Kingdom and it was called oil and its malignancy was spreading to every corner. Turbaned mullahs squatted on crimson carpets, sipping bitter coffee served by women in their austere chadors, and watched the infidels from the West who neither made pilgrimage to Mecca, nor seemed to pray, nor gave any visible service to God, and yet were infinitely more prosperous than the faithful. The Saudi Shia peasants and the workers in the Aramco oil camps saw excess in everything and they were suddenly hungry too. Doubts were created about those things of the spirit they had always valued. Few lost their faith, but many lost their devoutness.

The oil was pumping out of Saudi desert at the rate of ten million barrels every day, four hundred million gallons every twenty-four hours, and the enormous earnings from it slowly transformed the land of the Koran into something strange and hostile—just as they had in Iran, on the other side of the Gulf. Petro-dollars provided the Saudi rulers, eager with ambition, the means to transform a country that had known nothing but poverty into a thoroughly modern twentieth-century state. The world's largest royal family was earning over three hundred and forty-five million pounds a day every day in the year. There wasn't a global institution to match its purchasing power. Had it been on offer it could have bought out General Motors in a little over a week; British Leyland in two days seven hours, London's most prestigious store, Harrods, in nineteen hours and twelve minutes. Had Buckingham Palace been on the market King Fahd could have bought the residence to suit his ego in two days, twelve hours and eighteen minutes of pumping.

But no people could have been less fitted to receive the deluge of wealth oil thrust upon them. Wealth poured over them, deluged them, drowned them; wealth beyond all reason, beyond all need. Fifty years earlier Rockefeller's men had counted out thirty-five thousand British gold sovereigns and in return the Saudis had given them a sixty-year oil concession. Eventually the oil revenues gave kings and oil princes an annual income of over a million million dollars. This enormous explosion of wealth made multi-millionaires of over eight hundred Saudi princes and spawned an epidemic of corruption, extravagance and scandal. Fahd's half-brother Khalid had been a relatively inconspicuous spender, but he had had a two-hundred-foot yacht which he used only once a year, and a Boeing 747 jumbo-jet palatially equipped in gold fittings and Persian-carpeted with its own royal bedroom suite, bathroom and cinema, and an in-flight open-heart operating theatre.

The really big spenders, the young princes with more energy and lust, were known to gamble a million dollars a week in the casinos of London and the Riviera. Arab dandies would hire an entire ski-slope at Val d'Isère exclusively for a weekend so that their tumbles would not be witnessed. They stabled a dozen of the world's most expensive cars and flew the world's most expensive hookers to and from their villas in a fleet of the world's most expensive executive jets. The second casino on Monte Carlo's skyscraper waterfront had cost the Principality ten million dollars to build. In the first week of opening a Saudi prince of the Royal Family lost five million dollars at blackjack and roulette. They were still waiting for him to return to finance the other half.

The Saudi princes did things in faraway places with far-out people, enjoying excesses the rules of Islam back home denied them.

Their money was spread evenly in many capitals and enjoyed by many. All except those who needed it most, the Saudi poor. It had been estimated that if only one year's oil revenue was distributed evenly among Saudi's seven million population, every man, woman and child would receive fifteen thousand dollars each. Most would have been content with one hundred and fifty. Or failing that, five.

But that was small thinking in the eyes of the King and his ambitious brothers, sons and nephews. The House of Ibn Saud had grown big because, in the American vernacular, it had thought big. The Royal Family was grandiose and its projects reflected it, right down to the hundred-foot-square smoked glass windows shipped in from Hamburg or the forty-foot-square white marble table-tops flown in from Florence. Entire cities were being built block by block, new factories awaited adventurous investors. Free education was envisaged for every last camel boy and goatherd. And every son of every sheikh, prince and merchant banker flew first-class to the Sorbonne, Oxford, Cambridge, Yale and Harvard. Under the House of Ibn Saud, devout Saudi Arabia was a country on the make.

But oil brought more than gloss. It made two countries of one. The extremist devotees of Islam rejected the movement forward, spat at new thought, cursed the growing unstoppable dominance of Western ideas. Their murmur gained momentum and demanded the rejection of all things not of Islam. They spread their message loudly and menacingly and every Saudi was reminded of what was happening. Good Moslems winced at the dreadful probability that the evil of the West was contaminating Islam, the Koran itself; the writings of the great Mohammed were being defiled. But Islamic fundamentalism would resist.

Franklin paused and lit a cigarette, cupping his hands to hide the flame. He re-read his last lines of typing and wondered how much more he would need to write to describe the rigidity and devotion of the Saudi Sunni Moslems, the most conservative of all Moslems in the most severe and intolerant of all the world's religions.

He knew that already Iran, under the guardianship of

the Ayatollah Khomeini, had voted to turn back history and become an Islamic island within itself, and now Rahbar was encouraging the Saudis to do the same. On his own, Franklin thought, he could not have done it, but suddenly and unexpectedly he had support from fellow Arabs, fellow Moslems, fellow purists who, like him, denounced the contamination of Islam by the gangsters of the West. And if the West was too vague an enemy, too vague a target, then—as before, when Islam at last went into the attack in Iran—America became the focus for vilification. America was the West, Western evil was America's evil.

But no one in the West knew that in late October Ghaddaffi of Libya, that devout mischief-maker, had secretly met Crown Prince Abdullah, alias Rahbar, in the Iraqi capital of Baghdad. Waiting there too were representatives of the Palestinians, Jabir Sabah of the South Yemen, a strong and obedient ally of Moscow, Abolhassan Behesti, strong man of the Iranian Revolutionary Council and President Assad's own emissary from Syria. It took three and a half days of talking to finalize the plan. The infidels of the West would be expelled and a great wall would be built across the frontiers of Islam to protect its purity for ever. Radio and television stations would be destroyed, books not of the Koran would be burnt, arterial highways would stop in mid-desert, the ports would be closed to all but food and medical cargoes, airports would be shut. All but Moslems would be deported, schools and hospitals built with foreign money to foreign designs would have their roofs torn off and be filled with sand as monuments to Western decay. The sarced memory of Mohammed would be safe. God would be pleased and Saudis would be promised eternal grace.

Ghaddaffi had then outlined the military logistics. King Fahd had a large efficient army and air force, equipped and trained by the Americans. It was the most powerful war machine in the entire Middle East, following the demise of the Shah's. It was one thing, said Ghaddaffi, to call the prayer from the minarets but something else to take over the bases at Al Kharj, Tabjk and Mushalt and neutralize an active armed force of forty thousand men. It would take more than faith and devotion to ground Phantom and Mirage jet fighters. So Rahbar's agents began to sound out low ranking members of the armed services, men known to be devout Moslems and who, in a crisis of religious conscience, would defend Islam first and the King second. It was a delicate operation, and Rahbar's men trod carefully.

By mid-November the Baghdad War Council was satisfied that Rahbar had enough men in the necessary places to create confusion on the way, men who were in positions where they could cripple, if only for a few hours, the Saudi military machine. And this fitted into the scheme of things because, according to Ghaddaffi, a few hours was all that was needed. Then the other agents in the revolt, the Yemenis, the Iraqis, the Syrians, Iranians and the Palestinians, would move into the capital and sweep up new recruits at every street corner.

The Phantoms and the Mirages would be grounded by sabotaging their fuel, and the barracks and garrisons would be encircled by the mobs. But how would the tank commanders react? And the men behind the machine-guns? Would they shoot another Saudi in defence of their King? No! said Ghaddaffi. No! echoed Rahbar. Moslems would not kill other Moslems who were shouting the defence of Islam.

The War Council cleverly brought the forces together, quickly and at the right time. Thousands of Palestinians were already in the country working on the building and road projects, and revolution was as natural to them as eating, drinking and dying.

Over three hundred more Palestinians, mostly weapon instructors, arrived in Saudi Arabia in October and November and spread out among the resident Palestinian labour force to recruit and train.

The second force of fighters came across the southern border towards the end of November, one thousand three hundred men of the South Yemeni army, disguised as nomad tribesmen, sent by President Abdul Fattah Ismail with their camel sacks packed with arms and ammunition. They trekked across the Rub-Al-Khali desert by night and rested during the day, until they were finally spread along the southern city boundary of Riyadh.

By the second week of December the Baghdad plan was ready. The Palestinians, working with the Iranians and Syrians, were spread evenly throughout the capital with units in Jeddah and Medina. The dissident Hijaz and Majd tribesmen would support them there and the Shias would help in the east of the country around the oilfields. The South Yemeni force was stationed along the southern suburbs, close to the tank and artillery garrisons, ready to rendezvous with Rahbar's own army of military and political dissidents.

The Baghdad Council was satisfied that the explosive ingredients were now properly placed and primed, and all that was necessary was the detonation, a spark, something not necessarily of Rahbar's making, but something he could grasp, so outrageous that Moslem anger would be quickly and spontaneously combusted. It came sooner than Rahbar or the Baghdad Council expected, and at a place they would not have predicted. Jeddah.

Jeddah is Saudi Arabia's single commercial seaport, straddling the Red Sea on the country's Western coast. It is where all the goods bought by oil arrive. It is also where the world's Muslims disembark by sea and by air to attend *Hajj*, the pilgrimage to Mecca, forty miles up the road from Jeddah. Over two million pilgrims a year make the journey to the Prophet Mohammed's birthplace, Islam's holiest shrine.

Between the eighth and thirteenth day of the twelfth month of their lunar year—the Dhu-Al-Hijjah—these millions tumble into Jeddah, fifty thousand every day at the airport alone.

To cope with them, the Saudis had built a tented terminal, the modern marvel of the Muslim world. Here the devout could file off the airliners and be processed by health, immigration and customs officials in the shade of the world's biggest tent, protected from the sun and the flies and the dust, cooking their lamb and goat at the communal kitchens and praying as directed.

The tented terminal was not one, but many, tents strung

together over one hundred acres, an area larger than the Pentagon. Four hundred and forty steel pylons weighing eighty tons each and a hundred metres high supported those acres of tents. It was the Bedouin tent writ large, the tent of Arabia built in such enormous style and splendour as only the Oil King could conceive of. Or afford.

But the modern marvel of Islam had its defects. It was designed and built by the Americans; instead of Bedouin cloth, fibreglass from Rhode Island was used as covering, and the pylons came from the alien Japanese shipyard city of Tsu. So, among the fanatical and those who called themselves fundamentalists, this too was a symbol of Western contamination. It was evil. Simple, then, for the enemies of the Oil King to bring the tent down about his ears. Which was precisely what they did.

During *hajj*, thousands of Iranian and Palestinian pilgrims, ostensibly on their way to Mecca, demonstrated for two days and two nights inside the tented terminal, turning the pilgrimage by their unholy behaviour into a radical political theatre. On the evening of the first day, Saudi police moved in with venom and batons, determined that *hajj* should not become a political event nor their king be further embarrassed. The demo quickly became a pitched battle, Saudi baton against Palenstinian head, Iranian dagger into Saudi stomach.

On the morning of the second day of rioting the Saudis used tear gas, percussion grenades and rifle fire and by that afternoon a convoy of ambulances and lorries stretched almost bumper to bumper from the airport to the hospital in the centre of Jeddah. As the hours passed, the bodies began to swell and bloat in the heat outside the mortuary, already packed tight with the dead.

Four hundred and thirty-two people died. Eighty were Saudi policemen and Saudi airport officials. But their death did not end it. The Iranian and Palestinian survivors quickly spread their propaganda across the Gulf; the tented terminal became a symbol of oppression and, because of its American association, a symbol of foreign contamination. So it was the obvious target for the militant radical.

Eleven weeks later, over one thousand five hundred pilgrims on a charter tour, devout and without malice, quietly assembled themselves under the tent after completing Saudi immigration and customs control, and prepared themselves for the final coach journey to Mecca. The first light of the morning sun was tinting the tent pink as they queued patiently, shuffling slowly forward, some still praying, some still half asleep.

Later, eye-witnesses who survived could not remember what came first, the sound of the explosions or the crack as the pylons snapped. There were those who couldn't remember hearing any explosions, and there were those who were quick to persuade everyone that there never were explosions, only the horrible thunder as the eighty-ton pylons came toppling down, bringing with them the hundred tons of the fibreglass covering and the mesh of steel cables.

Those on the outside later described it as like a giant parachute billowing on to the ground, spreading out in slow motion, burying the screams and horror of the dying beneath it. Pilgrims and Saudi officials were crushed instantly by the pylons, or cut in two by the mesh of cables. And those who survived that were suffocated under the weight of the fibreglass.

When eventually the bulldozers and tractors pulled the debris away and after the rescue workers had separated torsos and limbs from the wreckage, they pieced together six hundred and twenty bodies. In earlier times the catastrophe might have been seen as a sign of God's wrath, an act of holy vengeance. But this was the twentieth century, and the two Iranians who had planted the bombs were well-practised, as were their accomplices in Teheran who had made them. The Saudis, and the American experts they employed to sift the debris, quickly provided evidence of sabotage and murder. Bits of the bomb casings were found and displayed. But no one in Islam wanted to believe it. Instead, the rumour spread that the pylons had collapsed because they were weak; because their design had been defective; because the Japanese steel had been inferior and because princes, encouraged by King Fahd, managing the contract had cut corners and taken bribes. The House of Ibn Saud was publicly accused by Islam of avarice and corruption, the consequences of which were evident in the carnage at Jeddah airport and the overflowing putrefaction at the Jeddah mortuary.

And suddenly, the streets of Jeddah and Riyadh overflowed with demonstrating Saudis sickened by the monsters who ruled them and made profit out of the devout. Rahbar's men moved quickly, adding mischief to the fire, and with them were the same Iranians and Palestinians who three months before had attempted to bring down the Oil King another way and had failed.

Within two days of the collapse of the tented terminal the revolution had begun. It was December the 20th.

King Fahd knew of the fighting at twenty minutes past two in the afternoon, when a 122 mm rocket hit the Eastern gate of his palace. By four o'clock, sitting in the fortified cellars, he was told that the armoured units of his Bedouin Corps had surrendered and that none of his jets had been able to take off because their fuel had been contaminated by water. At five o'clock he was told that eleven members of his Cabinet had been publicly executed, that the offices of Petromin were on fire and that four hundred and fifty-two Americans—men, women and children—were under siege inside the United States Consulate compound. By five o'clock, the King received a hand-written message from Rahbar advising him that the Islamic People's Democratic Republic had assumed government and urged him to wait in the palace until a way could be found to get him and his family out of the country. Rahbar assumed the King's co-operation, the alternative being execution. The King pressed the ring on his right hand into Rahbar's letter, indenting it and thereby signalling his assent. Before midnight he was flying away from his Kingdom.

The coup was more efficient and less bloody than the Baghdad Council of War had expected and they were well pleased. Threatened Islam was now safe again and the two vast countries either side of the Persian Gulf could together form a bond of Islamic unity that would never again be broken by the forces of Western evil. Rahbar announced over Radio Riyadh that the first Islamic Summit would soon be held in Mecca, chaired by him and attended by the Iranian Revolutionary Council.

That same evening, Rahbar, ever-mindful of his good friends in the War Council, sent them all a message of thanks and prayed that God would bless their souls. Immediately after hearing this in Tripoli, Colonel Ghaddaffi sent out his own cables containing the single word 'Yamani', the codename to signal their break from OPEC.

The OPEC members, who received the 'Yamani' cable were pleased and much relieved. After all, they had risked a great deal in capitals as far apart as Lagos and Caracas, pledging their money in secret support of Ghaddaffi's plan.

There was one member of the War Council who, having received his cable from Ghaddaffi, in turn sent his own, a carefully-coded telex to his masters in yet another capital, men who had been waiting more anxiously perhaps than the OPEC members for the outcome of the Saudi coup. Colonel Ghaddaffi had accepted credit within OPEC for originating the plot and ensuring its military success. But the seed of the idea had been planted on him by Saadoun Abdel Karim, member of the War Council, Iraq's Defence Minister, committed Communist and agent of the KGB since 1962.

It was Karim who, after many long briefings in Moscow, had carefully polished the plan that, left to Ghaddaffi, would certainly have floundered. Karim was the end of the long arm of the Soviets' ambition in the Persian Gulf to take control of oilfields.

For purpose of anonymity, Karim sent his telex from the General Post Office in the centre of Baghdad to an Import-Export company in Yugoslavia who in turn radioed the message to the Kremlin. Within minutes, following rapid decoding, the Soviet President and his Politburo had been informed and they were well pleased.

Franklin shivered. The sweat was now cold on his face and

his legs and back ached. It was twenty past four in the morning. The fighting outside had all but stopped. Occasionally a single sniper's bullet whined its way across the road from the open ground opposite, followed by the thump of a returning mortar. He could see from the glow in the sky that Riyadh was still burning, though it was probably from old fires that no one dared extinguish. Slowly he edged himself closer to the window and raised his head level with the sill. The cold air coming in through the broken panes of glass smelt strongly of cordite. It was hardly light but in ten minutes or so the open ground where the King's men had been hidden would be seen clearly, and those there who were not dead would soon be so. The Revolutionaries in the car park below had stopped firing and waited for movement, but there was none. Then, as the first rays of sun hit the rooftops, one of them—anxious to be the first to announce the end of the war—ran to the side of the car park, past the smouldering cars and coaches, to the gates. He was young, bearded and wore a camouflage tunic, a figure of revolution that had appeared in a thousand and more photographs. When he got to the gates, he jumped up on to one of the stone pillars and began shouting, waving his rifle above his head. And then Franklin saw him cut in two. Many times in the days that followed he wondered if he had imagined it, but it would always reappear in his mind's eye unchanging. The youth was suspended in mid-air, jumping two feet off the post, when the heavy calibre bullets from the machine-gun split him in two. And Franklin saw daylight between the halves.

He expected an immediate bombardment of the ground opposite, and he lowered his head. He waited a half minute but none came and when he looked up again he saw why. The machine-gunner, the lone survivor, had got up from his foxhole and was walking slowly towards the car park, his hands spread across his chest in a cross. He too was young, with a beard and in camouflage, and could easily have been the brother of the man he had just killed. Still the Revolutionaries below did not fire. Then, half-way across the road, he went down on his knees, a solitary target, and faced Mecca to pray. And as his head touched the road it exploded into pulp.

Franklin knew the young machine-gunner would not be the last to die in Riyadh that day. Nor the last to die praying.

'It's Iran all over again'

'How come we didn't know it was on?'

'No one knew, Mr President.'

'That wasn't my question, Johns. You had men there?'

'Yessir. We had men there. So had King Fahd.'

The President would not argue with the Director of the Central Intelligence Agency. It was his understanding that the CIA, with a budget costing the American taxpayer billions a year, was in the business to encourage coups and revolutions that were in America's interest and to prevent those that were not. Clearly the coup in Saudi Arabia was not.

'This rundown you've given me, Johns,' the President said, tapping the single sheet of paper on his blotter pad on the desk in front of him, 'is this all you can give me on Crown Prince Abdullah, alias Rahbar?'

'Yes, sir. It's the best our people could signal me—given the circumstances.'

'Given the circumstances, Johns, we should have had our people already out. Until they're out, we're paralysed. Whatever we want to do, whatever we decide today, we've got to wait until every one of our people is safely out of that hole.'

'Mr President. Arrangements for that are already well

under way.' General David C. Jarvis, United States Air Force, pulled at a hair in his nostril. 'Our planes are on standby in Cairo. We're only waiting the clearance from Riyadh and we can be in there in a little under two hours. Galaxies, sir, they'll take all of ours and any other foreign nationals the Saudis let go.'

'When they let go. If they let go.' The President stood up quickly and pushed his chair away with the back of his legs. He undid his shirt-collar button, loosened his tie and ran his fingers through his greying black curly hair, scraping his nails into the layer of dandruffed skin of his scalp. He tugged at the small curls of grey hair at his sideburns, looking at everyone in the room and no one for long. As they waited for him to speak, he dug out the dead skin from under his finger-nails with the tip of his silver ballpoint pen.

All five men there in the Situation Room in the fortified basement of the White House were now used to their new President's routine, concealing his anxiety with arrogance. But today the six knew, because each had been briefed by his own separate Intelligence, the political, military and economic implications of what had just happened in the Saudi desert capital seven thousand miles away.

'You say our people there are convinced it's religion and not Marxism, Johns?'

'Yes, Mr President. Absolutely certain. Rahbar, when he was Crown Prince, abhorred Communism. As religious leader of the country he must maintain that Islam and Communism are diametrically opposed.'

The President groaned out loud. 'Soviet Communism's diametrically opposed to everything in this world, Johns, even to other kinds of Communism. You told us, at least your predecessor in the Agency did, that the Ayatollah Khomeini was not a Communist. And we believed it. I still believe it, but it didn't stop him cutting off his oil to us. Seven hundred thousand barrels a day we were importing from Iran then, and it's nix, absolutely nil today. Just because their diseased little Shah tried to die on us, it cost us seven per cent of our oil imports, which is why we're so dependent on the Saudis. And that's why I want to know, Johns, whether this shit means to cut us out for good and sell instead to the Soviets.'

'Rahbar is no Communist, sir. He's a devout—extreme—Moslem.'

'He's popular?'

'He's in power, sir.'

'Balls, Johns! Don't play word games with me.'

The President slammed his fist down hard on the metal table and the little brass Stars and Strips on its little brass base jumped an inch with the shock. He tugged at his tie again, coughed, swallowed the phlegm and wiped his mouth with the back of his hand. A tiny haemorrhaged vein in his left eye began to spread blood across the yellowing white. Here, in this underground room out of the public eye, he could have been a bookmaker or a poolroom regular.

'It's Iran all over again,' he said. 'We've been caught on the hop just as Carter was with those student pigs. "Give them hell, Jimmy," we shouted then and for what? D'you remember the great phrases? How America had lost its clout, how everyone was still terrified by the Vietnam Syndrome, how America had lost its faith in the future for the first time in its history? Remember the burning effigy of Uncle Sam the students held up in our Embassy in Teheran . . . with a goat's skull for a head and collecting trash in Old Glory? D'you remember Vance trying to do the right thing? Remember his phrases? "We must strike a balance between timidity and provocation . . . American power is no longer the answer . . . not a sign of America's decline but a measure of America's maturity." Remember Carter—a hawk one minute, chicken the next?

'Well, let me tell you something you know already. That's not how I intend it. I won't play possum to some crazy dervish. They have broken all the rules, just as they did in Iran, and we are now going to play all the long shots. You say Rahbar is no Communist and I tell you that he and his mobs are doing the Kremlin's work even if they're not doing its bidding.

'Let's get it straight. He has closed down our oilfields, and we're going to sit here until we've decided how we're going to open them up again. Maybe the oil is his but the ways and means of getting it out of the sand have always been ours, our machines, our know-how, our men, our markets, our money.'

He left the table and walked to one of the wall-maps, a large-scale projection of Saudi Arabia. It was coloured yellow, a land of desert from the Red Sea on its western borders to the Persian Gulf on its eastern. And in between, the Great Nefud and Rubal Khali deserts consuming most of the Arabian peninsula, stretching a thousand five hundred miles from Jordan and Iraq in the North to the Yemeni States in the South. The President put his right forefinger on the capital of Riyadh and slowly traced the road travelling east to the Persian Gulf and the oilfields. He turned, half facing them.

'Six months ago a certain chief of a certain Allied European Intelligence Service stood just where I am now. You brought him, Johns. Remember what he said? It's all cinema, he said, all just cinema. Whatever the Soviets say they mean to do, whether it's about detente, or about strategic arms limitation, or about lessening the tensions, is just something they know we want to hear, just something to distract us while they set about their serious work elsewhere. Brezhnev kisses Carter on the cheek and initials SALT, and soon after Russian tanks rumble into Afghanistan. Remember, Johns, what our friend showed us on this map? Remember how he made a wide sweep of it? He pointed to Ethiopia where the Russians have got themselves a Red Sea port with access to the Indian Ocean, pointed across the Arabian peninsula, across South Yemen where they have anchorage refuel facilities and submarine pens on the Arabian Sea. And then he swung his hand around, completing the circle of Soviet ambition. And in the centre of that huge area he pointed to the Persian Gulf. This, he said, is the Soviet's objective, this is what they are after, this is what is real to them. They're trying to take over what he called the "rimlands" of the Middle East oilfields . . . as part of their strategy of denial against the West's energy sources; the creation of pro-Soviet oil states, including Saudi Arabia itself.'

The President raised his voice. 'Our friend ended with a simple warning, "If the Russians could get the Gulf oilfields by stealth and default, they would become masters of the world . . . and without ever having to go to war. The balance of advantage is already with them."

'So my question again, Johns. Is he popular? What is his Soviet connection? Is he there by demand, are they all with him? Or is there a chance, I don't care what the odds are, just a chance of shifting him right out again? Because if we cannot, this country can kiss itself goodbye and amen.'

'Mr President . . .'

'Let me finish, Johns. Without that oil we're not in the world-power business any more. You know it, I know it and by tomorrow, everyone from LA to Philadelphia will know it too. And they're not going to blame sonofabitch Rahbar and his Islamic People's Proletarian Revolution. They're not going to blame the oil companies and they certainly won't blame themselves. The President will be the kicking butt 'cause I'm supposed to look after them and I shouldn't have let it happen.'

Richard Johns, CIA, stood up again. His face seemed greyer than usual and his eyes were wide behind his spectacles.

'Mr President, with respect, and I want this put on record, if we put one invading American soldier anywhere on Saudi Arabian soil, Islam will explode. There is a unanimous belief that any semblance of stability there would be shattered by US military intervention . . . whatever the provocation. We must dilute, not aggravate, the situation. We do not know for sure how much control Rahbar has of the country . . . nor can we be certain Iraq, or Syria or Iran wouldn't go to its aid. We must assume Soviet complicity but at this time we are fighting Islam. By going in for that oil we may spark off a reaction in all Islam and set off a fire that neither they nor we could control.'

'That's a pretty speech, Johns.' The President said it slowly. 'I suppose this couldn't have come at a better time, you being such an Arab watcher. I forget that before you took to other people's crimes you did, what was it? Arab Affairs at Yale?'

'Islamic Studies, sir.'

'And Professor?'

'Yessir.'

'Well, too much knowledge is sometimes a dangerous thing, Johns. It narrows your vision, elongates comprehension, but gives it no breadth. Tell me, did Islam explode when Soviet tanks went into Afghanistan? Did it? I'm telling you to look beyond the Arabs and the prophet Mohammed. Look instead to the irreligious Russians, the apostles of Marx. I'd rather contest the Arabs now and put off later contest with Moscow, because that's what this is all about. Don't you see, Johns? They're probing again. They tried us on in Cuba and Vietnam and Angola and Iran and Afghanistan. They probed us on the neutron bomb and the B-1 bomber and they've come to the conclusion we're soft. So they probe and they find mush so they probe a little further. But God help me, I'm damned if they'll shove their filthy fingers any deeper into me. That's my answer, Johns, to your Islamic explosion. We'll set them on fire maybe. But we'll put out the flames soon after.'

He massaged his scalp for another twenty seconds and sat down again at the head of the long metal table in the centre of the Situation Room. The six men watched but said nothing.

The Situation Room is in the central basement of the White House, itself in the centre of Washington, so the little-known room could be said to be the centre of American presidential government. Or more concisely, the centre of crisis American presidential government, because it is in this long padded room, with its artificial strip lighting, its recycled air, its temperature and humidity control, that crucial decisions have been made by American presidents during the many and varied crises in the nation's history this century. And their secret conversations, controversial decisions, conspiracies and many deceits, are as secure in this room as a scream in a vacuum, because the doors, walls and ceiling of the room are sealed in a field of electro-magnetism.

The Situation Room is like Sir Winston Churchill's London wartime concrete bunker, though it has a newer sophistication. It is sealed against bacterial and nuclear contamination, and it is where the President and his family and the President's close friends and their families would run to in the event of the final bomb falling.

The Situation Room looks military, simply because so many military crises have been discussed there. Possibly because of the rows of maps and projections stretching along the walls explaining global strategies. It is the room where the Chief Executive of the United States changes coats and becomes Commander-in-Chief of the entire American military forces.

President Woodrow Wilson sat here contemplating the Somme and dreading Ypres. Franklin D. Roosevelt pondered on the American merchant convoys on their Atlantic way to besieged Britain and where he finally manoeuvred his countrymen into the Nazi war. Here, on this table, John F. Kennedy was shown USAF aerial reconnaissance photographs of the Soviet missile bases in Cuba and where a week later he decided his enormous bluff that took the world to the edge of war. From here fighting fit GIs were sent to South Vietnam, and from here, ten years later, considerably fewer were—in some ignominy—brought home again.

Presidents travelled down in their private one-man elevator from the Oval Office to make wars and later other Presidents returned to end them. The Situation Room was the room of lesion and lost causes.

'We're gonna have one helluva battle, Mr President, going on what Johns says. There's no way we're gonna get that oil unless we go in there ourselves and take it.' General Bernard James Browne, US Army, looked like a long-retired heavyweight boxer, though the broken nose and deformed left ear were the casualties of Korea, not the canvas. 'A limited action, sir,' he went on. 'Five thousand assault troops, paradropped, very feasible military-wise.'

'And unmilitary-wise, General?'
'Sir?'
'You're recommending, General Browne, that I send in a combat force. Okay, that's fine. Just give me one political excuse to do so. One is all I need.'
'But you said yourself, Mr President, that the oil is ours.'
'No, General, only the working parts on top. That's what we claim to own. Explain an invasion force of five thousand men to retrieve rigs and pumps worth less then ten million dollars.'
General Louis Wilson of the Marine Corps coughed and held up his hand to speak. 'Mr President, you said a short while back that we can't move against the Saudis until our people are safely away.'
'That's what I said.'
'Well, sir, might it not be better for us to use these people as the reason, the excuse, to go in while they're still there? Protecting our own?'
'George?'
The President looked across at General George Vernon C. Warner, Chairman of the Joint Chiefs of Staff. At sixty-two, he was the oldest man present, his hair completely white, his jaw square and jutting. He reminded the President of Spencer Tracy. General Warner clasped his hands together and held them out in front of him on the table.
'Mr President,' he said, 'we reckon to have upwards of a thousand military instructors in and around Riyadh with their dependants. I'm told the oil companies have another thousand men and dependants stationed there too. Plus all the Vinnell and Security people. So, over three thousand American citizens in Riyadh alone. Now, sir, we do not know at this time how or where all those people are distributed. Some are inside our Consulate compound, many are not. Many may have gone to the Vinnell compound, some to the Corps of Engineers. Given a sudden order to rendezvous at the Consulate or the airport, we have no idea—absolutely none—how many of these people would make it. We cannot even guarantee they would know where to go. We can only guess at the state they're in, and I dread

the problems these people may even now be facing. But, Mr President, we can be certain of one thing. If we land combat troops before our evacuation planes take off with all our people aboard, many, *many* innocent Americans, men, women and children, are going to die as a direct consequence. We cannot afford one civilian casualty. And, Mr President, with respect, it would be rash of you to think otherwise.'

The young President looked at the ageing general for a minute or more, than he slowly nodded and, very quietly said, 'Of course, George . . . you're right. You always are. It would be rash to gamble on the lives of non-combatants at the risk of losing that oil.'

But there was no conviction in the President's voice. It was dull, and it was something all those present in the Situation Room were to remember some days later.

Then he said, 'So we agree we evacuate as quickly as possible. Now let's talk on what we do after that.'

'The Rapid Deployment Force, Mr President. It has to be.' It was General Browne, US Army. 'We have men at Fort Bragg who have been trained for exactly this, top men raring to go. And we have the 101st Air Mobile Division at Fort Campbell.'

'How soon?'

'It's fourteen hours' flying time from Virginia to the Persian Gulf, Mr President,' said General Jarvis, US Air Force. 'We could begin to put ten thousand men immediately closer to the area—say Tel Aviv on standby. From there they'll be two hours from the dropping zone.'

'Not Tel Aviv, General.'

'Sir,' said General Jarvis, 'it's ideal. The Israelis will help all the way along the line.'

'You bet they will. An American invasion force from Israel paradropping on to the Arabs would be a dream come true for them. And a nightmare for us. We want no allies in this. They can't afford us.'

'But the evacuation planes are landing in Cairo, sir.'

'That's humanitarian. Anyway, it's still in the family, and helping refugee flights to refuel is not exactly the same,

General Jarvis, as refuelling war planes packed with US combat troops.'

'If we had the time, sir, we could mobilize out of Diego Garcia,' said General Wilson. 'We'd have full British co-operation.'

'Diego Garcia?' said the President. 'Wasn't that the idea for using the British base there, so we could have men on call close by to send in on just such an occasion as now? You told me yourself, General Wilson, that we have ten thousand men there with back-up supply ships on four hour standby.'

'Can't be done, Mr President.'

General Wilson stopped speaking and the others waited silently as he seemed to make rapid mental calculations. 'But we'd still be five hours' flying from the Gulf. The Soviets can be in there on the ground in three if they fly out from the Afghan border. Possibly sooner if they decide to move their fleet into the Gulf.'

'Christ!' said the President, 'and we talk of a Rapid Deployment Force. And there's nowhere else?'

'There's Turkey. We use the base at Adana. We've got a squadron of F-4's there already.' The voice came from behind them.

The President, the Generals, the Admiral and Richard Johns of CIA turned towards the low square soundproof door that connected the Situation Room to the Operations and Monitoring Rooms. Dr Tom Sorenson stood there smiling.

'Sorry, Mr President. Fog. Flight was delayed.'

'We got the message,' answered the President. 'Sit down, Tom; glad to have you here.' His anxiety during the past hour had been due, in part, to Sorenson's absence. No one knew the domestic scene better than the President, no one was better at managing the internecine fighting of Congress and Senate. He had been America's youngest Senator and had been scrambling, pushing, jumping and dodging in an upwards direction ever since. But his weakness, and therefore the weakness of his Adminstration, was his ignorance of international relations—a chronic defect of almost every American President since Roosevelt. So, like previous incumbents, he equipped himself with a strong team of

Foreign Affairs specialists, recruited from corporations and universities throughout the country—committed Democrats who found inspiration in their Camelot and fresh impetus to their own private political ambitions.

Dr Tom Sorenson was Head of the Foreign Affairs Special Advisory Committee to the President and the President did nothing, said nothing on matters outside of the USA before consulting him. The appointment of Sorenson continued a tradition of second generation Americans conducting American Foreign Affairs; what one critical political columnist had called 'the foreign monopoly of US foreign affairs'.

Sorenson, of Swedish stock, was to the President what German Kissinger had been to Nixon and what Polish Brzezinski had been to Carter. Like most of the White House staff, Sorenson was young; at forty-two, nine years younger than the President. A graduate of Cornell and the London School of Economics, Sorenson had been Dean of the Faculty of International Relations at Harvard before coming to Washington. His nickname among those he taught at university was Gung-Ho Tommy, for like his President, he was an extrovert in most things. Many previous Foreign Affairs Advisers to the White House had been insular to the point of being parish parochial, but Sorenson was in the new mould, intent on revitalizing America in the eighties at home and abroad. It had been the theme of the election campaign: 'We're on the march again.'

The President spoke. 'If all else fails, Tom, we're thinking of the Rapid Deployment Force.'

'Presidential Directive Eighteen, sir, a Presidential waiver, and your prerogative to invoke without recourse to Congress.'

'You agree we should use it?'

'Yes, Mr President, I agree. I don't see we can do less than that, if the Saudis refuse to negotiate. On the outside, Rahbar's coup is a simple spontaneous manifestation of the popular will. But it'll directly—perhaps violently—alter the world's balance of power. We have discussed this for many years, Mr President, you and I, almost as if we have been preparing for today, when the Arabs played their final bluff.

Their final hand we knew would be the simple demand to join the Super-powers. The Shah tried it and failed.

'Now the biggest of them all is going for it and, given the very special circumstances, the Saudis may well succeed. Seven million Arabs, Mr President, smelling of camel dung, sitting in mud huts, owners of a desert the size of Mexico and because of the slaphazard benevolence of nature, free-holders to enough oil to keep the States of Washington and New York alight forever. But the same people can turn those lights out. You ask me, Mr President, if I agree to a combat force should the talking fail. I say, we have no choice.'

There were five seconds or so of silence. Then the generals and the admiral applauded and the President tapped the table in accord. Only Richard Johns kept his hands in his lap.

'But one thing,' said Sorenson, holding up a hand. 'I wonder whether the Rapid Deployment Force should be sent first . . . on the initial landings?'

'Why not?' asked General Rogers.

'Mr President, Generals, Admiral, look at the logistics. Is it feasible? The 82nd in North Carolina are over six thousand flying miles from Riyadh. Can it be done quickly and secretively . . . even the dispatch of only a few units? Wouldn't someone leak it out . . . wouldn't someone tell mama? The problem is that we cannot arrive with any degree of surprise. We lack the airlift capabilities. We have only one Airborne Division in the entire United States Army, and that would certainly be insufficient. We just don't have the assets to drop that division by parachute assault. But we do have a brigade south of Naples and we could easily push them from there across to Turkey to Adana in a matter of hours, night-time, nobody would know. We have a lot of military freight transport air traffic between Europe and Turkey which we know the Russians monitor, but we could fill those transporters with troops. No one could tell his mama from there—we would seal it.'

'And use the 82nd as back-up?'

'Yes, Mr President,' said General Wilson. 'Have them on

their way just as soon as our initial force drops on the fields. I suggest we move the first units to Italy tonight. I reckon we can push, say, three thousand there without causing trouble, leakwise.'

The President looked around the table. 'Does that make sense?' The Generals and the Admiral nodded.

'We'll need technicians on that first drop, Mr President. Men who can get those wells pumping again.'

'And you have them?'

'Yessir, we have plenty.'

'Mr President.'

'Johns?'

'It's imperative we get King Fahd back as quickly as possible.'

'Look, Johns,' said the President in the flat voice he always used for his CIA Director. 'Let's talk first about getting our men in.'

'With respect, sir. Before we do that we've also got to find a way of getting them out again.'

'You still suffering Vietnam-phobia?' asked General Browne. But Johns would not be put off.

'I'm not a General . . .'

'That's right!'

'And I'm willing to believe,' Johns went on, 'that a task force can easily take and hold these oilfields. They're more than three hundred miles from Riyadh which is where much of the Saudis' artillery and many of their troops are, so our men could land without problems. But we're talking here of hours, sir. Rahbar could have his tanks and artillery up against our men in ten, maybe eight, hours.'

'Rahbar would not use artillery to destroy the derricks and pipelines,' said General Browne.

'We don't know he wouldn't,' replied Johns. 'Derricks and pipes can be repaired once an invasion force has been defeated.'

'Whose side you on?'

'Mr President,' said Johns. 'In military terms we will be able to hold our own depending on the size of the force we send in . . .'

'It's a relief to hear you say it,' interrupted General Browne, followed by General Jarvis, 'You're out of your depth.'

'Hey! Isn't this your area, Sorenson?' asked General Warner.

The Foreign Affairs Specialist nodded. 'If Johns would give me leg room,' he said. 'I'd be happy to outline what I have in mind?' It was put as a question to the CIA Director who nodded back and put his hands down in his lap again.

'Johns of course is right,' said Sorenson. 'We all know there is no military solution to this emergency, only a military expedient. The Rapid Deployment Force is that expedient. But, in the long term, we must have the Saudis' agreement to let us stay there. Our problem is, how do we survive the welter of international protests until that agreement is made?'

'You believe an agreement is possible, Tom?'

'Not exactly, Mr President.'

'I don't follow.'

'Let me put it to you.' He stood up and moved a yard away from the table. He folded his arms across his chest and addressed them like the Dean he used to be. 'I suggest, gentlemen, that the Government of the United States of America, by urgent and immediate appeal to the United Nations, recommends the entire Persian Gulf be declared an International Zone, controlled and policed by UN member states, in a similar way to the peacekeeping forces in Cyprus, Lebanon, the Golan Heights and the Sinai. We shall remind the world that the Gulf area produces over seventy per cent of the world's oil exports; Saudi Arabia alone has a quarter of the world's proven oil reserves. But it's an area that has become so politically volatile that free nations large and small, entirely dependent on Arab oil supplies, are fearful of that oil's being used for further political and economic blackmail. We shall stress by implication that the International Zone would not violate the sovereignty of any Gulf state and that the UN would guarantee those States their control of their own territorial waters, that is, up to twelve miles from their shores. The only exception will be the

Strait of Hormuz, the gateway to the Persian Gulf which is the only sea access to the oilfields. This narrow corridor of sea, only thirty miles across with deep water which is only twelve miles wide, will be under permanent UN scrutiny, patrolled day and night to ensure free access and movements to all ships, except ships of war. The Gulf then, under American sponsorship, will be a zone of peace, and the production of oil in Kuwait, Bahrein, Oman, Iran and Saudi Arabia and its transportation out on the world's tanker routes will be thereafter free from harassment. Oil-dependent countries can then plan their future accordingly. That, Mr President, is what I am recommending our immediate tactic should be.'

But the President was frowning. 'Tom,' he said, 'at any other time I would say it was a great idea and worthy of a good deal of effort on our part. But we do not have that time.'

'Correct,' said Sorenson.

'No way I can see the Gulf States agreeing to it,' said General Warner.

'That's right,' replied Sorenson.

'The Soviets would veto it all the way along the line,' said General Browne.

'Absolutely,' confirmed Sorenson.

'Do you realize the enormous difficulties facing sea patrols in an area the size of the Persian Gulf?' asked Admiral Holliwell.

'Yes,' answered Sorenson. 'Quite impractical.'

'Tom,' said the President. 'You're talking in riddles. You're seriously suggesting we put this forward to the United Nations and yet you say it hasn't a chance?'

'I am, sir.' They waited. He said nothing.

'I think we can do without the inscrutability,' said Admiral Holliwell after a half-minute had passed.

Sorenson looked at each of them in turn, smiling. Mystification was something he enjoyed. It was his most irritating habit.

'Mr President,' he said at last. 'If you send combat troops into Saudi Arabia, you as our President are going to need protection. This proposal of mine will provide exactly that. It's an umbrella that will give the Rapid Deployment Force some legitimacy. If we go in without it you are in trouble. This simple strategy will enable us to pre-empt the protests and keep you respectable for a time.'

'I like it,' murmured Johns from the end of the table.

'Much relieved to hear it,' replied Sorenson. He was still smiling.

'Genuine attempt to restore peace and stability to a vital economic area of the world—notification to Congress . . .'

'Exactly, Mr President, the War Powers Act.'

'It could just work.' Johns again. 'Not for long, but long enough.'

'The Soviets will know what we're up to,' said the President.

'Of course. Point is, Mr President, everyone will know what we're up to, including our friends, but by then our men will be on the ground. We give Rahbar and the UN simultaneous ultimatums, Rahbar to resume oil supplies, the UN to declare the Gulf an International Zone and bar the Soviet fleet. And we give them twenty-four hours to respond, knowing they can't or won't in that time. Then our boys drop on the oilfields, ostensibly to stabilize the area until the UN, or Rahbar, or both, make up their minds. It's not perfect, but it's the only gambit available to us, simply appearing to be seen to be doing what's best. A holding tactic to get us into those fields under the guise of a peacekeeping force—anything less than that and we can expect immediate Soviet response in a very physical way.'

'Meaning?'

'Mr President,' said Sorenson. 'You know that the seas south of the Persian Gulf are saturated with Soviet warships and re-supply ships. Remember those satellite surveillance photographs you showed us, Admiral, only a week ago? Eighteen ships of their Sixth Fleet anchored at Aden, eleven of their Third Fleet at Massawa in the Red Sea, including two battleships and a helo-carrier. At this very moment there's a convoy of twenty-two south of the Gulf of Oman on warm-water exercises.'

'That's right, Mr President.' Admiral Holliwell got up from the table and went to the wall-map of the Middle East to remind the others where Aden, Massawa and the Gulf of Oman were. The Admiral's hand swept the area. He said, 'This is the first time, Mr President, that they've had such a concentration of their fleets so close to the Persian Gulf. This convoy,' he circled an area with his finger, 'is certainly the biggest in fire and missile power we've ever seen in that latitude. The carrier *Minsk* is with them and it's their largest carrier. The *Ivan Rogov* is with her. That's an assault ship with helos and about a thousand combat marines aboard, battalion strength.'

'What do you read into so many Soviet ships being so close to the oilfields at this time?' asked the President.

'Well,' said the Admiral, 'Moscow let it be known ten days ago that their Seventh Fleet would be on exercises in that area. They do warm-water training every winter. Last year it was in the Arabian Sea, south of Karachi.'

'Extraordinary,' said the President 'that they just happen to be in there at the time of the coup. Are they close enough to be used against us?'

'If they moved into the Persian Gulf, yes.'

'What do we have there?'

'An assault ship, sir. The *Okinawa*. It's been on a show-the-flag visit to Bahrain but she's on her way out. Should be moving through the Straits of Hormuz some time tomorrow.'

The President beckoned to Admiral Holliwell to sit down again and turned to Sorenson.

'Tom, if we go ahead with your UN manoeuvre, how long have we got?'

'Four days, maybe. Probably less.'

'And then?'

'That's up to Johns, Mr President. I can buy us time at the UN, but it's up to the CIA to use that time to get Fahd back. Make no mistake, the success of this thing from the moment our boys jump on those oilwells depends on us taking the King back to Riyadh. As Johns says he's pivotal. I can get us into Saudi Arabia with the least damage internationally, but if we are going to stay there, it's got to be with the Saudis' okay and that means putting Fahd back on his throne. We have four days, as I've said—maybe less—but after that, combat troops of the United States army remain on foreign soil as aggressors and an army of occupation. And we can guess the consequences.'

The President looked at the man at the end of the table. 'Johns?' It sounded like a summons.

The Director stood up from his chair and pushed his gold rimmed spectacles further up the bridge of his long thin nose. He was slim and frail, looking almost as grey as his worsted flannel suit, more like a failing academic than the nation's Intelligence chief.

'Mr President, I agree totally,' he said in his clipped Princeton accent, reminding the President of familiar Boston tea-parties. 'If you want Saudi oil, you will certainly have to use American troops to get it. But you will have to use King Fahd to keep it. The Generals here, sir, tell us we can survive, despite the location and line of re-supply. But like Sorenson, I believe we cannot survive international reaction, or the protests here at home, and there'll be plenty, unless we put the King back in his palace. You may get those oil supplies moving again, sir, but without Fahd you'll not survive your presidency.'

Richard Johns sat down again and looked around the table for some endorsement, but there was none. The generals were looking at their President, their Commander-in-Chief. Very slowly, he did up the button of his shirt collar and straightened his black tie. Then he stood up and went behind this chair, his hands on the back of it, facing them. He coughed to clear his throat and, when he spoke, every one of them, there in the Situation Room, knew that the anxiety had left him. His voice was menacing. Advice had been given, strategies tossed around, and he had made up his mind. For good or for bad, country right or wrong, he had decided what he now thought best for America.

'Gentlemen. An hour ago I was briefed by Professor Nicholas Grüber of the Petroleum Institute on the simple facts of oil, not that I needed reminding, God help me! Grüber's conclusion, after forty minutes, was stark and simple. The United States of America needs that oil like a bleeding man needs plasma. Every fibre of our daily life depends on what Grüber calls hydro-carbons and we call oil, and which, by the saddest accident in God's world has lodged itself under the Arabs. Four million barrels a day we use of it, four million barrels, three hundred and sixty-five days a year. Our oil import bill is topping five million dollars an hour—d'you get that—every hour, that's over eighty thousand dollars a minute. Add to that the tankers, the truckers, the refineries, the marketing. And we reckon this is a crisis? By God, we haven't even started yet. At the moment we are only importing sixty per cent of our oil needs, but in eight years' time—let me repeat, eight years—all of our own oil will be used up. There will not, *not*, be a drop of claimable American oil left in the ground outside of Alaska. Who says so? The US Department of Energy says so. The American Petroleum Institute says so. Data Resources Incorporated says so. You want more? Because there's plenty who say so—here, in Europe, in Asia. And their figures tally. Conclusion? In eight years most—not all, but most—of the oil we want will be owned by the Arabs. Most of us will drive by courtesy of the Arabs. Most of the wheels that turn in this country will turn by courtesy of Arab oil. And by Christ! Do they know it!

'Ten years ago it was costing us three dollars a barrel and selling at the gas stations at eighteen cents a gallon. You all know what it is today. A twenty-five per cent increase in the past eleven months and the next OPEC meeting will push it even higher because they know, every single one of them, that we can't live without it. They're oil pushers feeding an addiction, feeding us addicts who demand more and more of it every day, whatever the price, whatever the conditions, whatever the humiliation!'

He paused and drank from the vacuum flask of iced water on the table. He wiped his lips with the back of his hand and the six men watching saw sweat on their President's forehead and saw that his left eye had become noticeably more bloodshot.

The President's voice got suddenly louder. 'But when a

pusher stops supplying, the clients get angry and rough it up, and that is exactly what I intend to do. I am President of the most powerful, most technically advanced, nation history has known, or will ever know, a nation that once fought a colonial war for its liberty and two world wars to keep it. And a nation that has sent its own men to the moon will not be brought to its knees by a few million Arabs who'd still be living in the Dark Ages, squatting in tents and eating camel shit, if we hadn't brought the oil up out of the sand for them. They have it. We need it!

'I've read all your reports and heard all I need to hear in this room, and I am persuaded that if we do not move fast to those oilfields, others will. You tell me that this man Rahbar is a devout Moslem. I say he has led a revolution and has used Marxists and Soviet-supplied weapons to do it. I don't care a monkey's ball whether the Jews or the Arabs, the Protestants or the Catholics, the Moslems, Hindus, Hare Krishnans or the Mafia own that chunk of desert. But I do care what they do with the oil in it, because we have a stake in it—a large and very vital stake, and if we lose it we will not survive. Our factories will wind down, our farms will go derelict, we will sit and go impotent. The lights would go out all over America. That oil is the stuff of our survival!

'It's something we have known about for a long time now. Five American Presidents before me knew about it, so did umpteen Generals, so did the Department of Energy, and the oil companies. But none of us care to think too long about it. Impossible, we used to say, that the wells would run dry. Even now, go out into the streets, ask a dozen people how much oil they think we have left and they'll guess at twenty, thirty, fifty years. And anyway, they'd say, there's always Arab oil—there's plenty around. And they would be right, two days ago. Two days ago we were just paying rotten high prices for it. Today it's not there to buy any more.

'Now the Soviet Union remains the biggest single oil producer in the world. With or without Arab oil it is self-sufficient and its war machine will continue to run. But the only guaranteed fuel we'll have if the Saudi fields remain closed to us is rocket fuel for our intercontinental ballistic missiles. D'you see? Without oil there is no such thing as limited conventional war. Without oil we have only the once-and-for-all nuclear warhead left. The Arabs are pushing us to our final option. As of this day, oil has a greater power potential than the entire American Military because without it there is no American Military. We know it. So do the Arabs. So does Moscow. And that is why I intend to go and get it. By persuasion if the Saudis can be persuaded. By force if they cannot.

'So, do what's necessary, Tom, to get our Peace Zone Resolution into the UN and, Generals, Admiral, get our men moving. I'm going ahead with an Address to the Nation and I'm going up to Camp David to write it. By the time I go on television I want confirmation that we have troops standing-by within two hours of their drop over those fields. And, Johns, you get going on Fahd. God knows how you'll do it in the time we have, but you're gonna do it, by Christ you are. I'll have him back on that throne if it needs a task force to put him there!'

He moved away from the table towards the one-man elevator that would take him into the public world of the Oval Office and to the bright winter sunlight overlooking the White House gardens.

As he got up the Generals, the Admiral, the Director of the CIA and the President's Foreign Affairs Adviser quickly stood to attention, men who would not stand that way for any other living American.

He turned. There was sweat on his forehead, his arms were stretched straight down the seams of his trousers with the palms open and the fingers splayed wide open. When he spoke his voice was almost lost in the hiss from the air-conditioning duct above him.

'An hour ago, I spoke to General Volney-Wagner at Macdill airbase. I asked him if he was ready. I quote him word for word. "I'm ready for anywhere, for any place at any time. You tell me where to put the x on the map and tell me what's under the x and I'll tailor my force and go there." Gentlemen, I'm putting that x right bang on those oilfields. I mean to get that oil . . . before the Soviets go in and get it themselves.'

December 21st

RIYADH

'But his soul goes marching on'

Fires were still smouldering in Riyadh, five hundred miles west of the *Okinawa*'s position in the Gulf, but the gunfire and the explosions of grenades and mortars no longer echoed through the narrow streets of the Saudi capital. There were still hundreds, possibly thousands, dead, but one by one, as their families claimed them, they were carried away in the half-light of dawn, sprawled across a camel's back or stretched out under a cloth in an open donkey cart. Makeshift flags of the new Islamic People's Democratic Republic had been quickly sewn together from remnants of red and black cloth and they hung limp from shuttered windows in the still cold morning air. Other bits of the same coloured rags had been hurriedly nailed to doors and on to the mud walls of the small squat houses.

At twenty minutes past five the sun rose above the desert horizon and shutters were carefully opened and doors were just as cautiously unlocked. The survivors of Saudi Arabia's first civil war nodded to each other, brought out their prayer mats and went down on their knees to touch the sand with their foreheads and thank Allah for their salvation. Loud-speakers on top of the minarets carried the same thanks-giving across the flat roofs and far away other muezzins relayed the message until all in Riyadh were down on their knees and elbows facing Mecca and thanking the God of Islam they were still alive to do it.

Within minutes of their prayers ending, as they washed their hands and feet again and boiled water for their coffee, they suddenly heard other loudspeakers proclaiming a message not of God. They went back to their doorways and windows and watched Landrovers turn the corner and come slowly down the street in convoy. The windscreens and sides of the vehicles had been smashed and ripped with bullets and youths stood in the back, holding rifles high above their heads, strips of red and black cloth streaming from the barrels. On a signal from the leading driver, the Landrovers stopped. A man with a megaphone began a new flow of propaganda, the youths in the vehicles jumped off and on walls and doors and shop windows they began spraying the initials of the new government IDPR, and the name Rahbar.

The youths shouted and danced and screamed abuse of King Fahd and spat phelgm at the ground. The people in the shadows of their doorways and those standing back from their windows watched silently for they knew with a simple wisdom that it was foolish to show commitment so soon. After all, today was only the third day in the week, and on the first day King Fahd had been their divine ruler. Was it not possible he might be again by the seventh? If he was not, then, and only then, would it be time to join hands with these young men with their Landrovers and rifles and their magic paint, who shouted obsceneties at the King and spat on the ground where the prayer mats had been only minutes before.

As the convoy accelerated away to other streets and other shy spectators, women went to their stoves to prepare the meal of the day and their men went to their Koran for guidance, astonished at Allah's ways.

Franklin was ordered into the open truck with fifteen other foreign nationals. Eleven were fellow Americans, all oil men, two were British computer technicians, there was a Japanese road engineer and a Belgian who had never confided to any one what his business in Riyadh had been.

They had been ordered at gunpoint from their bedrooms and told to leave everything except their passports behind.

As they crossed the downstairs reception foyer they saw the safe deposit boxes behind the cashier's grid blown open and thousands of US hundred-dollar bills were scattered across the floor, 'An expensive carpet even for the Oil King,' one of the British had said, but no one laughed. The soldiers in the foyer ignored the money, but the Belgian could not. He went down on his knees to scoop it up and the nearest soldier hit him with his rifle butt; then, as he sprawled across the dollars, others kicked him hard in his head and crutch. He was thrown up into the truck unconscious, blood and bile oozing from his mouth.

The Saudi driver kept the truck in first gear and they left the hotel car park, manoeuvring slowly past the burnt-out wrecks of cars, coaches and artillery pieces as a hundred or more soldiers saw them on their way with stones and spittle.

Just beyond the gate Franklin saw that the inquisitive had pulled the Swiss flag away from the dead family. They were covered in dust and flies and for a moment he thought the truck driver meant to drive over them. His gorge rose, but at the last second, laughing, the driver swung his truck away and the flies settled again. Except for a father who had been too frightened for their safety, Franklin thought, the two little blonde children would be here in the truck huddled in the arms of their mother on their way to the airport and freedom and home.

Whoever it was who had ordered their departure had worked fast and thoroughly because, as they joined seven other open trucks carrying other foreigners out, Franklin saw the route was lined with people, an avenue of thousands of hostile Saudis encouraged by their new party organizers to throw curses, stones, glass, camel dung and any missile at hand at these non-Moslems who had attempted to contaminate Islam, who had tried to impose their evils, their diseases, their greed, their blasphemies, even their own images of God, upon the guardians of Mecca in the land of the Holy Koran.

When the people saw their targets passing so close and so

slowly, they avenged themselves enthusiastically. The trucks had gone less than two hundred yards but already two of the older American oilmen were on the floor of the truck, their heads and faces bleeding. The little Japanese, terrified at first, not understanding the ritual, had hidden behind Franklin; but then, understanding the slogans and abuse, he suddenly and quickly moved to the side of the truck and faced them, hands by his sides, standing as straight as a ramrod. The Belgian was lying face down in a pool of his own blood and vomit—Franklin shouted to one of the injured Americans to pull the man towards him and turn him over. But as the blood and vomit ran off his face, Franklin saw that the eyes were open and unblinking.

He was dead. The American let him fall back again, face down. One of the Englishmen, his right eye blue and closed by a deep cut above the cheekbone, shouted as a pole spun through the air like a boomerang and hit him squarely in the throat and he fell backwards across the dead Belgian.

Then Franklin heard it, distant but unmistakable above the screams of the crowds: automatic gunfire—long bursts, six guns, maybe more—coming from the direction of Al Ahsa Road where many of the American families lived. He heard a siren, more long bursts of firing, then three explosions. And then nothing. He looked across at the tall American holding on to the other corner of the truck, a man of about fifty. His head started to shake as if he was saying 'No' to himself a hundred times. Stones hit him and a bottle split his cheek, but still he stared in the direction of Al Ahsa and still he shook his head.

'You okay, fella?' Franklin shouted at him.

'My wife and kids,' he said, not looking back. 'Our house is there—'

But he didn't finish. Something crashed him backwards, so fast and so hard that he took another three men down on to the floor with him. Hanging from a first-floor window, a heavy wooden barrel swinging from a rope backwards and forwards had caught the American in the full force of its swinging arc, breaking his ribs and forcing them into his lungs. Franklin went down on is hands and knees and began to crawl towards him, but one of the Englishmen who had gone down in the fall waved him back and turned his thumb to the floor. The American's face had turned blue and thick blood splashed from his mouth. Then he slumped to one side and was still and the blood flow stopped just as abruptly.

Youths were now running alongside the trucks, hitting the knuckles of those who were holding on to the sides and throwing handfuls of wet camel dung up into their faces. Franklin saw that the people in the truck in front were covered in cow's offal emptied from the window over an abattoir. Other youths were throwing cow pats, sending the discs baked hard in the sun spinning through the air, cutting through clothes with edges as sharp and as hard as rock.

They were driven from the Khurays past the roundabout into the Al Islam Road and the last half mile of city streets. Soon they would be turning at the giant Petromin Building and out on to the desert road to the airport. One of the older Americans, who had been sitting on the floor half conscious, held his hand out to Franklin to pull him up. Then, holding on to Franklin with one hand and holding his jacket, now sodden with blood, to his head, his grey hair turned red, he began singing loudly. And one by one, as the rest in the truck heard the tune above the screaming Arabs they joined in, the Japanese road engineer happy to sing the only American song he knew.

'*Tom Brown's body lies a-mouldering in the grave.*
'*Tom Brown's body lies a-mouldering in the grave.*
'*Tom Brown's body lies a-mouldering in the grave.*
'*But his soul goes marching on.*'

'I'm sorry,' shouted the old American as they went into the chorus of 'Glory, Glory, Hallelujah', but it's the only song I know the words to.'

'Except 'God Bless America',' Franklin shouted back.

'No, sir,' he said, 'I couldn't reckon to finish that entirely and anyway, I'm not exactly in the right mood for Thanksgiving.'

They were into the seventeenth verse—the seventeenth

repetition of the same verse—when the truck, moving fast now along the desert road, suddenly veered left off the main tarmac into Riyadh International Airport, swung left again past the main terminal building, past the fire-damaged cargo sheds and on to the concrete of the parking apron. And then they saw them, eight massive Galaxies, brilliant white, the largest air transport jets in the world, parked in line facing out towards the runway.

The turbine blades were turning inside the giant cowls and there was a shimmer of heat above the wings. Over three thousand people had been organized into eight queues, one to each of the aircraft. Men, women and their children shuffled slowly forwards, dirty, forlorn and silent. None carried any baggage, though some had a pillow case or a plastic laundry bag tucked under their arms, filled with the few valuables they could find in the scramble from their homes, before the mobs destroyed whoever was white, and whatever was not of Islam.

The truck stopped just short of the nearest queue and the Saudi soldiers banged the trucks sides with their rifle butts. Children in the queue began to cry and their mothers covered them with their arms as American medical orderlies came running.

Franklin lay still in his bunk. Only the shudder of the aircraft rising into the sky disturbed him. There were tight straps across his chest and knees and the surgical spirit they had used to clean the cuts and grazes were stinging. In the bunk above him he could hear the Japanese engineer still humming quietly 'Tom Brown's Body' and someone, a man, was sobbing, in the bunk below. Franklin raised his head. The aircraft was packed with the refugees from Riyadh. They had arrived months, even years, before at the beginning of their various contracts in style and expectation. Men of the United States Military Command, come to introduce the Pentagon's newest and most sophisticated weaponry and train the Saudis how to protect their oil Kingdom. Civilian Americans and their families who had kept the oil flowing from subterranean Arabia. American security and communication instructors. Civilian non-Americans, who had come to build the roads, railways, the Royal palatial annexes and the government office towers, blocks of glass and mosaic tributes to architectural ego. Civil engineers from Britain whose irrigation projects had brought water where they had been none for hundreds of millions of years. Agriculturalists from Ireland who had grown rice in the sand where nothing in the history of the world had ever grown before. British and Canadian doctors repairing inflamed lungs, removing cataracts, restoring sight and hope in hospitals newly built by the West Germans. Men and their families turning a remote feudal desert Kingdom into a twentieth-century nation enabling eight million Arabs who had known nothing but disease, poverty and anonymity to join the ranks of the all-powerful. Eight aircraft, now flying high over the desert, were carrying these people away as discarded, disgraced and humiliated refugees, arbitarily punished by Islam, for talents and ambitions that were not of Islam.

Franklin rested his head back on the pillow. The medical orderly had given him a painkiller. He had said it would make him sleepy and already the noise and friction of the people around him were beginning to fade into soft echoes. He felt his body shrinking inside the stiff white sheets, and he could no longer feel the straps holding him down, holding him safe as the huge transport jet shuddered through the air turbulence. He closed his eyes and relaxed. It was all over, he whispered to himself, all over. But as he sank deeper into sleep, another part of him gently nudged and told him that perhaps it was really only just beginning.

The Galaxies levelled off at forty-one thousand feet and turned on to a new heading north-west. Below was the vast empty Great Nefud Desert of Saudi Arabia. Riyadh was already two hundred miles behind.

In one hour and ten minutes' time, the pilots would check the radio navigational beacon over the Gulf of Aqaba, Southern Jordan, then turn their aircraft due west across the Sinai Peninsula, across the Gulf of Suez and begin their descent into Cairo.

'The House in Bonngasse'

The little man stopped at the corner and waited for the last cars of the night to pass. It was bitterly cold but he was always telling people the desert was as cold at night as any German winter. He watched the wind spiral the snow through the yellow light of the shop windows. It stuck like glue to his coat and like ice to his eyebrows and beard. He had watched it from inside the taxi, flying at the windscreen, building up each side of the wipers until it reduced their sweeping arc and the taxi driver had stopped to scrape it away, using German words he had never heard before.

He would protest later at being dropped off here like this, alone in the snow, but the instructions over the telephone less than an hour ago had been explicit enough. 'Stand with your back to the Rathaus,' the voice had said, 'and face the Marktplatz. Look left. That is Wenzlegasse. Walk three blocks and turn into Friedrichstrasse. Go another fifty metres and Bonngasse is on the right. Number thirty-five is the old house, just down from Beethoven's.'

He remembered the German voice. 'Once you leave the Marktplatz we'll be around you. Our security. Not yours.'

The house in Bonngasse in the West German capital of Bonn had been famous once in its own small way, which had nothing to do with the nearness of Beethoven's birthplace.

Fifteen years ago, an enterprising local photographer walking past it during the first fall of snow early one December evening had seen its commercial potential. He borrowed a small fir tree in a tub, bought a large wreath of fir cones and holly which he tied with a red ribbon to the old oak door and, using his own floodlights, completed a dozen colour photographs. The snow that evening was deep and fresh and it covered the steep roof of number thirty-five like great soft rolls of white dough. He was well pleased with the effect.

Later, in his studio, he superimposed another print: a carol singer he'd photographed at Christmas the year before, a small girl complete with carol sheet, lantern, bobcap and scarf. He completed his Yuletide composition with a negative from his print library, one of the Icon of Christ on the Cross taken inside Bonn's Münster Cathedral.

This gleamed from the dark December sky above the snow-covered tiles of number thirty-five.

Suitably mounted, it earned him an immediate profit and a contract for it to be reprinted in its thousands as Christmas cards. For a while the seventeenth-century house in Bonngasse, one of the very few escapees of the Allied bomber blitz, was famous and people came to take their own snaps. It became almost a place of pilgrimage, though visitors left disappointed because number thirty-five looked drab without the snow, without the holly and the red ribbon, without the little caroller and Christ in the dark December sky watching her. It looked vulgar in daylight, wedged between a sex shop and a coin-operated washerette, facing a used-car lot.

No one ever discovered the little girl's name, despite searches by national model agencies, but as it happened she later became very well-known in West Germany. This, however, had nothing to do with singing or Christmas or Christ. The pretty child grew up with a fierce dedication to international anarchy and the ability to kill very efficiently in its cause. She was also extremely lithe, with a body and a face men considered beautiful and desirable.

Anna Birgit Schneider joined the Baader-Meinhoff terrorists late. Already Fraulein Ulrike Meinhoff had killed herself in defeat in her solitary confinement cell. And Andreas Baader and his mistress Gudrin Ensslin had followed with double suicides in Stammheim. Anna Schneider then joined Verone Becker, Jorg Kranz, Wolfgang Hüber and Hanna-Glise Krobbe, collectively known as the Red Army Faction, a confused, desperate and lethal gang of young middle-class anarchists.

For more than a year, Anna's identity and membership of the Red Army Faction was not known to the West German police. She had grown up in a middle-class, inconspicuous district of Bonn, respectably, as befits the only daughter of widower Johann Schneider, Doctor of Medicine. Her lack of a police record was valuable to those in charge of the Red Army Faction who were working on the inside of it and to those lawyers and other young anonymous professionals promoting its aims on the outside. Schneider was used as a go-between, crossing international borders freely, carrying passports, letters, poisons, munitions, replacement spares for the Red Army's weapons, from one underground cell to another. And returning cash to the suppliers.

But the job as courier was frustrating to the young ambitious Anna. It was not enough for her to be assistant in the organisation. She was twenty-two years old and desperate for terrorist activity.

Her opportunity came on the fourteenth of July, 1979. Three Red Army members preparing to leave their apartment in the dock area of Hamburg to rob the Deutsche Bank in Jungfernsteg came face to face with three men of the Zielfahndung GS10, the West German Police Target Squad, who shot the three young terrorists—two boys and a girl—through their faces at a range of two metres as they left the front door of their hideaway, their weapons still in their holdalls. The sudden deaths were a great encouragement to the West German counter-terrorist units and a blow to the Red Army, but the bank had still to be robbed and three replacements were quickly assembled. Anna Schneider, caressing her newly-acquired Tokarev pistol, was one. Seven hundred thousand Deutschmarks were taken from the cashiers but then, even though the two others were on their way out of the front door, Anna shot dead two of the cashiers and a mother and her child lying face down on the floor. And she dropped her father's visiting-card by the bodies. Never again would she spend her time carrying messages. As of that day, in that one obscene act of terror, she became West Germany's most wanted terrorist and—in the logic of terrorism—the Red Army's most prized possession.

She had now come to thirty-five Bonngasse, but for one evening only. Fifteen years before, she had collected dozens of the famous Christmas cards and so had her father; it had been their secret. If Anna now recognized the house, she did not show it. She sat on the bare, stained mattress in the bedroom on the first floor, a sleeping-bag tied up to her waist to keep her warm, polishing her small black Tokarev pistol with a piece of muttoncloth. Anna Schneider, now twenty-seven years old, graduate of Leipzig University, disciple of Marcuse, Guevara, Morighelles and Habash, was waiting for a knock on the street door, a loud knock. She was waiting for someone who could tell her about a place called Ullswater in what was known as the Lake District of northern England, where King Fahd of Saudi Arabia was staying and where he was to be assassinated.

Schneider took off her gloves and from the breast pocket of her anorak pulled out a small silencer, screwed it carefully on to the barrel of the gun, placed the pistol on her lap, covered it with the sleeping-bag and waited for the Arab.

At that moment, three thousand miles away East in the Persian Gulf, an assault ship of the United States Navy began to change course in a slow three-mile-wide turning circle. Men aboard shielded their eyes from the low yellowing evening sun and felt the coolness on their faces as they turned into the breeze. The USS *Okinawa*, seventeen-thousand-ton veteran, had completed its goodwill visit to the Gulf and was obeying a signal from the US Naval Headquarters in the Pentagon, Washington, to make a new course south east, out of the Persian Gulf through the Strait of Hormuz, into the Gulf of Oman and the Arabian Sea.

'They're trying another Cuba'

Their faces were green and blank and entirely without contour, lacking the third dimension. Their eyes were wide and unblinking as if witnessing some dreadful evil.

The room was dark except for the luminous glare of the radar screens. It was also hot and humid, and the green faces glistened with sweat. The low hum of the ship's generators was the only sound.

The five men stood still. Occasionally one would ease his weight from one foot to the other, or lean forward to see the tiny moving blobs as the radar scanners swept clockwise around their dials, and each man in turn, every few minutes or so, would check his own wristwatch against the quartz digital above the main radar consul.

All five wore the light khaki uniforms of officers of the United States Navy—tropical dress—short-sleeved shirts, open necks. They stood in line behind the radar operators, or rather they stood at a slight angle, one slightly behind the other, as if service discipline made it necessary to stand a half-step behind one's superior officer, it being assumed leadership meant always being a half a step ahead.

Captain Edward James Hanks therefore stood furthest forward, nearest the radar screens. He had been in command of the *Okinawa* for nine and a half years and it was his last sea command. In four months' time he would take shore-leave and then a posting to Annapolis Naval College, Maryland pending his retirement from the US Navy, after forty-two years in the service. Life had come full circle. He had been fresh out of Annapolis on his first overseas posting as a ensign aboard the *West Virginia* and had come as close as he had ever been to losing his sea-legs and his life when a Japanese Nakajima torpedo-bomber took the side out of the bunk-room as he was sleeping off a night watch at Ford Island, Pearl Harbor.

Captain Hanks survived four years of the war in the Pacific. He was junior Gunnery Officer aboard the carrier *Yorktown*, had taken shrapnel in his back during the battle of the Midway and was with the *Enterprise* when McClusky went after Yamamoto. He wore the Navy Cross, the Silver Star, the Bronze Star, the Navy Achievement Medal and a breastful more.

He took command of the *Okinawa* in February, 1975, two months before the fall of Saigon. It was from this twenty-one-year-old assault ship he'd been given, forty miles out in the South China Sea, that task force helicopters took off for the US Embassy to bring refugees from defeated South Vietnam back aboard, thousands of Vietnamese who filled the *Okinawa* from bow to stern—living in their own stench and urine in the semi-dark of the hangars sixty feet below sea level as the ship steamed slowly to the Philippines and the promised New World beyond that.

Captain Hanks could still smell them, even though the hangars had been steamhosed and disinfected many times over since. On tropical nights, when the air maintenance crews opened the doors to the liftshafts going down from the carrier's deck and the air was still and warm, Captain Hanks could smell the stench rising and he would not eat his food and would refuse his coffee, and he would stand on the bridge in silence holding a clean white handkerchief soaked in aftershave to his nose.

And if a sudden breeze should come off the sea, Captain Hanks would hear coming up through the liftshafts the screams of young women, the coughs of consumptive old men and the cries of orphaned babies, and he would leave the bridge suddenly and go to his cabin to escape the ghosts of that miserable human cargo of that miserable American war.

Captain Hanks had many strange ways. His officers said he had been too long at sea and had survived more than his fair share of it, though it was not something he would admit to himself or hear from others.

His daily cliché was 'Workhorses are sent out to graze too early'—a reference, in case any one of his officers should forget, that he was only fifty-five years old, fit and with experience at sea second to none. And yet, despite it, he was being sent ashore before his time. The prospect had been with him all his sea life, yet it had always seemed so distant. Retirement was for old men, and he was not old.

It was the day he received the signal from Norfolk Virginia, telling him the date of the *Okinawa*'s scrapping that Captain Hanks suddenly realized it would soon all be over. According to successive medical examinations, he had been told he could expect to live another twenty years at least—and he knew that meant twenty years on land, alone.

He had never married and he had been an only son, so there were no nephews, no nieces, no grandchildren. Forty-two years in the service and never in one place long enough for a man so introverted to have time enough to make a friend. Not one. Without his ship, Captain Hanks would be on his own. Already he felt retired, and more and more he retreated into the past. He would stand silently on *Okinawa*'s bridge, and relive Pearl Harbor, and the Japanese KATE's divebombing that early December Sunday morning. Sometimes he would touch the shrapnel scars at the base of his back, tracing the ridges of thick skin of the badly sewn-up wounds, and remember the *Yorktown* lurching with the shock of the torpedo blasts and seeing his own blood mingling with the ship's oil as he floundered half-conscious in the water.

And that glorious morning in June as he had watched Lt Commander McClusky take off from the deck of the carrier *Enterprise* to attack Yamamoto's fleet. He remembered it all so fondly, those first days of victory in the Midway and the glory that attached itself to every man who fought there. Captain Hanks wore his service ribbons proudly and in these silent moods of remembrance and depression he would finger them, each one a separate gilt chapter of his long sea life.

The *Okinawa* had been anchored for three days off the Island of Bahrain as part of a 'showing-the-flag' tour of the Gulf states. The ship had been to Kuwait and was now sailing south-east to move through the narrow Straits of Hormuz into the Gulf of Oman for a two-day stay at the friendly port of Muscat. Captain Hanks would then take the carrier into the Arabian Sea, sailing further south into the India Ocean for a visit to Berbera in Somalia and on to Mombasa on the Kenyan coast. Then he would move into the commercial shipping lanes, past Madagascar, around the tip of South Africa at the Cape of Good Hope and into the Southern Atlantic. Then to the west coast of Africa and the Gulf of Guinea for a stop at Monrovia in Liberia. Finally he would head his ship due west for the final three thousand five hundred miles of Atlantic crossing to Newport, Norfolk Virginia, to the scrapyard of his career.

He watched the sweeping arm of the radar scanner pick up the small blobs and smear them as it swept on. In the last twenty minutes he had been in the operations room they had not seemed to move, but the radar operator sitting in front of him reported they had travelled one hundred and twenty-five nautical miles since they had first appeared during the night watch.

'Heading three hundred and fifteen degrees.'

'Bastards.'

'Sir?'

'I said bastards, coming this close at this time. Simple provocation.'

'But we're here, sir.'

Captain Hanks knew Lieutenant Ginsberg to be a Jew, a liberal and provocative, and he ignored him.

'I mean maybe they're coming, sir, because we're here,'

said Ginsberg, but the Captain still did not answer.

The dots on the screen had become more distinctive now, showing the formation of a triangle, the apex forward, each dot a similar distance from the next.

'Still eighteen knots?'

'Yes, Captain. Bearing and speed constant.'

'Assume they're making for Hormuz. How soon?'

'One moment, sir.' The radar operator reached across with his right hand and began typing on the keys of the computer. Almost immediately the answer showed up in red digits on the computer screen for everyone to see. Calculating that speed and bearing remained constant and predicting tide and wind change, the Soviet Seventh Fleet, led by the aircraft carrier *Minsk*—thirty-eight thousand tons and the pride of the Soviet Navy—accompanied by the thirteen-thousand ton assault ship *Ivan Rogov* and a flotilla of twenty other warships of various tonnage and capability, would be crossing the Tropic of Cancer and beginning their turn towards the Strait of Hormuz and the Persian Gulf in nine hours and ten minutes time.

Captain Hanks swore. 'Fucking provocation. With a rebellion going full steam in Saudi Arabia, and sending them in here now. Sheer goddamned fucking provocation.'

Lieutenant Vaduz, *Okinawa*'s Communications Officer, coughed. 'The latest satellite surveillance, sir, confirms twenty-two vessels. They're photo-wiring the pictures at this time, sir.'

'It's not photographs I need, Mr Vaduz, it's an order. I know what the mother-fuckers look like. In nine hours I'll be surrounded by twenty-two Russian warships and I want to know in good time—good time, mind you—what I'm expected to do.'

'We must assume, sir,' said Lieutenant Ginsberg, 'that they mean to anchor somewhere in the south of the Gulf. There's nothing north for them. So to avoid confrontation we need only change course a few degrees south.'

'You assume, Mr Ginsberg?' said Captain Hanks through his teeth. 'Only a few degrees south, for Christ-sake? I am here on a goodwill visit, a peaceable tour and well advertised as such. I have my signal to exit and I have set my course and I do not intend to change my mind or my bearing, if there were a hundred Soviet ships out there!'

'The *Minsk* is equipped with torpedoes, and Forger vertical take-offs, sir, and the *Ivan Rogov* has a battalion strength of Marines aboard with support helos and Sam-2 or Sam-4 missiles.'

'Why do you pick this exact moment to tell me that, Mr Vaduz? You assume I know nothing about two of the best ships in the enemy's navy?'

'With respect, sir, I simply remind you that this is the largest and best equipped naval task force the Soviets have ever sent to the Persian Gulf.'

'And?'

'Well, sir, according to my logs on all signals received from SATCOM, three days ago the *Minsk* and the *Ivan Rogov* were refuelling at Aden, South Yemen.'

'For warm-water exercises in the Gulf of Oman,' said Captain Hanks. 'So?'

'Sir, if the computer prediction is correct, they must have been ordered to leave their exercise area fourteen hours ago, which means—'

'Which means,' interrupted Commander Daniels, *Okinawa*'s Executive Officer, 'that the Soviet Seventh Fleet was ordered to the Persian Gulf before the Saudi coup had begun.'

The Captain's eyes narrowed as he absorbed the arithmetic and its implications. The arms of the radar sweep on the green screens had made another seven turns before he spoke again, and so slowly and so softly that the officers at his side had to lean forward to hear and wonder later whether they had heard it correctly.

'They're trying another Cuba,' he said. 'On another Kennedy. By Christ they are. And this time they may even make it.'

'One helluva story'

It was 87 degrees Fahrenheit and still Egyptian women covered them in blankets and forced hot cups of coffee into their hands. Egyptian immigration officials demanded passports from the sick on stretchers, ignoring the shouts from the American medical orderlies to let them be. The tired, the injured, the frightened and the wounded who had arrived in Cairo aboard the USAF Galaxies, sedated and comfortable, were suddenly confused and in pain again. Walking wounded sat down in one place and were asked to move to another only to be moved on again. A stretcher was put down in one corner of the airport arrivals hall and seconds later picked up and put somewhere else. There were a dozen different men in a dozen different uniforms and each was in charge. An American stood on a chair and shouted out names and instructions to American citizens but no one could hear him and the tension and anxiety increased so that women suddenly screamed and sat on the floor and sobbed as their children lost themselves, and scattered across the hall. Men wandered in no particular direction hoping to be stopped and told what to do and where to go, and the sick on the stretchers stared at the ceiling and at nothing as flies settled on the caked blood of their bandages. And all the time the women of the Egyptian Red Cross put their blankets around hot and sweating bodies and held scalding mugs of coffee to broken parched lips.

Franklin sat by the air conditioning unit. The cuts in his head and face had been cleaned again with new dressings but the after-effects of the painkillers given him aboard the evacuation plane had made him dizzy and every now and then he could feel his gorge rise. He had to stand up and walk some yards then sit again as his legs began to shake. He watched Egyptian immigration officers stand on the seats shouting out passport numbers and names.

'Franklin?'

The man went down on one knee close to him and held out the slim green American passport. A second man stood behind him.

'You Franklin?

'That's right.'

'*New York Times*?'

'That's me.'

'I have a letter for you. It's a kinda introduction.'

'From New York?'

'From Washington.'

Franklin looked up. The man was dressed in a lightweight wash'nwear tan suit. His face was the same colour. The man behind him could have been his brother. Franklin took the envelope, held it up to the light to see the shadow outline of the letter inside and tore open the end. He pulled out a single sheet of paper, headed United States Cairo Embassy. It was from the State Director of the Washington Bureau.

> 'Glad you are out. Good rovers never die, they say. The Mid East has gone sour and our advice too lately accepted. It's now spreading and need immediate conversation with you so call me from Embassy soonest. Cheaney will explain. Regards, Heinzerling.'

Franklin held out his hand and the man helped him up. 'You Cheaney?' And the man nodded.

'You've something to tell me?'

'Sure,' said Cheaney. 'We have a car for you. Let's talk on the way to the Embassy. This is Joe.'

'They always are.'

Joe smiled back.

'Can I get a shower?'

'Sure. Just about everything here my friend, except tail, but I reckon we could manage that at a push. D'you know Joe here tells me he can even get pretzels nowadays. Can you imagine pretzels in Cairo? They'll be selling baskets of fruit for Yomtov next.' He grinned. He had a fat shiny face as if it had been regularly polished and small bullet eyes deep set and green. His paunch fell over his trousers. Joe ate pretzels. Cheaney looked as if he was fond of Budweisers.

'I'd be happy,' said Franklin, 'with a shower and a change of clothes. And perhaps a quick call home.'

'You betcha,' said Cheaney. 'Joe here will look after everything. Leave it to him.' Joe smiled again, the same broad grin on the same fat, polished face.

Joe manoeuvred the black Embassy Chevrolet through the mass of bodies in the road outside the arrivals hall. Passengers hauled luggage away from porters, taxi drivers hawked their girlfriends, tin-chinking beggars masqueraded as totally blind and terribly crippled. He swung the car through a gate marked in English 'SECURITY AREA. NO ENTRY' then through another with the same sign, halting only for a moment as the red and white painted barrier was raised by a saluting security guard. Then on to the tarmac of the apron, within fifty yards of the refuelling Galaxies, past the cargo shed and a sudden right turn on to the main Cairo road. Joe knew the airport, and the airport security men knew the Chevrolet.

'You know the President's going to make a speech?' Cheaney asked. He lit a Camel cigarette and handed it to Franklin.

Franklin inhaled and then filled the car with heavy purplish smoke.

'Yes?' he said, inhaling once more. 'Be one helluva lot of bullshit.'

'Maybe,' said Cheaney.

'Five months in office and already playing the odds.'

'Finding his feet, perhaps,' said Cheaney.

'He reckons the Saudis are going to be frightened off? Who's advising him?'

'Who's advising the Saudis?'

'Meaning?'

'Somebody is. This Rahbar guy is not doing this on his own.'

There was a pause before either man spoke again.

'How much does the Agency know?' Franklin turned in his seat to face Cheaney.

'We're still struggling, but it's piecing together. One helluva jig-saw, though.'

'How much d'you know?' Franklin asked again.

'We know who started the coup. We know that Ghaddaffi did the footwork and we think we've got most of the names who met at that hotel in Baghdad. What we don't know is which one of them is working for Moscow. Do you?'

Franklin drew on the cigarette again and Cheaney's fat face, wet and shining now with sweat, was hidden for a moment in the smoke.

'Yesterday, Cheaney, I had an audience with the King. The Agency had given the Saudis my cover, so he called me in. He was a very worried man.'

'That OPEC planned Rahbar's coup?'

'Yes.'

'But that it really wasn't OPEC? That somebody else was behind it?'

'That's right.'

'Who?'

'Karim, Iraq's defence minister. He's been with the KGB since 1962. It's been Moscow's idea for a long time. Suddenly they found a way using Ghaddaffi. They had a man in Lagos who's been pushing the Nigerians. Same in Caracas. It's a big operation, Cheaney. They've been working on this for years. They knew Afghanistan was as near as the limit of their confrontation. From then on in it had to be done underground. Iran, Oman, Iraq, Saudi Arabia, working from the inside out. But the Royals had Saudi Arabia all tied up and Moscow couldn't find a way in, until the Crown Prince became an Islamic freak.' Franklin then repeated what Fahd had told him.

Twenty minutes later Cheaney said, 'You got all this from Fahd?'

'A couple of hours before the start. The first rockets hit the place about midday.'

'How did he get it so wrong?'

'Wrong?'

'So late. How come he knew all this but didn't splash it sooner? Expose them?'

'Very simple, Cheaney. So simple it breaks your heart. He got his timing wrong. His family had been in charge for so long they reckoned they controlled time. His service reports were coming in, intelligence was being slowly put together, the fingers were being pointed. Fahd thought he would choose the time when he would come down on them and wipe them out. He got it wrong. He was behind time, not in charge of it.'

Cheaney lit another cigarette, took the half-smoked one from Franklin and gave him a fresh one.

'You always so agreeable, Cheaney?' But Cheaney didn't answer. For a minute or more he looked ahead, over Joe's shoulder, his chubby face lit up by oncoming car headlamps. Then he turned in his seat and faced Franklin.

'You heard of Schneider? Anna Birgit Schneider?'

'Sure. West German. Red Army.'

'Ever seen her?'

'No.'

Cheaney touched his arm. 'She's on her way to kill Fahd.'

Franklin drew on the cigarette. It was too strong and was beginning to make him feel sick again. Some miles ahead he could see Cairo, the city's lights reflected in the pollution haze, hanging over it like a low yellow cloud.

'Is Schneider on her own?'

'We don't know,' said Cheaney. 'If we did we'd be halfway there already.'

'And where are you exactly?'

'Nowhere, Franklin. Shit scared and nowhere.'

'Where is Fahd?'

'England. Somewhere north called the Lake District.'

'So why the Agency? It's a British problem.'

'Wrong, Matt. It's everybody's problem, but most especially it's an American problem. Director Johns wants Fahd back in Saudi Arabia and he wants him back there quickly.

'Johns is mad. If he understood anything about that country he wouldn't bother. The King's gone, like the Shah, like King Farouk, like King George out of Boston. There's been a special revolution with some very special backers and Johns mustn't imagine we can pull the strings any more. Rahbar is not Thieu or Lon Nol or anyone of the Agency's puppets. Fahd has lost. So have we. It's history. Rahbar and his Revolutionary Council have taken over and there's nothing Johns or the President of the United States can do about it.'

'Wrong again, Matt. There's a lot the President can do, you can bet on it. And there's a lot he will do. None of us know exactly what, but we're guessing and the prospects are bright. What we do know for sure is that getting Fahd back on his throne is vital to whatever the President has in mind. You wait for his speech.'

'I said it'd be bullshit.'

Cheaney leant forward in his seat, rested his elbows on his knees and clasped his hands so that the tips of his fingers touched his nose. For a moment Franklin thought he might be praying.

Then he said quietly. 'Let me tell you about Schneider.'

'Not for publication?'

'Most certainly not for publication. In this car, Matt, you're an Agency man—but we'll talk about that later.' He lit another cigarette and wound down his window and threw out the match. A narrow blast of warm air hit them.

He said, 'West German police in Bonn have picked up the body of an Arab. Shot once in the head at close range.

Through the left ear. Seems he once worked for the Saudi Embassy in Bonn as a cypher clerk and got fired for drugs four months ago. The Germans found him by a fluke. He had been dumped inside a mould for one of the concrete supports of a new building, but there was bad frost overnight and the workmen had to break open the scaffolding because the cement had cracked. The Arab fell out.'

'The Saudis sacked him four months ago and he was still in Bonn?'

'Yes.'

'Schneider's bullet?'

'Yes.'

'How can you be sure? A cypher clerk with info is dangerous on the loose, especially one on dope. Could be the Saudis.'

'No,' said Cheaney. 'That's what the Germans thought at first until their ballistics checked the bullet. It was from a Tokarev 762. It's the one Schneider uses. There's a defect on the ejector. Leaves a scar on the shell. The one in the Arab's head matched others they'd had from Schneider's gun. Same scar.'

'Cheaney,' said Franklin. 'Why are you telling me this? Why am I interested in a German terrorist who kills an unimportant Arab?'

'Not unimportant, Matt. He'd been fired for drugs and for sure he ought to have been back home. But instead he's been selling information and codes to anyone who wanted them, including the East German Abteilung and the KGB. The fact he was killed by Schneider means the Red Army made contact for a special bit of information.'

'About Fahd?'

'About Fahd.'

'He knew where the King had gone?'

'He knew that if he went to England he'd go to his Lake District hideaway.'

'How would he know?'

'He worked in cyphers, and he was into traffic between Riyadh and Europe, particularly between Riyadh and London, so he knew government interests there, especially the King's. When Khalid bought his estate in the Lake District, he ordered a complete security checkout and turned it into a fortress. Now, most of the detailed plans went in the diplomatic pouch; but later alterations, and the King's changes of mind, were passed on to the London Embassy by coded telex and he was clever enough to know their value. He took photostats of those telexes and when he was fired he kept his cypher book. It's all been changed since, but whoever shot him has the photostats and the cypher decode book. And knows the layout of Fahd's little fortress.'

'Schneider will kill Fahd?'

'Without him the Saudi Royal Family stand no chance of a comeback and Rahbar is safe. That's contrary to our plan. 'We've got to get the King back on his throne—for reasons I don't know about yet—but he's vital, absolutely vital to us.'

'Cheaney,' said Franklin. 'I think you'd better know that—'

'Another thing,' interrupted Cheaney. 'We reckon Schneider's already on her way, probably via Greece and Italy. Security's lax at those places and she'll try and slip through. Again, she may want us to think exactly that and fly direct to London. There are a dozen routes she could take and I wouldn't bank on us stopping her at any of them.'

'Cheaney—'

'Let me finish. We—that's you and us—have one thing going for us. Schneider speaks English with a strong accent; and, okay, so do a million Germans in and out of London. But she has a new scar, the West Germans are convinced of it. They had a shoot-out with her last September in Leipzig. They don't think they hit her, but they did hit a doorframe where she was standing. Took out a large piece of wood. They found a long splinter, covered in blood, from the doorframe taken out about shoulder-neck level. Their forensic said there were no cloth fibres in the splinter, just tears of skin, which convinces them that she was torn in open flesh and the wound will show, possibly her face or neck, and on her left side. A bad gash. So we're looking for a tall thin blonde German who speaks like Mai Zetterling with a scar and carries a Tokarev 762.'

'That's all, Cheaney?'
'For the time being.'
'You want me to find Schneider?'
'No. There are a few thousand police doing that. We want you to go to Fahd.'
'Why me? I'm not a regular. I'm not even Security.'
'It's got to be you. The Brits can cope but the Director wants our own man on the inside. He's got a plan. You get it later, but you're very much part of it.'
'I said why me? You've got a thousand younger, better-trained regulars, so why push me in?'
'Fahd has met you. He likes you. Better, he trusts you. He won't take anyone else, not someone he doesn't know, not at a time like this. It's got to be you.
Franklin shook his head slowly. Then he stubbed the cigarette on the heel of his shoe and let it fall on the carpet.
'Have you explained all this to the *New York Times* or have you just put my name in the obituaries? Christ! D'you think I can just wander off—'
'Listen. You're not the only thing that's going for us, but you are one of them. Your paper knows nothing yet, but we'll give them something—a medical report—saying you've gotta be kept under medical surveillance, best attention, not terminal. We'll have something for them, don't worry.'
'You reckon they'll swallow that crap? They'll expect to hear from me.'
'They will. You can file to them tonight out of the Embassy We'll see it first, of course.'
Franklin began to laugh quietly, which made Joe in the front seat look back over his shoulder.
'You want fat and flabby Franklin who hasn't seen action or anything like it in years to go chase Mai . . .'
'Before she kills King Fahd.'
'You know Cheaney, it's guys like you that give the CIA a bad name. Okay, so it's not you, it's Washington. So I blame Heinzerling, and he blames Johns. Now you just telephone one of them and tell them that I'm leaving here all right, but not for London and wherever the goddamned Lake District

is. I'm catching Pan-Am to New York, and if you want me after that you'll have to send a snowman to get me out of New Hampshire. I'm back in the news trade, Cheaney, and I'm staying there. You just tell them that.'

Franklin sat back and let his head fall against the cushioned headrest. He stared at the patterns made by the oncoming car headlamps on the vinyl roof lining. Then he closed his eyes and thought of a shower, and a shave and clean clothes. And then perhaps a steak from the Embassy freezer. Then file. Then sleep. And no dreams.

'Franklin.'

'Forget it, Cheaney, I'm not listening.'

'Then hear this. Heinzerling told me to tell you something just in case our conversation went the wrong way.'

'Not the wrong way, Cheaney. The only way.'

'He said that if you let the Agency down, he'll blow your cover with your paper. He'll blow it to the Correspondents Association. You'll never work again. You'd be disgraced. That's what Heinzerling said.'

Franklin kept his eyes closed. In the blackness there was suddenly a ball of red, like a revolving meteor that was coming away at the edges as it spun, tiny bits of matter exploding in the blackness. Then it spun out of the corner of his eye and just as suddenly he was standing on Brooklyn Bridge and the steel girders were flashing brilliantly. Through the steel mesh he saw a raft floating downstream, then the raft became a Swiss flag and, huddled on it, the Swiss father, mother and children from Riyadh. They waved, and he opened his eyes and the car was passing through the iron gates of the American Embassy and into the floodlit compound. The car doors were opened each side by tall white-capped Marines in white gloves who saluted as Cheaney got out.

'Take it easy, Matt,' he said. 'Easy. I've got to get through to Washington. Tell them all you've told me. Joe here'll get that call to the *New York Times* for you, just as soon as you've had a wash-up. We'll get you through as fast as we can. Christ! You've got one helluva story to tell them. One helluva story.'

'When the chips are down'

The President jogged until eight, took a cold shower, and in his blue towelling dressing-gown breakfasted on grapefruit and yoghurt.

By eight forty-five he had shaved and dressed and sat on the terrace of Aspen Lodge drinking his second pot of black bitter sugarless coffee. He looked out across the lawns towards the copse of brown and orange maples. The overnight frost had covered the ground in a thin skin of white, and he watched a couple of woodcock beyond the gravel path tugging at a thin crust of toast one of the security men had thrown to them. Beyond them, as the lawns sloped away, he could see squirrels sitting on their haunches peering back.

Camp David, perched high on the Catactin range of mountains in the State of Maryland, is thirty minutes' flying time by Presidential helicopter from the White House. It is where American Presidents traditionally go in retreat, sometimes to escape political blunders, often to pause and prepare political offensives. It is a luxury estate made entirely of local wood stained in various shades of browns and greens, set in twenty acres of electrified wire-enclosed woodland. Here the air is clear and clean. Here a man can believe he has vision.

The President had made a private departure from Washington and flown in just after midnight. Instead of taking off from the helipad in the White House grounds, in full view of the press who worked in shifts like sentries watching every coming and going, the President and three of his security staff had driven out of the staff gate in a Volkswagen Beetle belonging to someone in the typing pool. Then over the Potomac using the 14th Street Bridge, past the Jefferson Memorial to the busy and anonymous helipad at National Airport. The President, all enquirers were later told, was working in his private rooms and could not be disturbed.

The ruse was necessary. The American and International news media had been placated by Press Secretary Peter Schlesinger's initial press release, quickly followed up by a television briefing to two hundred accredited journalists inside the White House by Foreign Affairs spokesman Tom Sorenson. But there were pressmen with a nose for the impending, who smelt something bigger on the way, and those who had followed the President's career for twenty years and more thought they knew what it might be. So it would not have been wise for the President to be seen flying to Camp David because Camp David spelt crisis and crisis and an hysterical press were something the President had to avoid.

He had this one December day to prepare. The Generals had convinced him it could be done, and Sorenson had endorsed his own fears of what would happen if they didn't take the initiative, and take it quickly. The phrase the oil boffin Professor Grüber had used in that first briefing in the Oval Office kept repeating itself in his mind. He had gone to sleep with it. He had woken up and it was still there. 'Oil now has a greater power potential than the entire American Military because without it there is no American Military.'

Units of the Rapid Deployment Force were ready, waiting for his order to go. What he had to do now was to sell it to the country.

He turned to the sound of footsteps on the gravel path.

'Hey, Peter, I didn't hear you come down.'

'Morning, Mr President. We landed way over there.

Didn't want to disturb you.' The Press Secretary, Peter Schlesinger, came on to the terrace.

'You can take it from me,' said the President, 'that I've been disturbed for a day now and I'm likely to remain that way for some days to come.' He poured himself more black coffee. 'Want some?'

'No, thank you, sir.'

'What you got?'

'You're booked nationwide, live tonight. The Nets are satelliting direct to Eurovision and to Asia. Moscow will take it off the European feed. They'll be seeing you late by their time, but we'll warn them through a Priority Release your Address to the Nation is of major importance.'

'Don't overplay it. Sorenson's right. We've got to appear as if we're only just realizing how few options we have left.'

'I understand.'

'You've booked me after the news shows?'

'Yessir. If we went on before them we'd face immediate reaction, immediate analysis, and inevitable criticism. This way they'll have to wait.'

The President heard more feet. It was his secretary, Mrs Baines, who would type the speech and speechwriter Theodore Austin who would help him write it.

'Morning everybody', the President said. 'I've got a message. Is anyone going to help me deliver it?'

'Morning, Mr President,' the two answered together. As the president rose and they followed him from the terrace into the study they found the housekeeper already lighting a fire.

The early morning sunlight from the east was being overtaken by grey clouds coming from the north-west and with them the beginning of a wind. A gust caught one of the woodcocks unawares, throwing it off balance as the other took the crust of toast and disappeared quickly up into the trees. The squirrels were already back in their boltholes in the oaks, and the boughs of the maples and chestnuts shook and carpeted the groundfrost with leaves.

Within ten minutes each of the three new arrivals to Aspen Lodge had gone to their separate rooms to resolve their separate problems. The President was alone at his desk, sideways to the log fire, facing the windows that looked out across the terrace and the lawns. In front of him, neatly laid out on the desk, were the transcripts brought by speechwriter Austin, transcripts selected by him of all the most famous and most persuasive of Presidential speeches over the past forty years: Roosevelt, Eisenhower, Kennedy, Johnson, Nixon and Carter. All the speeches had a common denominator, what Austin had called their 'spirit'. The President looked at each title in turn, the dates, the subject matter. They were all crisis speeches. Roosevelt's 'Four Freedoms' speech enticing the American people to go to war against the Nazis. Eisenhower's January 1961 speech on his retirement, warning the free world of new Communist aggression. John Kennedy on Berlin and Cuba. Lyndon Johnson on widening the Vietnam war, Nixon on getting deeper into that war by bombing Haiphong, and on getting out again leaving the South to its despair. And Carter's State of the Union address in February 1980 on Soviet aggression in Afghanistan.

The only one missing, he thought, was the Gettysburg Address. He picked up the red pencil Austin had brought with him. 'Ring what you like,' Austin had said, 'even if it's only a word. Write in the margins, an idea or a paraphrase. They are model speeches, and they did the trick, did what they were supposed to do at the moment they were delivered. They won over a suspicious America, and granted to each President separate permission to move in the direction he wanted to go.'

The President did not question his speechwriter. Austin knew his business well enough. He had worked magic for lesser men in less plausible causes at less critical times, and anyway, if the President had any doubts, he had to forget them. He couldn't possibly write the speech himself.

He pencilled a line under Roosevelt's '. . . those who would give up essential liberty to purchase a little temporary safety deserve neither liberty nor safety.' It was short but powerful, and captured the spirit as no other had done until J. F. Kennedy had come along.

He dropped it on the floor by the desk and began thumbing through Eisenhower. '. . . throughout America's adventure in free government, our basic purposes have been to keep the peace and foster progress in human achievements.' Five minutes later Eisenhower was lying on Roosevelt.

Then he reached for Lyndon Johnson, defending the use of B-52 bombers on Hanoi—the first time since Korea that American warplanes had been used against another nation. 'We must stop Communist aggression,' he had said, 'before it stops us. And ask yourselves what kind of world are we prepared to live in in five months or five years from tonight?'

A good speech, delivered with all of Johnson's melodrama. But it had done the trick. It won over a suspicious America.

Johnson followed Eisenhower and Roosevelt on to the carpet and the President reached across the desk for the transcripts marked John F. Kennedy. He smoothed out the paper and ran the tip of the red pencil slowly along the famous Kennedy lines. 'Ask not what America can do for you. Rather ask what you can do for America.'

He ringed boldly in red '. . . the United States cannot tolerate deception or threats from any nation, large or small . . . let every nation know we shall pay any price . . . bear any burden . . . for the survival and success of liberty.'

The President shuffled the Kennedy transcripts together and he placed them back on the desk to the right of the last transcript marked Richard Nixon.

He picked up the Nixon transcript and saw that speechwriter Austin had already ringed some passages. On part of a television address on Nixon's reasons for going into Cambodia to attack the Ho Chi Minh trail, Austin had ringed in red twice and had written, 'This is it.' The President read:

'If, when the chips are down, the world's most powerful nation acts like a pitiful helpless giant . . . all other nations will be on notice that, despite its overwhelming power, when the real crisis comes the United States will be found wanting.'

It was ten minutes past twelve. The President had been through the speeches and had drafted his own simple outline. Austin would add to this all the relevant data concerning oil imports and energy prospects given him by Professor Grüber. Austin would then write the first draft adapted to the President's vernacular, making it the President's own. When corrections and modifications had been finalized, the President would deliver it in front of the mirror above the fireplace, watching himself as Schlesinger and Austin watched him, correcting faulty intonation or over-emphasis, or an important line not stressed enough, until they were satisfied. Then the President would speak it uninterrupted into a small pocket tape recorder and, during his after-lunch walk in the garden, he would listen to his own voice through the tiny earpiece clipped to the lobe of his ear. He would hear himself a dozen times over until he was confident enough to speak it out loud repeating word for word what he heard in his ear, following exactly its speed and style. This was how he would deliver his address to the nation tonight. It would appear unprompted and spontaneous for maximum effect.

The speech would be beamed live from one satellite twenty-two thousand miles high in space to the next, across the Atlantic to the European capitals and to Moscow, across the Indian Ocean and the Pacific to Peking. By ten minutes past seven, Central Eastern Time, the President's ultimatum would be known to the world.

He got up from his desk, ready for his lunch, and waited for Mrs Baines to take away the marked transcripts, his notes and the empty coffee pot. He opened the French windows to go out on to the terrace for exercise and fresh air, stopped and then drew a cross with the red pencil on the back of his left hand.

He walked slowly down the steps on to the lawns and a security man, dressed in a winter Burberry and brogues, followed twenty yards behind. The President knew him as Jed and recognized him as the man who had driven the Volkswagen to National Airport, a conspicuous man, he thought, to be in security—with bright ginger hair and freckles on his face the size of golfballs.

It was freezing again and there was snow in the air. The morning cloud had now come together, and everywhere was a dull grey with the wind constant from the north-west. The wind and the smell of snow were the usual forerunners of a blizzard.

He liked Camp David, but like every other American he associated it with crisis. Presidents only came here in trouble. Except Eisenhower, who had come simply because he liked the place and liked it so much he had had a nine-hole golf course built, with the first tee a ten-yard walk from the breakfast room of Aspen Lodge. The camp had been named after his son. Presidents now, with a greater sense of urgency, used the green instead as a convenient helicopter pad.

The holly bushes were covered in berries promising a good winter—or was it bad, he could never remember. The holly and the ivy and Christmas so soon. He picked a dark green shiny leaf and, one by one, nipped off the prickly corners and flipped them in the air with his finger and thumb. If he could survive until Christmas he knew he would survive another seven Christmases as President.

The air was suddenly icy and as he turned back to the house for the housekeeper's pea and bacon soup, the frost crunched under him and he saw his own footprints. In an instant he was back more than forty years with his two brothers, lying on the ground, playing with their toy lorries on such a frozen patch, cutting trucking routes with their fingers through the frozen wastelands of a child's Alaska in a wintry Boston suburban garden.

It was dark before time. The snow clouds were almost touching the peaks of the Catactins and the wind was shaking the blades of the small Bell helicopter parked on the green by Aspen Lodge. The floodlights picked out the small Presidential insignia on its nose and the two crewmen standing by the open door slammed their arms around their bodies and jogged on the spot to keep themselves from freezing. Five minutes before they had been drinking hot chocolate in the warm kitchen. Then came a message that the President was leaving for Washington before the weather closed in. The President's bodyguard stood by the rotor arm at the tail, the collar of his overcoat up to his eyes, covering the golfball freckles.

The upstairs lights had just been switched off and the only lights in the lodge now were in the kitchen and in the President's study. The curtains had not been drawn and the crewmen and the bodyguard could see him clearly, standing in his shirtsleeves, his tie half way down his chest, in front of the fireplace. He was talking to himself in the mirror, waving an arm, clenching a fist, snapping a finger. They watched in the dark, fascinated.

At fifteen minutes past five, the curtains of the study were drawn quickly and the house lights went out. The bodyguard ran across the lawn to the terrace and the crewmen began their start-up procedures. Seconds later the President appeared in a heavy fawn mohair overcoat and long multi-coloured hand-knitted scarf wound high around his neck.

The helicopter turbine screamed at near full power, waiting for the pitch of the blades to lift. The President reached out and grabbed the supports of the door to pull himself up. He saw the first flakes of snow on his overcoat sleeve and, on the back of his hand, a cross drawn in red. He remembered the pocket tape recorder needed new batteries.

'The Americans are going strong'

The Foreign Secretary smiled back as the policeman saluted, a habit of many years acknowledging subordinates. His face dropped again as the door of Number Ten shut firmly behind him. He walked the twenty yards across Downing Street, through the arches of the Square and into King Charles Street. Usually at this time of night, when the last bus had left Whitehall and the traffic had faded into the London suburbs, he would hear the clip of his steel-capped heels on the cobbles, but tonight there was a soft crunch of snow and by the time he had reached the wide swing doors of the Foreign Office his head and shoulders carried a layer of it. He stood still and to attention while the night porter brushed it away. He wiped his spectacles dry with the yellow duster that hung by the radiator for just such emergencies.

The Foreign Secretary was neither a tall man, nor as young-looking as his press photographs and reputation indicated. His photographs also showed a smiling, pleasant man, genial almost, with humorous owl-like eyes behind the bi-focals. He was none of these things either.

He was short-tempered and vindictive. He came from a long line of aristocrats, an illustrious English family who had been bequeathed thousand of acres of fertile Norman England by a generous and grateful Conqueror, wealth compounded many hundreds of thousands of times since.

The tea tray was already on his desk. By it was the vacuum flask of hot water and next to that the small black plastic travelling clock. It was thirteen minutes to midnight and the Foreign Secretary stood dripping by the two-bar electric fire, tired after a four and a half hour Cabinet meeting followed by two hours with the Energy Committee. His office was cold and smelt damp and he was irritated.

'We must get some cocoa powder, Simmonds.'

'Drinking chocolate?'

'Get some. Difficult taking tea this late at night and we're going to have a lot of late nights.'

Simmonds poured hot water from the flask into the floral-patterned china pot and stirred, as the Foreign Secretary eased himself slowly into his chair. Simmonds covered the teapot with its knitted cosy and pushed it carefully towards him on the tray.

'Bad news, sir?'

'It's not good.'

'Unanimous?'

'Absolutely.

'How long do we have, sir?'

'Tonight. Just tonight. She's going to announce it at ten tomorrow morning, won't even wait to do it in the House. Shame. It would have given me something to work on, something for the French especially.'

'She's not afraid of expulsion, sir?'

'She's afraid of bugger-all. Couldn't care a tinker's! Wondered tonight whether she wasn't delighted at the prospect. She's never been very keen. But whatever they do doesn't matter. We keep our oil to ourselves until the Saudis sort themselves out.'

'Or the Americans sort them out for us.'

'Meaning?'

'The Americans might use military action. Go and take the fields.'

'Wouldn't dare. They'd have the world on their backs. They'd do nothing unilaterally.'

'The President is new, sir.'

'And rash?'

'Yes.'

'Checks and balances, Simmonds. Essential to the American Administration. He may shout. But he can't do. This is awful!'

The Foreign Secretary pushed the tea tray away and wiped his lips with a large white monogrammed linen handkerchief.

'Will there be a vote in the House, sir?'

'No. No vote. We can't go through that kind of palaver at a time like this. She'll do an Order in Council. Privy Councillors will meet at nine, statement released at ten.'

Simmonds moved in closer with relish.

'King Fahd is safely in the Lakes, sir.'

'Damn! What bloody news! As if we haven't enough. Why on earth did he pick us?'

'He does own a lot of England, Sir. And Scotland. And you did promise.'

'What?'

'Eight months ago, sir. In Riyadh, during your visit. You said you would—'

'Be delighted to be host in return. God! Did he ever think we would? He was the Almighty then and we could buy his oil. Now he's not and we can't. Will he stay long?'

'Hard, sir. It's an immense estate, the whole east side of Ullswater. And very secure, which is what he wants. There's a risk, of course, sir.'

'Risk?'

'That they'll do to us what the Iranians did to the Americans over the Shah. Take British hostages. Demand Fahd back.'

'Possible. But improbable. The Shah was a crook and unloved. Bloody shame, though. Used to go to Ullswater myself once. Lovely place. Disgraceful it should go to an Arab. His brother's with him?'

'Sultan's dead, sir.'

'What about Yamani?'

'He was out of the country during the coup.'

'The clever ones always are.'

'The President's televised address is coming live from the White House.'

'Be saying the same as us. Conserve stocks, domestic restrictions, rationing, possible new impetus for alternative energy research. Usual thing. Always the same solutions to the same repeating crises and never venturing beyond a promise of intent. It'll hit the Americans hard even if this Saudi thing ends in a month or so. But it'll do them good. Austerity. No harm in it.'

'They'll ask for our oil to bide them over.'

'Maybe. But I'm not certain they'll get any. It was talked about tonight but we couldn't see how we could suspend oil exports to Europe and then sell to Washington.'

'All our exports?'

'All. As of ten tomorrow morning not a drop will be sold. All pumping operations will be suspended. The PM will order it to be left in the sea. Royal Naval patrols in all areas, and the military aboard the rigs, until the Saudis come to their senses. We have enough oil already ashore for two months, once domestic rationing is imposed.'

'When is that, sir?'

'Tomorrow, too. All be in the same Order in Council.'

'When will the Community know?'

'The PM wants it done tonight. Has to be. They all know we've been in Cabinet They're all expecting something, probably guessed already. Hate to think of the revenge being planned at this very moment in Bonn, Brussels and Paris. You take Paris first, then the Germans. I'll wake up the Community Chairman. Tell them there's a temporary suspension of contracts pending clarification of the Saudi embargo. We renege on the Treaty of Rome—with mortification of course, but national law, like national interest, is paramount.'

'They will expel us?'

'Possibly suspend membership. But we'll survive. We can do without them but we can't do without oil and that's our message tonight. We're keeping it until further notice.'

It appealed to him. The traditional, routine diplomatic protocol had always appalled him despite his apparent subscription to it. It belonged to another age—if it had ever belonged to any, and he doubted even that. The Age of Diplomacy had been when ambassadors and emissaries had needed to talk and present credentials in time-consuming pomp and ceremony because, while they were doing that, battalions and fleets could be moved slowly and laboriously to new advantage and new adventures. Diplomats parried and delayed in foreign ministries to give their own generals time to outflank in the field and their politicans time to design alternative strategies, prepare new ultimatums. In the age before the intercontinental ballistic missile and the neutron bomb, diplomatic manoeuvres were essential preludes to war or peace, but the Foreign Secretary thought such luxuries were no longer relevant today, and it surprised him that there were still people in government and the Foreign Service who were only now just beginning to complain that the traditional rules of international conduct could no longer be taken for granted. The world is changing, they'd say, as if it was something sudden, new and momentous, and their naïveté appalled him. The world was not changing. It had changed. The metamorphosis was already complete. There simply were no rules any more, the unpredictable had become commonplace The world was a gangster.

The description appealed to him because he knew that privately many of his colleagues and as many of his opponents considered him also to be outside the rules. But then, he would argue, how effective was a man who used yesterday's techniques today? Oil was the newest and most efficient fulcrum of power so why shouldn't the British Government use it as such? Thankfully he and the Prime Minister were in accord. It had, after all, been very much her idea.

The red telephone, the direct line to the PM's private secretary, began its soft buzzing. He picked it up and grunted. Then, very suddenly, he sat erect and grabbed his pen. His lips pursed inwards and his yellowing teeth began chewing them. For one full minute the room was silent except for the faintest buzz from a faulty bar of the electric fire and the pattering of snow on the window panes outside.

Slowly he kneaded the loose folds of skin in his neck, pulling at the ridges with his finger and thumb, the pen in his hand moving as if he was writing, though it did not touch the paper.

Without a word of acknowledgement, the Foreign Secretary replaced the red receiver, leaned back in his chair, rested both hands on the table, his spectacles reflecting the red in the glow of the fire.

'Simmonds,' he said in a quiet voice. 'The American President is making his address in ten minutes. Make sure you record it.'

He stood up. 'I'm going back to the PM. She's just had a call from our Ambassador in Washington. He knows what's in the President's speech.'

Simmonds helped him on with his heavy overcoat and, for the cold return to Downing Street, the Foreign Secretary put on a knitted woollen scarf and wrapped it around his neck and head. At the door he turned to speak again, and Simmonds thought he looked ridiculously like an old granny.

'Don't bother with those calls to Europe,' he said. 'They're not important for the moment.' He paused. 'Things have changed, Simmonds. Drastically. Appallingly. The Americans are going strong. The President is issuing an ultimatum as a prelude to a military invasion.'

In the four minutes it took the Foreign Secretary to walk from the swing doors of the Foreign Office to the shiny black door of Number Ten, snow covered his scarf and water dribbled from his long, thin nose. The policeman, now a snowman, saluted again, but this time there was no smile, and the door opened to the Minister without a knock.

'An assault will be repelled'

'The light's gone.'

'What d'you mean, gone?'

'I mean gone. Out. Bulb in the left back flood's busted.'

'You've got five lights up—Christ! you can manage.'

'I can manage on one, but the President of the United States is going to lack something behind.'

'So we'll have a dim Stars and Stripes. You should worry.'

'I should worry? I'm not worrying. It's your problem. You're the director. You want the President shot in half light you got it. The networks will think they've bought themselves a Fellini on the cheap.'

'Don't be crude!'

'Fellini, crude. Not fellatio. He's Italian, uses natural light—Christ! You should know these things—you're supposed to be in the picture business.'

'I'm in television. That's not the picture business.'

'So where's a new bulb?'

'So where's your assistant?'

'He's parking the van.'

'Move one of the lights round.'

'And lose his shoulders? The President will have head, flags and no support?'

'How come he's still parking the van? We've been set up an hour already.'

'So he's having problems. He brought someone with him. They're saying goodbye.'

'That's sad.'

'Sure it's sad. They've been together a long time. He came home last night and found another man in the apartment. Coming out of the bedroom. Just his socks on.'

'That's bad.'

'Sure it's bad. Real friendships are a treasure.'

'*Schmaltz*! Where d'you pick up that crap? Anyway he'll find another bit of tail. There are plenty of nice girls around.'

'Girls? Who said anything about girls? C'mon, you got him all wrong. He's not like that.'

'Turn that second flood around a bit, spread it. It'll cover shoulders and the flags. No problem.'

'Problem? So who says there's a problem? Hilton Smilton in Yonkers says the President hasn't got shoulders. So we shouldn't worry about the customers?'

'Christ! Where is he anyway?'

The President was running late. His live insert into the Network was timed for forty-five seconds after the early news shows had finished, forty-five seconds made up of four ten-second advertisements and a five second introduction off-air. There were now three minutes and those forty-five seconds to go. On the television monitors in front of the floor manager, the three separate national news shows were moving into the last of their reports. Don Rather, in his own nightly address to the nation, was summing up the day's events and promising viewers that CBS would extend their late-night news bulletin for analysis and comment of the President's speech 'if it was so called for'.

Peter Jennings, ABC's anchorman in London, was reporting a demonstration by Saudi Arabian Islamic extremists outside Buckingham Palace demanding the return of King Fahd to face trial in Riyadh. And NBC's Gavin Uckley was reporting on the anti-American demonstrations by Libyan students outside the besieged United States Embassy in Tripoli.

The floor manager looked over his shoulder at the

director and shrugged. The President had still to be made up and he would want to read his script through a couple of times, they always did. They hadn't even got the auto-cue script yet. Presidents had run late before, but never like this. Network master-control always insisted that Presidents were in their chair, ready to go, five minutes to insert time. The floor manager checked his watch with the director. They were on in two minutes and forty-five seconds. Over his intercom he could hear the master-controller in New York screaming abuse at the White House director, which was where the buck stopped. He knew well enough that to cue the President of the United States live into the Network was a coronary risk. To cue a President who wasn't there would cause national hysteria and a million heart attacks.

There were eighteen technicians and seven production assistants in the room and everyone of them now realized, with one minute and forty-five seconds to go, that such a thing was suddenly a probability.

The tension would not help the President. Tension was infectious, it even affected the pro's who did it live every night. He would look anxious on the screen, he would peer at the auto-cue and fluff his lines and people wouldn't remember anything he had said, just the dismal way he had said it. The floor manager bit his lip and smiled at the camera operator and the lighting man and his production assistant who stared blankly back. Ninety-five seconds. There was sweat on the top of his nose and he took off his headphones and wiped the moisture from the pads. Network master-control was now threatening to pull out. The director screamed abuse back.

The floor manager pulled out the plug on the intercom cable and began speaking quietly to himself. 'There's going to be cosmic disaster, millions sitting out there, waiting to see the President, and then they don't. They'd know it was assassination just like the other two, Christ!'

'Lights back on . . .'

'Fuck your lights,' he shouted and looked up into the face of the President.

'Evening, gentlemen—how long have we got?'

'Fifteen seconds, sir. Jesus!'

But the President was already in his chair with make-up girls dabbing his face with powder puffs as he adjusted the tiny earpiece of the pocket tape recorder.

'Five seconds.' The floor manager held up his hands. 'Quiet please. Three, two, one . . .

'Good evening. You will have seen on the television news, you will have read in your newspapers and you will have heard on the radio reports from the Saudi Arabian capital of Riyadh of what has happened to that country in the past forty-eight hours. You will also know how Americans working out there for the Government and for private corporations have just been evacuated by the US Air Force and who, with the co-operation of the Egyptian government and President Mubarak, are on their way home.

'You will also know that the Revolutionary Council in Riyadh has closed down the oilfields and has placed a moratorium on oil supplies to the West for at least one year. Tonight I want to tell you what the consequences of that decision will be for the United States and the free world.

'The problem that faces us now is as grave as any America has faced since World War Two. It poses a national security threat of such scope, of such complexity, that it threatens to radically transform our economy, our political consensus, our accepted way of life. Jeremiahs are already speaking of an inflation-plagued recessionist economy for a generation to come, with drastic fuel shortages that will stake city against suburb, farmers against truckers, East against West, North against South, in a regional, racial and economic divisiveness not seen since slavery and secession.

'This country, the greatest and most powerful nation in the history of the world, runs on oil. That was never a problem when we had plenty, but since the first oil embargoes in 1973, our problem has been our dependence on an uncertain monopoly source, a dependence on that thin line of oil tankers stretching from the Persian Gulf, one of the world's most politically volatile regions. And as you well know since the Shah of Iran was deposed and Iranian oil denied us, that dependence and that uncertainty has rapidly grown.

'Now, with the benefit of hindsight always available to us too late, we realize that we should not have depended so much on such people. That years ago we should have served notice on the Arab oil producers that we, the world's biggest oil consumer, were no longer willing to soak up their production at any price on any condition. But we didn't and that failure has cost America a terrible price.

'Let me now tell you just how much. In the last ten years, the nation's bill for Arab oil has risen from three billion dollars a year to nearly fifty billion. That's an increase of at least fifteen hundred per cent. To pay this price, there has been a massive taxation on your consuming power which in turn has reduced economic growth, spurred inflation, sent the balance of payments deficit into orbit and subjected the US dollar to regular and humiliating depreciation. Until yesterday we were importing just over four million barrels of Arab crude every day, an unbelievably staggering five million dollars an hour, twenty-four hours a day—three hundred and sixty-five days a year. The Arabs have had us on the rack and little by little they've been tightening the screws, selfish little people who would clip the wings of the American Eagle to feather their own nests. Tonight I address myself on your behalf to them and say Enough! We will not be made fools of any longer.

'This evening I've been given the list of twenty-seven American dead who were murdered by mobs as they were driving out of Riyadh. Men, women and children, innocent non-combatants, shot down by savages pretending to be disciples of Mohammed. American families who had gone to that land to help build a better and more prosperous life. Tonight those families are on their way home in coffins.

'I have also, within the hour, received a signal from one of our ships at present in the Persian Gulf. I want to read it to you: "Tonight at 18h30 Greenwich mean time twenty-two Soviet vessels sighted by radar proceeding northwards towards Strait of Hormuz, Persian Gulf. Speed constant at seventeen knots." That was sent by the Captain of the USS *Okinawa* and it confirms our satellite surveillance reports which has identified them as warships of the Soviet Seventh Fleet. The Soviet aircraft carrier *Minsk* and the assault ship *Ivan Rogov* are in that fleet. Both those warships have vertical take-off aircraft, both are equipped with missiles, both carry combat troops and helicopters to carry them to land. Furthermore, we have established by satellite observation and from our intelligence sources that this fleet, which was conducting operational training exercises a hundred miles south, received their new orders two days ago to enter the Persian Gulf. That was before the Saudi Arabian coup. Our conclusion is that Moscow knew what was about to happen there—indeed may have been directly instrumental in its success.

'Further reports from our Embassy and Military personnel in Saudi Arabia confirm that the weapons to overthrow King Fahd were Soviet built and were used by Marxist Palestinians and Marxist South Yemenis.

'Now, according to my advisers, Rahbar, former Crown Prince Abdullah, abhors Communism as much as we do. I'm told that his coup against the King succeeded because of the Saudi people's faith in him and their belief that Islam was being contaminated by the West. But I say this. Whoever is now in charge of that country, whatever the religious credentials of the Islamic People's Democratic Republic, Communist ambition will attempt sooner or later to take it for itself. Because it is the Soviet's economic and military strategy to deny the United States Saudi oil. They know in Moscow what so many of us here in the United States refuse to face up to, the harsh and unpleasant fact that American oilfields are dying. They are running dry.

'You should know that according to all the specialist data available to us from the Department of Energy, the American Petroleum Institute, Data Resources and others, our oil will run out in less than ten years' time at the present rate of our consumption. And when the last barrel is filled, the United States will be entirely dependent on imported oil. From Venezuela. From Nigeria. From Mexico. From the

Arabs. Is it hard then to understand why the Soviet Union should do everything in their power to prevent us getting it? Without that oil the American Eagle is crippled. It will not fly again.

'But there is another reason for the sudden Soviet activity in Saudi Arabi and the Persian Gulf. It is this. Moscow needs that oil as much as we do.

'The Soviet Union is the biggest oil producer in the world. Once it was pumping six hundred million tons every year, but in the last two years its production has fallen by half and it is now buying all that Libya and Iraq and other pro-Soviet Arab states can provide. It has cut its own oil exports to dependent Soviet block Comecon states in Europe to conserve stocks. But despite this, its industry has been reduced to a three day working week because of fuel shortages and the Soviet government has been forced to introduce severe petrol and diesel rationing.

'Moscow has read the writing on the wall. It must have more oil, for its factories, for its farms, for its ever-expanding war machine. Arab oil has become as essential to the Soviet Union's survival as it has to ours.

'It is for these reasons that I believe the Soviet Seventh Fleet is now sailing towards the Persian Gulf. It is for these reasons that we in the United States, as leaders of the free world, must be prepared to act.

'As your President, I believe that it is not our power but our will that is being tested. And the question all Americans must ask and answer tonight is: does the strongest nation in the history of the world have the character to meet a direct challenge by people who ignore our warnings, trample on agreements and violate innocent people? If, when the chips are down, this powerful nation acts like a pitiful helpless giant, the forces of totalitarianism and anarchy will threaten us and all free nations throughout the world. If we fail to meet this challenge, all other nations will be on notice that, despite its overwhelming power, when the real crisis came the United States was found wanting.

'But tonight, let it be known that the United States will no longer tolerate deception or offence from any nation, large or small.

'Events now force a change, and I quote, with respect to his memory, the words of John F. Kennedy. "Let every nation know, whether it wishes us well or ill, that we shall pay any price, bear any burden, meet any hardship, support any friend, oppose any foe to assure the survival and success of liberty." I will not be made impotent. I will not sit back when our oil supplies are cut off and watch Soviet warships sail into the Persian Gulf to lay claim to it.'

'Fellow Americans, tonight I have sent a message to Rahbar, leader of the Islamic People's Democratic Republic, telling him that the United States is resolved to preserve peace. I have also told him of our resolution to have the oilfields reopened and oil supplies to the United States resumed forthwith, and that contracts regarding those supplies signed in good faith by American corporations shall be honoured, notwithstanding the new political situation that now exists. And I have told him that my Government expects full and early reparation for all damage to American property sustained during the fighting there.

'I have also expressed alarm at the prospect of a Soviet war fleet in the Persian Gulf, I consider it an obstacle to peace in the area, and for this last reason I have, as your President, tonight sent an urgent appeal to the Secretary General of the United Nations, asking for an immediate meeting of the Security Council. I am proposing that the entire Persian Gulf, from latitude 26 degrees North be declared an International Zone under United Nations' administration, policed by a UN peacekeeping force.

'As President of the United States, I give notice to all parties concerned that I will stand by here at the White house, ready to offer counsel and material aid should it be asked for. I will wait twenty-four hours as of this time. If there is no positive response to my appeals by that deadline, I will do whatever I consider to be right and proper in the best interests of my country. The choice of the alternatives available will be mine. The timing of that choice will be mine. The responsibility for any American initiative will be mine and mine alone.

'Let our position be made absolutely clear. Any attempt by outside forces to gain control of the Persian Gulf region will be regarded as an assault on the vital interests of the United States of America. And such an assault will be repelled by any means necessary, including military force. To make this warning more credible I hae asked Congress to authorize the registration of young Americans for the draft.

'The path we have chosen is full of hazard, as all paths are, but it is one most consistent with our character and courage as a nation. Our goal is not the victory of might, but the vindication of right; not peace at the expense of freedom, but both peace and freedom. God wiling, we'll achieve it.'

December 22nd

'We're on the march again'

Captain Edward Hanks had stood in his corner of the bridge of the *USS Okinawa* and heard the President's speech live at 0510 hours local time, via the Satellite Communications link that connects all US Navy ships at sea directly and at all times with Navy Command at the Pentagon.

The Captain had ordered all the six hundred and nine officers and men aboard to stop all but essential duties and be out of their beds so that they should hear what their Commander-in-Chief had to say.

Captain Hanks, just as soon as the President's broadcast had ended, did the most extraordinary and uncharacteristic thing. He was never a man who needed much sleep, often boasting that he could manage on three hours in every twenty-four. But, the Washington speech over, he ordered the officer on deck to reduce the *Okinawa*'s cruising speed of eighteen knots to four, just enough to keep her manageable. Then he went to his cabin and, fully dressed, lay down and slept like a child.

When he woke he felt reborn. He casually showered, shaved, put on newly-laundered shirt and trousers and lunched on tuna fish salad. Then he called up the bridge and ordered full speed ahead on bearing 042 degrees, which the officer on watch, Lt Vaduz, knew was the course that would take them to the Straits of Hormuz at the southern end of the Persian Gulf.

After his light lunch Captain Hanks sat at his table, staring at the row of books on the shelf above the rack which held his logs and charts. The President's voice still echoed, his words and phrases still exploding in a speech that perfectly captured the spirit of all those things American Captain Hanks thought had long been ridiculed into oblivion by the new generation of Americans, those children who mocked everything and to whom nothing was sacred. And yet here was a man of that same generation, and a Democrat, resurrecting what Hanks was certain had long fallen and been lost—the spirit of America past. He sat there, his hands in his lap, staring but seeing nothing. He was trying to grasp what was happening around him, physically around him, here in the Persian Gulf. He had heard the President quoting the signal he, in command of the *Okinawa*, had sent. He had heard the President's own reaction to that signal, the President of the United States publicly responding to the warning that Soviets were about to barge their way into the Gulf and take it the way they took everything. How closely in tune he suddenly felt with this young man seven thousand miles away, his President, his Commander-in-Chief, who now promised to restore to all Americans their pride and dignity.

Quickly, like a mushroom spore pushing its way through black peat, the psyche of Captain Hanks began to assume a new situation and a new ambition. A state of war or something like it now existed around him. Russian warships were now sailing towards him, approaching the narrow sea corridor that would bring them into the Persian Gulf and the oilfields. But the President of the United States had suddenly and unexpectedly said *no!* He had said *enough*! He had issued an ultimatum, just as John F. Kennedy had done—the last time, as Captain Hanks remembered it, an American leader had shown spunk. He knew it because he had heard his President say so.

A band of sweat had formed across his forehead, darkening the grey hairline, and his jaw muscles hardened, flexing the powerful bunches of sinew at the sides of his face. He reached across the desk and from an ashtray in which there had never been a cigarette, he picked up a squash ball and began to turn it in his right hand, kneading the hard black rubber with his short, stubby, powerful fingers.

The brass ship's clock above the bookshelf clicked as the minute hand went past the half hour and the Captain's right eyelid twitched in response, though he heard nothing. He was suspended in excitement, relief, anticipation. He was on the move again and there was no going back, not for him, not now, not after such a speech promising so much so earnestly. No land duties, no early retirement, no scrapyard, no twenty and more years of loneliness. He was back in the business he was best at. Back at war.

He began to grind his teeth, crunching the molars sideways, contorting the jaw muscles and twisting the skin at his temples so that the beads of sweat collecting there formed tiny rivulets and ran down the hairline of his grey sideburns, across his chin, through the folds of loose skin on his neck and on to the open collar of his khaki shirt.

He leaned back in his chair, raised his head backwards and turned it slowly from side to side to relax the neck muscles that nowadays tightened up more and more, making him hunch his shoulders with the nagging ache. As his head rolled, his eyes scanned the framed photographs screwed to the wall each side of the brass clock. The *West Virginia*, the first ship he had served on; the *Yorktown* and the *Maryland* of the Phillipines campaign. And the *Okinawa* now, as he saw it, girding herself to defend US interests in this newest arena of the continuing American war against Communist aggression. Against the Russians in the Persian Gulf.

With his left hand he pulled a ballpoint pen from the breast pocket of his shirt and began to bend it between his thumb and finger, keeping his eyes on the photograph. It would not, as he saw it, be a contest of strength but a show of courage by a single US vessel, a declaration by him to the Soviets on behalf of his President that the game of hide-and-seek was over for all time and that the Russians' attempt at a sea monopoly was at last being disputed. Hadn't he seen it—hadn't everyone?—the certain gradual build up of the

Soviet fleets in all the seas around the world, dropping their anchors in more and more of the ocean's ports, challenging the sanctity of the West's established sea-lanes? For years now he had been warning people and they'd told him to go and shout 'wolf' somewhere else. But now at last the US Navy had a President who had decided to kick against the pricks.

Suddenly the plastic ballpoint broke between his fingers, and the noise seemed to wake him as if a hypnotist had snapped his fingers. He was alert and he looked quickly around the cabin. He got up and opened the door to the lavatory and then the door to his wardrobe. He looked puzzled, as if he was trying to remember why he was where he was, why he was wet with sweat and why there was a growing throbbing pain in his back molars.

By the time he had reached the bridge, the tension and the pain had gone. He had washed the sweat from his face and had put on his peak cap and, as he entered the bridge, the helmsman stiffened with a 'Good evening, sir', and Captain Hanks smiled back, something neither the crewman nor anyone else could ever remember him doing before.

'Say your head,' the Captain said to him.

'Maintaining constant 042 degrees, sir, at 23 knots.'

'What time is it, son?'

The crewman looked at the large clock immediately above the gyro compass to the side of the Captain's head. 'Just on 1800 hours sir.'

Captain Hanks leant forward to the control consul and spoke to the radar room. 'Cap'n here. Position of *Minsk*?'

'26–02 degrees North by 56–45 degrees East, sir.'

'Expected time at the turn?'

'Standby one, sir.'

The computer went rapidly through its wind-tide-speed calculation.

'The leading ship should begin its turn west on to a new heading opposite the Musandum Peninsula in forty-five minutes, sir.'

'Is that the narrowest channel of entry into the Straits?'

'Yessir. The deep water channel is only two miles across at that point.'

'Thank you, radar.' Captain Hanks turned back to the crewman. 'What time's sundown?'

'18h33, sir.'

'Completely dark about ten minutes later?'

'Normally, sir. But tonight there's a full moon and we should have good visibility.'

'All the better to see them with.'

'Excuse me, sir?'

But Captain Hanks was already walking to the forward window of the bridge on the port side. He looked out across the angled flight deck to the stub-nosed bows and the sea, gold with the low evening sun beyond it. Thirty men or more sat half-naked at the edge of the bows, their feet touching the safety net and watching, two hundred feet below them, hundreds of flying fish criss-crossing their way in front. There was a sudden cheer as a school of dolphins leapt from the water less than a hundred yards away to starboard.

Immediately below the bridge towards the stern, Captain Hanks saw the neatly parked rows of Harrier vertical take-off aircraft, the tips of their hinged wings pointing to the sky, exposing on their undersides the racks that carried their bombs and rockets and behind them Sea King and Sea Stallion helicopters. Squads of men in singlets and shorts were on physical exercises and beyond them in the gun turrets on the edge of the deck, men in green helmets turned the barrels of their three-inch guns left to right and back again, sweeping the sky and sea in silent gunnery practice. Every few minutes, gaping holes sixty yards square would suddenly appear in the flat deck aft as lift platforms sunk down into the hangars below to reappear with another Harrier or another helicopter, manoeuvred by men in blue helmets and jerseys. Ordnance crews wore red, the re-fuellers the purple, the plane captains brown, and the flight directors yellow. From the bridge a hundred feet above the flight deck, they looked like an army of techni-coloured roving ants, moving rapidly in irregular directions, touching but never colliding, and to anyone not of the sea, the activity might have seemed frantic and unco-ordinated and without discipline.

Captain Hanks seemed not to see or hear any of this.

Perhaps after so many years he noticed nothing so routine, saw only the exception, the irregular, only that which was out of place. But on his ship, nothing was ever out of place. He stood where he always stood on the bridge, the Captain's corner they called it, quite still except for the squash ball slowly turning in the fingers of his right hand. The clock above the gyro compass read 1805 hours. In forty minutes the leading ship of the Soviet fleet would begin its slow turn, ready to pass through the narrowest part of the Straits of Hormuz, the deep water channel between Kuzari Point and Resuradam Island, the tight sea corridor into the Gulf. And in thirty minutes, ten minutes before them, the *Okinawa* would be there too.

Lt Vaduz, the ship's Communications Officer, came on to the bridge, bringing the warm, sticky evening air with him. He held a signal.

'From Command, sir,' he said.

Captain Hanks stretched his arms behind him and braced his shoulders. The little black rubber ball slowly revolved in his right palm.

'Yes?' he said without turning.

'It reads, sir, "Ships of Soviet Seventh Fleet in your area 18h45 local. You will remain in Gulf but will proceed immediately South to 24 degrees 30 North, 54 degrees 100 East, remaining off Abu Dhabi until further notice. Confirm new co-ordinates. Repeat – confirm immediate receipt of this signal."'

Captain Hanks did not move. Lieutenant Vaduz watched the squash ball turning. It was the barometer of the man's moods. As anger and anxiety rose inside him, his fingers would spin the ball faster and faster until it was squashed flat by his short, powerful fingers, and his anger would explode in vicious and obscene language. But as he watched, Lieutenant Vaduz saw no change, the fingers turned slowly. He waited. 'Shall I acknowledge, sir?' Still no reply. 'Shall I confirm change of course, sir?' Another thirty seconds passed. Then Captain Hanks answered. His voice was low and quiet and even.

'How far is Abu Dhabi, Mr Vaduz?'

'Navigation say it's two hundred and fifty miles, eleven hours sailing, sir.'

'Not exactly eyeball to eyeball, is it?'

'Sir?' Lieutenant Vaduz looked at his Captain and then across to the crewman, who shrugged.

'Give me the signal, Mr Vaduz.' Without looking away from the window, Captain Hanks held out his hand and Lieutenant Vaduz gave him the piece of paper.

'You have a copy?'

'Yessir. For logs, sir.'

'Bring it.'

'Sir?'

'I said I want the carbon, Mr Vaduz.'

Again the young lieutenant looked across to the young helmsman, but this time the sailor was looking dead ahead. From this point on, he decided, he would hear nothing, see nothing of the conversation between the Captain and the lieutenant.

Vaduz hesitated. He looked down at the squash ball. The fingers still caressed it slowly.

'Shall I send confirmation of receipt, sir?'

'No, sir,' said the Captain. 'You will do no such thing, sir. You will send my own reply shortly—just as soon as I've written it. Goddamnit! Don't you see? You see, don't you?'

Suddenly he swung round at them. His face was on fire. The evening sun was now red and large and sitting low on the western horizon and it lit up the Captain's head and shoulders; he was no longer grey, not his skin not his hair. He was crimson and sweat sparkled red on his forehead, and his eyes were wide and so bright they looked as if they were burning.

Then he whispered to the two of them as if only they should be party to his conspiracy.

'Maintain our course, boys. Get me there before them and give me time to turn broadside. We'll not go south, not us, not the *Okinawa*, not the United States Navy. We've finished running and you'd better thank God and the President of the United States for it. We've turned about at last. Keep engines full ahead. Godamnit, don't you see? We're on the march again.'

'With the help of young Kieran'

Just as Cheaney had promised, Franklin got his Cairo Embassy shower and his Embassy change of clothes and his Embassy steak and onions. He also got his call to the *New York Times* and dictated fifteen hundred words of copy. His night editor was ecstatic and promised him a Pulitzer.

The story was syndicated to a hundred newspapers worldwide and used as the lead by all the News Agencies. Television networks coast-to-coast ran it at length. The ex-Mrs Franklin saw it, watching the ABC evening show from her bedroom in Tamworth, New Hampshire. Quietly she packed her bags and just as quietly left the house, leaving the large man asleep in her bed, snoring and smelling of sweat and Jack Daniels.

Franklin left Cairo in the Embassy Lear-jet for Rome a little after three in the morning and arrived at Leonardo da Vinci airport in time for breakfast and the Alitalia flight to London Heathrow. But there the Agency's forward planning did a turnabout. Agents began running, Embassy phones began ringing, deputies began chattering.

Forward Planning dealt with the untoward and were proud of how well they manoeuvred with the unforeseen, but there's nothing more untoward than fog at London airport and nothing more unforeseen than visibility below a hundred yards. So Franklin was requested to remain in transit at Heathrow.

Anna Schneider bit the plastic sachet and spat into the bath. The she squeezed the rest of the bath oil into the hot water and lowered her body until only her nose and eyes showed. She felt the current of water from the slow-running hot tap move inside her thighs like an eel and rest on her stomach. She closed her eyes, slid her hands along the enamel of the bath to her thighs. She gently fingered her pubic hairs and as steam descended like a warm cloud she began luxuriously to masturbate.

Her Dublin flight had been delayed and then cancelled because of fog at London's Heathrow. So, like many hundreds more in the departure hall that afternoon, she had been shepherded into a convoy of buses and distributed to the nearby tac and tinsel hotels which depended on the cussedness of British weather, unable to make their money any other way.

This was not something her own people or those at the other end would have taken into account. European weather could not be. The Irish, used to such things, would simply wait for the next day's flight, but she hoped he would take trouble to cool the Arabs. They were the anxious ones, the ones who would do the wrong thing in panic. The Irishman would have to stay with them. There was nothing she could do.

That was the rule when things went wrong. No contact outside the list. No unilateral initiative. She could not move until London's fog lifted. People would simply have to wait until that happened.

Her years as a courier with the Reds had taught her patience at such times, had taught her not to side-step, not to detour. From her early revolutionary reading she remembered that George Grivas, the Cypriot EOKA leader, worked the opposite way. If anything went wrong with his schedule, however small, however apparently insignificant, he would cancel the entire plan. A late car, a plane delayed, an appointment made too early or kept overdue, and he would revise. It was, he had written, his way of reducing anxieties and keeping alive.

She preferred her own strategy, such as it was. At moments of alarm, at times when fate or man's stupidity forced her to move sideways or not at all, her own chemistry took control of the situation. She became sexually highly charged. Enormously so. She understood from what she had heard and read that such a thing was not unusual. Men and women in the Reds had spoken of it during the drugs and drinks in the early days—but listening then she knew none felt it her way. It was after her first bank raid, and the elation that follows survival, that to her surprise she had taken the most energetic role in her first sex orgy. Three men, all since dead, and four women, three of them also dead, had been astonished at her inventiveness. But the men, despite their initial enthusiasm, had tired too easily and the other women had crept away after their orgasms. Only she was left alone, still waiting to be exhausted. She had tired of men so she had tried women and had tired of them. So eventually she took to herself, frequently, sometimes violently and often in the most absurd places, wherever the urge took her. As it did tonight.

The hot tap was still slowly running and the gurgle of the overflow mixed with her moaning as she suddenly surged. Her body arched out of the water, her hands lost in the foam covering her stomach and thighs. Her legs twisted and her hoarse shouted obscenities were suddenly lost as she turned over gurgling 'Pappa, Pappa' in the tiny voice of a child.

An hour and ten minutes later she woke, chilled. The hot tap was trickling cold and the bath oil covered the water like a slick. She got out, covered her shoulders with a towel, and stood shivering in front of the mirror. The cold had turned the scar on her neck a dull blue, a thin curved slightly raised purple line contouring from the clavicle three inches up towards her left ear but after a minute using her make-up stick the scar might easily have been a varicosed vein or something just as comfortably explained. She combed her straight blonde hair tightly back, squeezing the ends dry. Her crutch ached. She had not enjoyed it. She had had orgasm but the cold water had denied her satisfaction. She went into the small bedroom, as grey and as blank as the television screen that dominated it. Outside she could hear the droning of diesels as the coaches queued to drop off more despondent passengers from the emptying airport halls. She read the single-card room service menu, then dropped it into the waste-bin. She could feel irritation rising to anger. The tension had not been got rid of this time. She dropped the damp towel and wrapped herself in the quilted bedcover and sat on the warm air vent by the dressing-table. She picked out a cigarette from the Benson and Hedges packet, lit it and inhaled slowly with a hiss. The scent of sweet marijuana filled the room. She had broken the rules for the first time. Others smoked it regularly, some even during a job to keep themselves easy. But she had never done that. She had always insisted you were never properly in control.

Recrimination fired anger and she wanted to crush the cigarette. But the longer she delayed doing so the easier it was to smoke, and the easier it was to cope. She knew she could not sleep until she was tired and she would not be tired until long after midnight, four hours away. She drew in, a long pulling of air through the sides of her mouth. Malawi Gold they had always called it, to be distinguished from the rubbish. She felt its warmth inside, mingling with the growing warmth coming up from the vent and spreading inside. She was beginning to feel the fire again, distant and remote but still there. She shook her head and dry warm hair fell across her face and she sucked some into her mouth to tickle her tongue. Success was so near now. Two days and she would be done, safely away and lost.

There was an inch of cigarette beyond her fingers. She threw her head back and blew hard to the ceiling. Then slowly she inhaled its last pleasure, watching the dark paper turn to ash in the side mirror of the dressing-table. And she focused on herself as the inner warmth moved into the tips of her, the skin on her knees, her ankles, her toes, her nipples.

For the first time in many many years she felt irrational, almost careless. She broke the burning ash between her forefinger and thumb and felt the tingle of pain. She would not wait alone tonight. For once she would not be on the outside. Tonight she would wait with the bourgeois for the fog to lift and enjoy bourgeois things, a gin, a steak and the warmth and light of their idiot noisy bars.

Franklin was into his fifth large whisky and soda and eating peanuts from a bowl when she sat down at the bar, leaving an empty stool between them. He had watched her in the mirror opposite. He turned, smiled, and nodded to the stool.

'You mustn't let a little thing like this come between us.'

Without a word, she stepped down and then stepped up again to sit next to him.

He looked astonished and grinned. 'That was real Yankee corn and I didn't expect it to work.'

She nodded back. He held out his hand.

'I'm Matt Franklin. Can I get you a drink?'

She nodded again.

'What'll it be?'

'Is that bourbon?'

'No, it's Scotch.'

'I'll have bourbon.'

'American style?'

'With rocks.'

Franklin laughed loudly, much encouraged.

'On the rocks. Great.' He caught a passing waiter's arm and held him. 'One large bourbon, one large Scotch, lots of ice, separate glasses.' The small man smoothed his sleeve and went away whimpering.

Franklin swivelled his stool and faced her.

'You're Swiss?'

'Yes.'

'And if I'd said you were German?'

'Yes, too.'

'But you're not Australian.'

'Recently emigrated.'

'I like your humour.'
'Swiss-Germans have none.'
'Is the fog going to damage you much?'
'Damage?'
'Upset your plans. You on business someplace? Holiday? Visiting?'
'Yes.'
'Sorry. It's an American habit. We tell everything about us. You tell everything about you.'
'You are Mr Franklin and you are American. What else?'
'Fire away.'
'May I drink first?'
Franklin swung round and hit the bar hard with the fist of his hand. 'God help me. Can somebody pour a drink, or do droughts follow fogs in this goddammed city?' He banged his glassful of Scotch on the counter and ice cubes fell into her lap.
'Christ, I'm sorry.' He reached down to pick them up and she felt his hand move clumsily on her thigh. She brought her knees together quickly and trapped it.
Franklin looked up. 'I was going after the ice, lady.'
'It can do little damage there,' she said, picking his hand up with both of hers and placing it back on the bar.
The Scotch and bourbon arrived immediately, the barman anxious to avoid noisy scenes with foreign strangers.
Franklin lifted her drink to her and chinked glasses. 'Chow!'
'Chow!'
'If I ask you a direct question will you knock me off the stool?'
'Yes.'
'Are you a hooker?'
'Do you not usually talk to ladies in the bar?'
'No. Are you?'
'No. Disappointed?'
'No. Encouraged.'
'Because you might get it free?'
'Christ! Are all Swiss-German-Australians like you?'
'All of them. It's just they travel so little it's not known.'

'Dinner and bed?'

'Dinner and bed.'

'I never thought it could be so easy.'

'It may not be.'

'You're what we call a cock-teaser.'

'It's a nice idea.'

'Christ again!' He watched her forefinger and thumb move slowly up and down the neck of his bottle of soda. 'Jesus! One helluva movie. Can we eat and bed before the lights go up again?'

She held out her hand to steady him as he got off the high stool and he was mildly astonished at her strength. He grinned. 'There's an American joke that ends: "Gee, that was great, what did you say your name was?"'

'I know that joke too,' she smiled back. 'And you're supposed to ask that afterwards.'

He held on to her elbow and pulled her closer. 'Ma'am, no offence, but if I'm going to fuck you I ought to call you something.'

'I'm sure you will, Mr Franklin. You will.'

Anna Schneider had her steak. And Franklin persuaded her to take one glass of champagne with it. The fillet was small and over-done and the Moet Chandon had lost its chill, but they were in no mood to trouble over such things. Franklin sat close to Schneider with many Scotches and most of the champagne inside him, her right hand in his left trouser pocket, and cared not at all.

Schneider found it pleasurable and felt safe in his company. She had broken a rule formerly cherished, one of many that had kept her safe. But at this time, in this place, she could persuade herself there was good reason for an exception to be made. Tonight she was marking time in fog. Tomorrow she would be on a flight to Dublin. She moved as time moved and stopped as it stopped. There was, she mused, sipping her champagne, a soothing inevitability about it.

She had made no other concession. She'd told him nothing, relying on any man's assumption that a one-night stand values anonymity. He had called himself Franklin. She could have invented a name just as readily.

He knew nothing, suspected nothing. Afterwards he would remain behind long after she had left. At first she had thought that it might be better that he never left the hotel alive, but decided the risk did not match the convenience. So she would delay him, and he would only blame the drink.

When they finally came to wake him up he could remember very little. He didn't recall her room number, only that she had insisted they went to hers. They had smoked pot, very strong and very good. She'd called it 'Gold'. He remembered her sitting on the warm air vent smoking it, naked except for a thin twist of red silk around her neck. She'd joked about it but he couldn't remember what or why he'd laughed, except that he had laughed for too long and she stopped him by sitting on his face and he'd thought that funny too but couldn't laugh any more.

And then he'd been woken up fourteen hours later with why and what the hell! At first he'd blamed it on the fatigue of a middle-ageing man not used to it. And who the hell could ever get used to her and her enormous enthusiasm, whose contortions and appetite and sheer bloody strength had threatened to tear him apart!

They'd started by blaming the drink until they checked the glass she had given him and found the tiny deposits. And then they stopped blaming and started questioning. But what to tell? A one-night stand to end them all. Beautiful, blonde, green eyes, with a body you only see in make-believe. A Swiss-German—German-Swiss? Or an Australian emigrant. No. Certainly German or Austrian, about twenty-four years, 140 pounds, five feet ten. It was a pick-up, and you don't ask for curriculum vitaes. Anyway, when she'd done she took him back to his room. How about that? And she knew as much about Franklin as Franklin knew about her. Drink or no drink.

So they'd left to go back to the American Embassy to write their report. And he'd been given orders, *orders* this time, to catch the 1730 hours flight to Dublin that evening. Their contact would be rearranged to rendezvous as before. Meet him, they'd said threateningly. This time meet him!

He went into the bathroom to shower. He washed and rinsed gingerly in cold water, and went to the mirror to shave. He saw his neck. In places it was red raw where she'd bitten him and sucked blood to the skin. Then he remembered her, provocative and naked, with the red twist of silk around her neck. And somewhere in the hung-over and drugged recesses of his memory he remembered in their convulsive orgasm his tongue reaching inside the silk and touching a ridge of skin that could have been a scar.

One hour and ten minutes later, with the capricious English winter sun making his forehead tingle with a slight sweat as it beamed into the departure lounge, Franklin was sitting exactly where he'd been ordered to sit, reading the book Cheaney had given him for the occasion: *The Ruined Cities of Mashonaland* by J. Theodore Bent. He was about to finish his seventh cup of coffee when the man sat down at the table.

'Keen on African archaeology?' he asked.

'Not at all.'

'You're Franklin?'

'That's right.'

'*New York Times*?'

'And sometimes Washington.'

'How d'you do. Your people have told us. My name's Howard.'

'Pleased to meet you,' said Franklin. 'Is that your first or second name?'

'Sorry. Surname. John Howard.' They shook hands.

'It's warm,' Franklin said.

'Amazing December, really. Very warm. I'd loosen that scarf, old lad. Hate you to explode. You're looking really rather all-in.'

'It's been quite a time,' Franklin said, loosening the scarf he had bought at the hotel to hide his bruising. Her red silk twist plagued him. And again and again his tongue moved inside it to caress the ridge of hard scar from the wound she'd received at the shoot-out at Leipzig. And he'd remembered too late. Too late to stop her. Too late even to catch her. By the time he'd called the Embassy she would have been in Dublin for six hours and might well have flown out of it again. He had told Cheaney they should use a professional. Now they knew what he meant.

'You flying with me?' asked Franklin.

'Only as far as Dublin.'

'Then?'

'You make it on your own to the Lakes. They're expecting you.'

'Why do I go to Dublin? Why not straight to Fahd?'

'I want you to meet someone there. Won't take long. He's a . . . he's a fellow terrorist, a Provisional from the north but very active internationally, a go-between, Ghaddaffi, the Palestinians, the Syrians. He's been involved in gunrunning with the Red Army. We got some movements from him. We're hoping to get more. We'll know when we arrive. They're still working on him.'

'You made him talk?'

'Not me, old man. We. Quite a lot, actually.'

'And he's still alive?'

The Englishman laughed. He brushed aside his blond straggling hair from his forehead.

'Look,' he said. 'They'll be calling our flight any minute.'

'Yes?'

'May I pinch your coffee? It'll take half an hour in that queue.'

'It's cold.'

'Love it cold. Drives my wife mad. Once she poured cold water on to the Nescafé thinking I wouldn't notice. Silly ass.'

'I'm surprised you're married.'

'Good heavens. Why not? You mustn't think the English are all gay. Not all of us.'

'Kids?'

'Yes. Two. Boys. May I show you?'

He pulled a wallet from his inside breast pocket and

opened it to Franklin. Two small faces smiled from behind the square cellophane window.

'They're good lookers,' said Franklin.

'Thank you. Very nice to say so, I must say.'

He drank cold coffee.

'You were telling me about the man you tortured,' said Franklin.

The Englishman's blue eyes twinkled over the rim of his coffee cup. Very bright eyes. Small pupils. His face was thin and his nose was long and very straight. He looked as if he had come straight from the *Herrenvolk*.

'If I hadn't been so punctual,' he said, 'this coffee would have been perfect. There's our flight.'

The departure board clicked its computer way through the letters and numbers until it showed the Aer Lingus flight departing for Dublin at Gate 14.

The Englishman stood up from the table and watched Franklin gather his things together. He made the scarf more comfortable and then picked up a small shoulder bag, supplied by the Cairo Embassy, containing a shirt, a pair of socks and underpants. And Theodore Bent.

It was dark when they got to Dublin. The man they kept in the long squat grey building had talked some more, just as the Englishman Howard had expected. Irish Intelligence had had the most extraordinary luck—as they put it. Once the Americans in London had alerted them to Schneider they had checked with their airport watchmen who remembered a known and as yet unconvicted Provo at the airport about the time of the London flight. As far as they knew he met nobody and left on his own motorcycle. It was only after Schneider's description reached them that one of the younger watchmen remembered the Provo stopping a tall blonde for a light. Innocent enough, until it was recalled that the young Provo didn't smoke, and never had.

'You did this?' asked Franklin.

''Fraid so,' said the Englishman. His blue eyes smiled.

'You've crippled him.'

'Apparently.'
'Bastards!'
'Don't be absurd. Your people want Fahd back on his throne. We gather he's rather vital, and we mean to keep him alive for you. With the help of young Kieran here I think we will.'
The Englishman raised his hand and the guard by the door switched off the ceiling light. For five seconds or more they stood in the dark. Then an intense beam of light from the Englishman's torch shone into the prisoner's eyes.
'Good evening, Kieran,' he said softly and pleasantly. 'I've brought someone here to see you. From America. I am going to ask you some of my questions again and I want you to answer them just the way you've been doing. D'you understand, Kieran? Just the way you've been doing.'
The grey eyes looked into the beam of light, wide and unblinking. Morphine, injected to ease the enormous pain between his legs, had dilated the pupils and they were so grey and so empty it was like looking directly into the brain behind.
'Kieran, you met Miss Schneider at Dublin airport?'
'Yes.' It was a whisper from the back of the throat. The eyes did not move.
'And you took her back to your rooms. To meet others?'
'Yes.'
'And what did Schneider want from them? What did she ask for?'
'A plane.'
'To?'
'Fly to Carlisle.'
'To refuel?'
'Yes.'
'And then?'
'Newcastle.'
'Why?'
'A ferry to Stavanger, Norway.'
'Was she flying anywhere in between Carlisle and Newcastle?'
'Ullswater.'

'Why, Kieran? Why Ullswater?'
'To drop a bomb.'
'A bomb, Kieran? A bomb?'
'Canister.'
'And where did Schneider get this canister?'
'Brought to my room.'
'When?'
'Two days ago.'
'Who brought it?'
'Arab.'
'From? Where from, Kieran?'
'Iraq.'
'How did you know?'
'Searched him.'
'A passport?'
'Yes.'
'And the canister? What was in the canister?'
'It was sealed.'
'Made of?'
'It was heavy.'
'Metal?'
'Lead.'
'A canister made of lead, Kieran. And what was inside?'
'I don't know.'

The grey eyes quickly closed and the young man squeezed his eyelids tight and held his breath.

'Don't be afraid, Kieran,' said the Englishman softly and gently. 'I believe you now. When you say you don't know, I believe you. I didn't before, did I? But I do now. Really I do.'

The grey unseeing face slowly relaxed again, and the grey eyes opened.

'And the Arab, Kieran? What happened to the Iraqi?'

'He stayed.' The voice was so small that Franklin moved a step closer. He smelt the man's sweat and his excreta smeared across the chair. And the clinical alcohol splashed across the man's bruised genitals.

'He stayed with the canister, Kieran, until Schneider came?'

'Yes.'

'And then he gave the canister to Schneider?'

'Yes.'

'And then you killed the Arab?'

'Yes.'

'And Schneider left?'

'Yes.'

'With the canister?'

'Yes.'

'But we don't know where she went, do we Kieran?'

'No.'

'Thank you. Now you can sleep again. Goodnight, Kieran. Goodnight.'

'Goodnight.'

'Lights, please,' said the Englishman loudly, suddenly, pleasantly.

In the sudden brightness Franklin held his hand to his eyes and turned away from the torture chair and the dull grey shape slumped in it. The guard held open the door and stood to one side for them to pass. The Englishman smiled to him.

'You can clean him up now and put his trousers on.' He stopped and touched the guard's arm. 'If the doctor agrees, of course. Only if the doctor agrees.' He walked out into the corridor and Franklin followed.

The Englishman stopped half-way down the narrow corridor and leant against the wall, hands in his trouser pockets. Everything was painted high gloss green and there was a strong smell of floor wax. There were no windows and no doors other than the one they had just left. It was like a long narrow prison cell.

The Englishman smiled. Franklin looked away to the blurred image of him reflected in the shine of the green wall opposite.

'A lead canister, Franklin, stolen from the Al Ahrish laboratories in Baghdad, containing twenty grams of plutonium, highly radioactive and, you understand, a deadly contaminate. Schneider intends to deliver it to King Fahd. It's a fantasy, Franklin, except the reality is that we know that canister was brought to Dublin and that it is now somewhere en route to Lake Ullswater.'

'And Fahd dies.'

'You miss the point. There are simpler ways to kill a king than plutonium. If that canister is opened, its radioactive contamination could spread twenty miles in every direction from its centre point . . . forty miles depending on the wind and weather. That's an area of two thousand square miles. It will destroy the lakes and the land and every living thing. It would be a biological desert for half a century or more. Schneider's target is Fahd, but more than ten thousand people live inside that circle. Can you begin to imagine what would happen if it became known that the canister was somewhere in England? Can you? On its way to kill an Arab and every living English thing just because he had become their neighbour in exile?'

'So either way Schneider gets Fahd.'

'Exactly. Dead by her hand or that of any one of a million English. The threat would be enough to force the British Government to deport him. And where could he go with such an assassin for company?' He went on, 'I'm told flights between here and the British mainland have just been grounded, but I've a feeling the bird has already flown. Nothing goes within sixty miles of Ullswater, even the scheduled flights must detour. RAF Fighter Command is patrolling.'

'She needn't use a plane,' said Franklin.

'All roads are being sealed off. Everything, even the mountain tracks. And we'll have special army units patrolling. And helicopters.'

'She doesn't have to go by automobile.'

'Oh yes, she does. That canister weighs over thirty pounds and it's three feet long. Schneider is young and strong, but not strong enough to carry thirty pounds of lead very far.'

'Couldn't she ride?' asked Franklin.

'Ride? Ride what?'

'A horse! No plane, no automobile, how else could she carry thirty pounds deadweight? How did they do it before cars and planes? And it would be easy by night without the helicopters. And silent. The night patrols might come across her but then again they might not. She stands a chance. She doesn't have any other way.'

'What extraordinary fantasy, Franklin. A German terrorist on horseback riding through the Lakeside dales by moonlight carrying plutonium to kill an Arab king. Improbable, but not impossible, I suppose. When you have dismissed the improbable only the impossible remains, as the famous detective said.'

'What will you do?'

'Put guards on every stable and farm around the cordon area.'

'She may already be inside.'

'Yes, Franklin. But it's all for nothing, because we're already evacuating. Army and police and civil defence have been on the go now for three hours. It's a slow job, farms are miles apart and some without telephones, but with luck we'll make it. As you say, she can only move at night so that must mean tonight and by then, please God, we'll have everyone well out of the contamination area.'

'Fahd?'

'Out first, what did you expect? Your people came in for him as soon as we alerted them.'

'Schneider will know.'

'She can't. Nothing on radio. Nothing.'

'So we're safe?'

'People are. But not Ullswater, not the land. Not the animals. It'll be a desert, Franklin, untouchable. God, d'you see the panic once it happens? Where next? What ransoms will we pay in the future if this one comes off? It's too horribly fantastic.'

He moved to the door at the end of the corridor and held it open. He said, 'Your people will meet you in Manchester before you go on with the police to Ullswater. You, plus nine of our own with radiographic metal detectors to give you something on the lead canister. And you'll have suits. Anti-contamination suits. You'll be safe.'

'My people said I go?'

'Yes.'

'But I'm not even a regular.'
'Meaning?'
'I mean I'm not a regular. Not a professional.'
'You really do write for a newspaper?'
'*New York Times*.'
'Good Lord!' Howard was not smiling. 'How much do you know about the Fahd thing?'
'The Fahd thing?'
'About Ghaddaffi. And OPEC?'
'I know all about it. I got it from Fahd himself. And I gave it to the Agency.'
'Good Lord!'
'Good Lord what, Howard?'
'A newspaperman? And you know so much?'
'What are you getting at?'
'Nothing,' said the Englishman, 'really nothing.'

But it all suddenly made sense to him. He had wondered why the Americans in London had been so insistent it should be Franklin who went into the cordon area for Schneider. Franklin was the risk . . . a high risk. He was not a regular and yet he had information that no non-regular should have. So they were sending him in after Schneider, and into an area where the odds of coming out were very slim indeed. The Americans in London knew that and so presumably did Washington. Now Franklin was to be put out of the way, and the ends to be neatly tied up—very neatly indeed.

The Englishman smiled what he considered to be his last smile at Franklin. 'Come,' he said. 'Let's get you off. You Americans,' he said, patting Franklin on the back, 'sometimes show style. Wonderful style.'

December 23rd

'Let the bastards freeze'

Already the President's Ultimatum, as it was now being called worldwide had backfired—just as his adversaries in Washington, Riyadh, Moscow, Paris and Bonn had predicted it would. The first intimation was the signal relayed to him from Naval Headquarters in the Pentagon, received via the surveillance satellite SATCOM that the LPH 3 Assault Ship *USS Okinawa* in the Persian Gulf had suddenly increased its speed, slightly altered its course, and was not responding to orders to sail south-west.

Had there been a technical fault, the President had demanded?

Was it possible the Soviets were jamming communications? Surely, said the President, there must be other ways for US Navy Command to contact one of its vessels at sea? No, sir, was the answer. Not if the ship cannot or will not answer. Will not? What is the implication, the President had asked. None at this time, was the answer, but we are investigating with utmost vigour.

Not for the first time in his short Presidential career, suddenly intimate with the nation's most precious military secrets, the President realized that the military machine, working properly, is one colossal marvel. But faulty circuitry can reduce its many parts to sudden impotency.

Readiness Command at Modill Air Base in Florida co-ordinated a twelve-thousand-million dollar world-wide military control system—WIMEX for short—which was supposed to tie up the whole of the United States global electronic intelligence-gathering network. It had satellites twenty-two thousand miles up in space and submarine-listening buoys down on the floor of every ocean, all linking up with that telephone on the President's desk and he in turn was linked to all the twenty-seven major US Commands around the world.

Yet at that moment, a warship of the United States Navy, fully armed with a variety of missiles and a full complement of men, steaming through the waters of the most politically volatile area in the world, was suddenly out of touch. And approaching it, according to the satellite photographs, were twenty-two warships of the Soviet fleet. And all the Pentagon could do was to investigate with utmost vigour.

The President's attention was quickly diverted to the immediate domestic crisis. He had expected the nation's support, but on the morning following his address to the nation, it became clear to him that he had underestimated his fellow-citizens' panic and their fury at the loss of their God-given right to mobility.

Some Governors in the North-Eastern States had already taken precautionary measures in anticipation of it. In Massachusetts, where the overnight temperature had fallen to a freak fourteen degrees Fahrenheit below zero, a ban was placed that morning on the sale of all fuel, except for domestic heating. The Governor, who had held that office for twenty-seven years, reckoned he knew his constituents like his own family, and was convinced they would accept that he had done what had needed to be done for the general good.

He was wrong, and petrol bombs thrown through his windows reduced his pretty New England wood-shell house to charcoal.

Across the nation very rapidly that morning, from East to West Coast, from the Canadian to the Mexican borders, lobbyists besieged Washington with charges of incompetence, nepotism and corruption. 'There is,' said one Congressman, 'energy McCarthyism at work.' It was quickly and generally agreed that the fair sharing of available fuel stocks would be impossible to achieve, and the consensus was that it was quickly going to be every man for himself and the lobby with the most punch would be the winner. The President had appealed the night before for sacrifice; he had also spoken of the Jeremiahs who, in the President's words, had predicted a regional, racial and economic divisiveness not seen since slavery and secession. He was not going to get his sacrifice but for sure he was getting the rest.

Shortly after the television breakfast news shows, spelling out the fuel crisis were over, a crowd of over a hundred in Freemansburg, Pennsylvania, attacked the manager of a gas station, beat him unconscious, filled up their tanks and drove off.

In Levittan, an estimated two thousand militants and thrill-seekers began systematically wrecking those stations that had either run out of fuel or pretended they had. At one of the largest, in the centre of the town, they used a lorry to knock over the pumps which then began spewing hundreds of gallons of gasoline on to the streets, like the original gusher. In an attempt to cut off the electricity to the pumps, a policeman pulled out the power line. It earthed, accidentally, and the flash set the lake of gasoline alight; the policeman and twenty-two rioters went running hysterically around the centre of the main street on fire.

The Governor of Georgia declared a State of Emergency which gave him wide powers and he applied them in the way Southern Governors traditionally do. Dusk-to-dawn curfews were imposed in Alabama after widespread rioting, and national guardsmen were given authority to shoot to kill anyone on the streets during curfew hours and to arrest, during the day, any people who gathered in a public place in groups of five or more.

There was the same extreme emergency law enforcement in Ohio when men came on to the streets, armed with shotguns, to confront policemen who were trying to prevent a mob from taking over a Gulf Oil fuel depot containing one hundred and eighty-two thousand gallons of high octane gasoline.

And in the oil-producing states of the South, Mr America was reminded of what the Jeremiahs had meant when they had promised 'regional divisiveness'. Masked men had shot dead a security guard and critically wounded three more in an attack on the pipeline taking oil north where it crossed the state border. Then they sabotaged the supplies by blowing up the pipeline and the pump relay station. And when police arrived by helicopter, they saw scrawled in the sand in oil, 'IT'S OURS. WE KEEP IT.'

There were also attacks on the refineries at Galveston and Houston, Texas, because refining more heating oil for the chilly north-east meant less petrol for the auto-dependent West. And diesel for the farmers of the mid-West meant less for the truckers who carried east and north most of what the farmers sold.

The truckers, promised diesel by Federal decree, found they were suddenly having to pay four times the price for it, and even if they filled their tanks they were still immobilized by traffic jams with the highways strewn with abandoned vehicles and throughways clogged by motorists queueing for fuel. In Florida, troopers were flown in by helicopters to force motorists off the streets at gunpoint so that a stranded convoy of meat trucks could pass through.

Stickers started to appear in the the back windows of cars in the southern oil states with the simple, provocative message addressed to their fellow home-heating consumer Americans in the North: 'LET THE BASTARDS FREEZE.'

In California preparations were made to plough under hundreds of thousands of acres of ripe tomatoes, lettuce and melons, because there were no trucks to take them to market. Ten and a half thousand head of beef cattle waiting in the abbatoirs in the mid-Western States of Iowa, Nebraska, Oklahoma and Minnesota were shot dead and burnt because it was too expensive to feed them. There were no trucks to take the meat off to their markets and the freezers were already full to capacity.

People thought of building their own fuel reservoirs in their back gardens, but for most it was already too late. There were plenty of plastic tanks, but where was the fuel to fill them? Wherever fuel supplies were moved, by train or by road tankers, they were heavily guarded by army and state troopers. Gasoline was now better watched than Fort Knox gold simply because it was now more scarce.

'They drink camels' piss'

'PETROL RATIONING . . . IF WE'RE LUCKY!' The headlines were splashed large. The story dominated the media, reporting in detail Britain's newest and most unpleasant economic surprise, the consequence of a decision taken that morning by the Privy Councillors at Number Ten Downing Street, in reaction to another earlier one taken in a hot desert capital four thousand miles away from bitterly cold London.

The Prime Minister had been in Cabinet ever since the Privy Councillors had left Number Ten. She was expected to emerge in the early afternoon to make a statement to the House of Commons.

But as it happened, neither she nor her Foreign Affairs advisers knew all the developments. It was later described as 'a communications lapse'.

An Admiralty signal of priority classification had been received early that morning from the British Naval Intelligence Unit stationed on the coast of Oman, reporting the arrival in the area of twenty-two warships of the Soviet Seventh Fleet which, according to earlier information, had been undergoing warm-water exercises south in the Arabian Sea. The signal reported the Soviets headed by the carrier *Minsk* and the assault ship *Ivan Rogov* cruising towards the Strait of Hormuz, presumably to enter the Persian Gulf.

The signal was considered important enough to be forwarded immediately by Intelligence at Admiralty to the First Sea Lord for him to acknowledge and advise the Prime Minister accordingly. Unfortunately, although it was considered by him of much relevance, it was not, because of the immediate domestic emergency, thought crucial enough to worry the Prime Minister immediately. But then he had not been told, nor would he be, of the presence of the American assault ship *Okinawa*'s position at the entrance to the Persian Gulf. Neither could he have known the character, or mental instability of the *Okinawa*'s Captain. So the Oman signal was acknowledged as received by the First Sea Lord's personal secretary, logged by him and then placed in a file marked 'PRIORITY' on the right-hand corner of his desk, where it was soon covered by Orders of the Day concerning vital fuel supplies to the Combined Services pending the implementation of fuel rationing in the country's private and public sectors.

The Prime Minister's decision of an immediate and total embargo on all North Sea oil exports received, after some debate, unanimous Cabinet approval. Most of the Ministers present, sitting in the cramped Cabinet room overlooking a snow-covered Horse Guards Parade, voted enthusiastically for it. They knew it would most certainly lead to confrontations with the EEC and in turn Britain's probable expulsion from the Community, and they were not displeased at the prospect.

They argued that every one of the Member countries would do exactly the same, given similar circumstances, given that they too had oil to barter with. The British Government, they insisted, would ride the protests and the charges of infidelity and selfishness from the super-critical Germans, and the hypocritical French. And anyway, as the Foreign Secretary had argued so reasonably, oil had suddenly become a scarce product, and the prospect was that it would become even scarcer; and Europe was nothing without it. If Britain was expelled from the Community and the time came later for readmission, who among the member governments would object? The Foreign Secretary was right; oil had become a powerful weapon and Britain should use it.

The Prime Minister agreed, as it was expected she would. It was, she said, a crisis of such proportion that extraordinary decisions had to be taken. She reminded them of the urgent need for strong purposeful leadership, and the commitment Ministers had to collective responsibility. She concluded, as she always did at moments when her will and her office were liable to be questioned with a warning. Because of the nature of the present crisis and the need for quick Cabinet consensus, she would have to consider taking certain Ministerial portfolios to herself.

The vindicatory was understood by all and there were no objections, and that evening the Prime Minister went on television on all four channels simultaneously to explain why her Majesty's Government considered the British oil embargo and fuel rationing essential to survival. She ended her statement to the nation with phrases similar to those used by the American President in his; appealing for the support of 'each and every one of you, confident you will rally'. And like the American President, she was wrong.

The petrol bombs were thrown through the first-floor window of Number Ten Downing Street one hour and ten minutes after the Prime Minister had left for her house in Chelsea. No one was injured, but the fire spread quickly and extensively, damaging curtains and carpets. The worst damage was done by firemen whose water jets pierced the smoke and ripped apart two canvases hanging on the wall of the first floor landing, a Turner and a Sisley on loan from the National Gallery.

At first the IRA was blamed, they being held responsible for all black mischief in the United Kingdom. But an anonymous telephone caller to the Press Association claimed responsibility and promised there would be more. His ration of petrol, he said, wouldn't move his car out of his garage so the petrol would be put to better use. Within the hour there were similar attacks on the Home Office, a hundred yards down Whitehall from Downing Street, and another on the Department of Employment in St James's Square.

The last flaming bottle went through the swing doors of the Foreign Office and hit the night porter in his chest, severely burning him. There were no further incidents that night and no further calls to the Press Association, and it was hoped the fire-bomber had used up his ration of petrol.

Squads of workmen from the Department of the Environment began screwing steel-mesh fireguards over the windows of all important government buildings at ground and first-floor levels and it was hoped the protest and demolition would end. It did not. It became far more spectacular.

The Saudi Arabian Embassy was hit at ten minutes past two, the Lybian and Iranian Embassies at twenty past. The techniques of these explosions were identical and simple, using—with macabre irony—Arab oil to do it.

In the basements of the three West London Embassies were large storage tanks containing fuel oil for the central heating boilers. It was an exceptionally cold London winter, and special care had been taken to ensure that the tanks were always kept full. At the time of the attacks, the tank at each of the three Embassies contained one thousand, two hundred gallons of highly combustible fuel oil.

The central heating system in all three embassies had been installed by the same national central heating company so the design was identical. At the Saudi Embassy, leading from the underground storage tank was the inlet supply pipe, three inches in diameter and fifteen feet long, coming up just above ground level on the outside wall at a convenient height for visiting fuel tanker lorries to connect their resupply hoses to. The tank's supply pipe was sealed by a heavy brass cap and secured by a single padlock.

The petrol-bombers, as the press catch-named them, operated in teams of three. Dressed in blue overalls with the initials 'BP' on their backs, and passing for British Petroleum maintenance engineers, they broke the lock on the brass sealer cap and emptied four five-gallon cans of petrol down the pipe. Being lighter than the heavy fuel oil, this floated on top. Then they rolled down the pipe three small balls, two inches in diameter, each containing a phosphorus-based compound sealed in a thin layer of hard wax. They sank into the fuel oil and as they floated back to the surface the petrol dissolved the wax. Within three minutes, and with the bogus BP engineers safely away from the area, the phosphorus was exposed to air and ignited. The flash set the petrol on fire and within another four minutes the fuel oil had been heated to five thousand degrees Centigrade, the temperature at which it combusts. Sealed inside the tank, the heat and pressure generated by it was enormous, and the blast took the steel-plated top of the storage tank up through the basement floor, the super-heat instantly killing twenty-four Saudis queueing at the Home Affairs desk for air tickets home. Their bodies, immediately sealed in burning oil, were then forced twenty feet through the wooden floorboards above and into the First Secretary's offices where the scorching heat and the burning oil took their second round of victims.

Fifty-four Saudis died in their Embassy, thirty-eight Libyans and forty-one Iranians in theirs. The just-living casualties, survivors so badly burnt and so deformed they would never walk again, would drink their food through pipes and would never close their eyes to sleep again, totalled, for the three Embassies, eighty-eight. That evening, the terrible casualties made television viewers throughout the world forget for an instant their own separate woes and they joined the outraged protests. But then, just as quickly, fuel rationing, the President's ultimatum, United Nations' confusion and Soviet naval activity—lumped together by the media as the 'Gulf Crisis'—took back their attention, and the dead and the slowly dying who had been brought out of the three Arab Embassies in London were quickly forgotten.

It was hoped that the outrage would dissipate the accelerating anti-Arab sentiments that were now being promoted on street corners, in pubs, bars, Parliament and clubs, but it did not. All kinds of British Nationalist Movements under many titles and for many reasons began quickly to spread anti-Arab propaganda and the Arab suddenly supplanted the West Indian and the Pakistani as the targets of racist attacks. This caused much relief in London's Southall, Lewisham, Brixton and the country's other Black immigrant ghettoes and, almost in a sense of gratitude, the Black and the Asian became as quickly and as vehemently anti-Arab.

The Monday Club, a select association of wealthy right-wing racist-xenophobists, demanded the immediate nationalization of all Arab investment and property in the United Kingdom, including the sequestration of Arab money held by British banks and Arab stocks and shares held by British brokers. 'Do what they did to us', became the Club's shibboleth, reminding people of Sir Anthony Eden's loss of the Suez Canal to Nasser in 1956, and his futile attempts to bomb the Egyptians back to submission.

The Monday Club clarion was quickly taken up by others. There was much to fire Mr Ordinary Britisher's hatred of the Arab. 'Wog' was reintroduced to his vocabulary of abuse and 'A-rab' became the vilest term of derision in school playgrounds and factory shop-floors. Overnight it had become a physical hazard for anyone dressed in djellabahs to hail a taxi, let alone walk Regent's Street. Arabs were advised by their Embassies to stay indoors and they did. Harrods, long called 'Arabs' by Londoners, seemed suddenly bare without them and the chain department store, Marks and Spencer, wondered, looking at the West End daily sales returns, whether Arabs had been their only customers. There were empty waiting rooms in Harley Street and exclusive doctors and dentists bit their nails and wondered whether the replacement Porsche might not have to wait a while. In quick retreat from the sudden antagonism the Arabs created something of a vacuum.

The anti-Arab rantings across the entire spectrum of the British Right was given much exposure and therefore much encouragement by the media. The long-dead Lord Avon, Prime Minister Sir Anthony Eden at the time of Suez, became the hero of the day and, taking the precaution of informing Fleet Street picture agencies and the television news networks, the League of Empire Loyalists draped the Union Jack over his grave at Alvediston cemetery, near Salisbury in Wiltshire while a bugler sounded the 'Last Post'.

Like their American cousins, the British found it easy to despise the Arabs, who had created a dozen crises in as many years; taking the Israelis repeatedly to war, causing recession after recession in Western capitalism with their insatiable demand for petro-dollars, hijacking and destroying aircraft, killing innocent people for some non-existent never-to-be-gotten Palestine. Bombing, bullying, hostage taking, machine-gunning and hand-grenading their way to the world's attention. They were the makers of mayhem with their unique Moslem intolerance in a world that possibly deserved better treatment. Western eyes made no distinction. Palestinian, Kuwaiti, Saudi, Iranian, Iraqi, Yemeni, Lebanese, Jordanian, Egyptian, Syrian: they were all Arabs and they were hateful. They were Moslems. They were filthy. They fornicated with goats and ate sheep's balls. They drank camel's piss. They were to be despised.

Again, like their American cousins, the British did not take kindly to the new and very severe restrictions caused by the fuel rationing, caused by the Arabs. Until petrol coupons could be printed, all petrol stations were closed and, until the government had decided how coupons could be distributed equitably, only public transport would be available. Request for permits to obtain petrol had to be applied for at local magistrate's courts, and they were not expected to grant them freely.

As always, many thousands of motorists refused or were unable to look reality and the law in the eyes, and on the evening following the Prime Minister's decree the roads and motorways of Britain were littered with cars and lorries, abandoned wherever the needle had finally crossed '*empty*'.

And that night, on the separate main news bulletins, Mr Britain saw live, via satellite, what extraordinary and increasingly outrageous things Mr America was doing to keep himself mobile. And they saw too the extraordinary outrageous thing their President now seemed willing to do to keep it that way.

The patience of the British, like their apathy, is well known, and, in the tradition of the British in times of crisis, it was widely believed that it would all blow over, despite what they saw on their screens, in spite of what they heard on their radios and read in their newspapers. The President's ultimatum would do the trick. Anyway, there was always North Sea oil. Nothing could touch that. Which, as it happened, almost proved disastrously wrong.

It was a force nine and gout in the skipper's right foot that prevented it.

The *Pegasus* was a converted Scottish motor trawler operating out of Aberdeen on the West Scottish coast. Once a week it sailed from that port eighty miles out into the North Sea to the giant oil drilling rig *Constellation*, supplying the one hundred and five men working there with essentials like kippers and smoked bacon, cigarettes, bread, water and a regular assortment of expensive rig equipment to replace the worn and the faulty. And once a month the *Pegasus* would bring out a new shift of men and take the tired ones back for a fortnight's shore leave.

But on this morning, the *Pegasus* had been held up in Aberdeen harbour because of the pain in the skipper's foot, long diagnosed as gout, symptom of a high uric acid level in his blood, the result of sixty-two excessive years. He should have been at the wheel at three am, but the pain was such that when he had swallowed the last of his Brufen painkillers, he realized he could not sail without more. He would wait for his doctor's surgery to open, get a new prescription and sail at nine. But in the meantime the wind turned around from south-west to north-east and the waves began hitting the breakwater twenty feet high. For three hours the *Pegasus*, deep in the water and full of supplies, rode the swell inside the protected harbour, tugging at her ropes, with her skipper—the painkillers having dissolved the pain—striding back and forth along the quay then looking at the sky and cursing the cussedness of Scottish weather. He did not know it but the north-easterly and his gout caused what was possibly the most fortunate delay in recent British history.

The *Pegasus* should have tied up at the rig at eleven that morning but instead she eventually came alongside at ten that night. It meant that the two men, hidden in the forward hold of the supply vessel, had either to abandon their attempt to blow up the rig or do what they could despite the late hour, and despite the tide that was now running from slack to ebb.

They knew that the one hour of slack tide had been crucial to their operation, so meticulously planned. Sitting there in the dark, sick with the sea's buffeting and the smell of diesel oil, they talked in whispers. They could go back to Aberdeen and report to their superiors that the attack had had to be abandoned. Or they could do what they had come all this way to do, in spite of the tide and the odds against them.

They had come aboard in their black neoprene diving suits, carrying their compressed airbottles, the previous evening while supplies were still being loaded into the *Pegasus*' holds. They had taken it in turns to sleep during the night, but they had both heard the wind turn and felt the rise and swell of the water inside the harbour and they knew before they heard the skipper's curses that it was going wrong and there was nothing they could do to change it.

Their own people would ask later why, knowing that the delay in the harbour made it impossible for the attack on the rig to succeed, the two went ahead with it? Why didn't they abandon *Pegasus* and report back and wait for new orders? There was never to be an answer.

The rubber tyres on the supply boat's sides prevented the teak boards from being splintered in the sea's buffeting and after much manoeuvring the skipper got his lines securely tied to one of the rig's tubular steel legs. The hatches were then opened and through the icy, stinging spray supplies were slowly hoisted to the main platform a hundred and twenty feet up, the rig's floodlights making harsh daylight on *Pegasus*' deck. All eyes were on the work, so no one saw the two divers emerge through the forward hatch and slip overboard, though had anyone seen them they would have been taken for maintenance divers going below to carry out any one of a hundred routine checks on the drilling gear. They carried across their chests toolpacks identical to those used by the rig's diving engineers, and the same weighted orange coloured torches. But they did not carry tools in the chest packs. Neatly arranged inside them were seven pounds of plastic high explosive, two electro-magnets, nylon lines and detonators that could be activated by a radio signal sent from the radio transmitter carefully concealed between the timbers of the *Pegasus*' forward hold.

Before they began their dive through the black sea, they tied a cord to the steel tow-ring at the base of the boat's bow, a bright orange nylon cord that would guide them back up. Slowly they began their struggle down and, every few minutes, each man shone his torch at the depth gauge on his wrist. Only these occasional flashes through the blackness assured the other he was not alone. Still they carried on down, hoping the current would ease. At eighty feet they came together, facing each other, their torches alight so that the one could see the other. One passed his hand sideways across his throat in a cutting motion, but the other shook his head and pointed downwards indicating that they should dive deeper. There was a moment's hesitation. Then the other nodded, the torch lights went out and the orange cord unwound further.

At one hundred and twenty feet beneath the hull of the *Pegasus*, they stopped diving, their torches came on again and they checked the depth gauges on their wrists. Their faces were only a yard apart and in the brilliant glare they saw each other's eyes through their masks. They had hoped that at this depth the strength of the running tide would not prevent them doing what they had come to do, but they were still struggling to keep their position against the leg of the rig, twisting to stop their air bottles turning them upside down. They felt the vicious tug at their goggles and mouthpiece and they knew, even as they began to undo their chest packs, that they had failed.

Their target was one of the four huge legs that supported the rig above water and the series of underwater bearing supports that held the drill in position. Both men had been employed on oil rigs as construction divers, so they both knew exactly what could be sabotaged with a little explosive. It was impractical to blow the drill. Any malfunction in the drilling mechanism itself or any blow in the pipeline and the oil outlet on the seabed was immediately and completely sealed by what oil men call the 'Christmas tree'. To blow the Christmas tree meant going down three hundred feet or more, and that could only be done in a diving bell. It was decided that the quickest and easiest sabotage was to collapse one of the legs at its weld seam, the weakest point, so the entire rig would topple into the sea. There was an even chance that as it went over it would pull the Christmas tree up with it, freeing the pressure of oil and spilling it out at the rate of a thousand gallons a minute. It had been estimated by the planners who had hired and trained the divers that it would take between eight and thirty hours to cap the well again, an operation delayed and hampered by the oil and the need to rescue the survivors who had gone overboard. In that time, they calculated, nearly ten million gallons of crude oil would have spilled into the North Sea with the tides and wind spreading it fast to the eastern Scottish coast, the Norwegian and Danish coasts and, with the wind constant from the North East, oil would enter the English Channel, the Thames Estuary, and touch the Normandy coast.

But *Pegasus* had been late, the divers had lost their one precious hour of slack water, and the tide was now running fast and quickly, sapping their strength. Yet they had come this far, had risked so much, and the reward promised was so great that, struggling in the darkness at a depth of one hundred and twenty feet, they decided to continue.

Holding on to the nylon line with one hand, they unzipped their chest packs, took out one of the two electromagnets and clamped it to the leg. On the magnet was an eyelet and, as one man held the other steady in the surge, he threaded half-inch thick nylon cord through it and through that he threaded the small round doughnut-shaped packs of explosive and the detonator rings. They struggled to keep their position as the sea surged this way and that, turning them and pulling them away from the steel leg. But the magnet was now clamped tight on to the steel and the divers used it to keep themselves steady. For another five minutes they slowly threaded the explosive doughnuts and the detonators on to the cord, every effort harder than the last, until fifteen had been secured.

Then, pulling the second magnet from his chest pack, the senior diver, took hold of the end of the cord and began to swim around the twenty-five foot circumference of the huge leg, so that the explosives were evenly spread around it. But at that moment, as he let go of the orange safety line, a current of sea pushed its way through the maze of steel struts and he was suddenly caught in its flow. Desperately he began clawing for the safety line but as the other watched in the flood of torchlight, he saw the black body tossed up and down and smashed against the steel, and he saw the man's airpipe torn from the valve and a burst of bubbles shoot from the bottles. Then only the blackness, only the nylon cord carrying the doughnuts shaking violently around him with the heavy electro-magnet on the end of it. Quickly he tugged in the orange safety line and began to pull himself up, forcing his flippers down in an effort to lever his tiring body away from the explosives, away from the heavy magnet that spun around him in the swirling current. But just as he felt he was free the cord and the explosives whipped around him like a dozen lassoos, tying his arms tight against his body and then there was the sudden and terrifying thump on his back as the electro-magnet clamped itself to his steel bottles.

The rig's maintenance divers found him the following morning, his head torn off by the whiplash of the underwater current. He was trussed up like rolled mutton, the nylon cord wrapped tightly around him, secured at one end by one powerful electro-magnet to the steel leg and held by the second clamped to his bottles.

The headless torso, the explosive doughnuts and the

detonators were brought to the surface, the body to be examined and its finger-prints taken, the detonators to be disarmed and the plastic to be taken away by a Royal Air Force helicopter to Kinross. By the time the *Pegasus* had arrived back in Aberdeen, eight police in uniform and three men in civilian clothes were waiting on the quayside. With apologies from the police Superintendent, the plain clothes men, led by a middle-aged man the other two referred to as Colonel, went into the boat's holds. They stayed down there searching for forty minutes and when they reappeared, the Colonel was carrying what looked to the skipper like a small portable radio transmitter, though he had seen nothing quite like it before.

When they had left, with casual apologies, the skipper took the *Pegasus* around to the dry dock for inspection. The portside screw had been fouled up and he saw that it was bound in a bright orange nylon cord that someone, for some extraordinary reason unknown to him, had tied to the forward tow shackle on the underneath of the bow.

Nothing was made public concerning the *Constellation* rig or the headless diver, tied up in explosive, who had been found one hundred feet beneath it. Nor was much interest shown locally when the skipper told his story over his evening beer about the plain-clothes man called Colonel who had found a radio in *Pegasus*' forward hold. And, as no organization claimed the diver's torso, the incident was for ever to remain a secret.

Only in Dublin, Belfast and New York did the lack of radio and television news that morning confirm that the sabotage attempt had been a failure. The divers must be dead. They would have made contact otherwise. Shortly after midday a call from Dublin to the Irish Revolutionary Party offices in New York, relaying an eye-witness account from their agent in Aberdeen, confirmed that the *Pegasus* had returned undamaged but with a headless passenger.

It was the end of a plot to aggravate, in the most outrageously sensational way, the British oil dilemma and had been masterminded by sophisticated Irishmen in New

York who would only have found need to advertise themselves had their attempt succeeded. As it hadn't they were content to sip their dry Martinis high above Manhattan, just as ready to try something else, just as sensational another time.

That night the towns and cities of Britain experienced something they had forgotten existed. The Government not only suspended sales of fuel oil for domestic heating, but at the same time also suspended the Clean Air Acts which had banned the use of any but smokeless fuels in built-up areas. So that night people warmed themselves with coal and wood in open grates, and looked out of their windows on the first smogs for more than twenty years.

'Two horses and a saddle'

Franklin sat in the front passenger seat of the Range Rover driven by the Chief Constable of Cumbria, the administrative county that encompasses the Lake District of northern England. They were travelling along the M6 motorway towards the Penrith turn off that would take them on to the road to Pooley Bridge and Howtown at the eastern end of Lake Ullswater, bordering King Fahd's estate.

For an hour he had been listening to the news bulletins over the car radio, reporting the panic that was now sweeping the United States—the same panic that now threatened Britain and Europe. The British Government had reneged on its oil contracts with its North Sea oil embargo. In response, the French President closed French airports to British airliners, the West Germans had begun recalling short-term loans off British banks, and the Belgians were stoning the British Embassy at The Hague. Even an England v. Netherlands football match in Amsterdam was cancelled.

'Your President's waving the big stick,' said the Chief Constable. He was a burly man who had outgrown his jacket and Franklin saw that his shirt-cuffs were frayed.

Franklin nodded back. 'He reckons that's just about the most threatening weapon in the Pentagon's armoury,' he said.

'Will he invade?'

'He can't. We just don't have the capacity. The Russians are already there, all around the Gulf. It would take America two weeks to set up a force big enough to land there and stay.'

'Dangerous then, to issue such an ultimatum.'

'Right.'

'And frightening. You're our leaders too, you know.'

'You're right,' said Franklin. 'It's frightening.'

The Chief Constable looked into his driving mirror. The car in the police convoy behind him was flashing its headlamps.

'They want us to speed up,' he said.

He leaned across to thumb down a switch and Franklin could just make out the revolving blue light reflected on the car's bonnet. There was a quick burst of siren and cars in front of them in the fast outside lane, travelling at the regulation seventy miles an hour, quickly moved left to let them pass by.

'You've no doubts about Schneider?' asked the Chief Constable.

'She's here.'

'The canister too? It's fantastic.'

'That's what Howard said.'

'Howard?'

'Someone I met. One of your people in Dublin.' Franklin pulled out his cigarettes and the Chief Constable pushed in the lighter button on the dash, but shook his head as Franklin opened the packet to him.

'It took him a day to make someone talk before he got to know about Schneider's arrival and the canister. I think that one day delay could cost us a lot.'

'Fahd is that important?' asked the policemen.

'Without him back on his throne, we're apparently all in trouble.'

'Why?'

'I don't know myself. It's an Agency operation, that's all I know, and it's moving on a Presidential directive which means it's big. For whatever reason they want Fahd back we've gotta believe it's a good one.'

'I believe you,' said the Chief Constable. He paused. Then he said, as if he'd suddenly lost interest. 'D'you know, I think it's going to snow again!'

Franklin could see the mountains of the Lake District ahead, rolling black and white shapes, like sleeping dinosaurs. And touching them, sprawling over them, snow clouds, like dirty grey tablecloths, coming in from the north-east. He had never been this far north of this tiny island before and it struck him, watching the face of the countryside change as the sky changed above it, that there was possibly no other country he had ever visited where the weather could alter the character of the land and its people so rapidly. Britain and the British he had always been told were so constant. He found them both flimsy and volatile.

He saw the motorway sign and the convoy of police cars turned left towards the motorway junction. An army road block was ahead, three Scorpion light tanks and a Scout helicopter were parked on the grass verge. Identities were exchanged.

'I've a message for a Mr Franklin, sir.'

'I'm Franklin.'

The army captain leant forward closer to the car window. 'It's from one of our patrols, sir who've been scouting along Martindale, that's on the south-west corner of the Lake, sir, about three miles down the valley. A farm's been attacked . . . man and his wife shot dead.'

'Is that all?'

'No, sir. We've had orders from headquarters to let you know of anything to do with horses.'

'Yes?'

'Two seem to have been taken from the farm, sir. Two horses . . . and a saddle. Nothing else missing.'

The Chief Constable of Cumbria, already briefed by Franklin on the preposterous possibility and the sudden extraordinary relevance of horses, accelerated away down the winding road between the high hawthorn hedges lined with oaks towards Lake Ullswater.

She led the horses carefully through the tight gulley, wet from the small waterfall that splashed its way through the crevices and bounced off the boughs of alders, trees that had curled and spread over it forming a ceiling of leaves. The first horse tugged at its halter to drink from a small pool that had collected in the indent of a boulder and Schneider waited until it was satisfied. Then she pulled them further down into the shade and tied their halters to the root of a sapling giving them enough strap to eat.

She had made it just in time. Snow was beginning to fall, and the clouds were heavy. Within an hour it would be inches deep and every footstep, every hoof mark and rabbit's paw, even the pattering of woodcock and pheasant, would be seen by a trained tracker. But she had left no tracks and in an hour's time the snow would be a help. It would muffle sound and hamper the army patrols.

She held the map towards the late afternoon light and with her finger traced the line she had drawn on it above Martindale church through the stream and up the side of Hallin Fell following the sheep tracks, beyond Sandwick Village still climbing to the Knab. Her finger stopped with the tip of her nail touching a small black square over-printed Howtown. She planned to stand on the top of the mountain looking down to the small estate, certain to see the lights of the house a thousand feet below. And there, as the mountain sloped towards the edge of Ullswater, she would leave the horse with the lead canister strapped to it. There she would cut its hamstrings, there she would set the timing device of the detonator that would explode the soft lead and release the plutonium. And the mountain's downdraught would take its death rapidly and inevitably to Howtown and the King.

She had given herself only fifteen minutes to ride the second horse away from the explosion, estimating that the wind off the mountain would be constant and that the flow of radio-activity would not begin to change direction until it had reached the warmer turbulent air of the valley. Even if the lower winds did begin to take it south, she would be ahead of it and outside the contamination area before it could reach her. If she was wrong she would die by her own devices. For this reason alone the small black pistol was in her breast pocket.

She folded the map and looked up towards the mountains a mile the other side of Martindale. Through the falling snow she could see figures three thousand yards away moving along the skyline, men with back-packs and rifles. And she knew the dead farmer and his wife had been found.

'Four miles and approaching'

Captain Hanks stood in his favourite corner of the bridge, forward port side, looking out across the three thousand square yards of flat grey deck. His hands were behind his back, and the small black rubber squash ball turned between the fingers and thumb of his right hand.

Below him, blue-overalled aircraft handling crews manoeuvred vertical take-off aircraft into neat lines, six of them abreast, guided by marshallers in yellow flight helmets communicating with the hangar below by two-way radios strung across their shoulders. And in the mess rooms below the flight deck, pilots sat drinking coffee and Coke and wondering why on a good-will tour they should suddenly be on standby alert.

In the gun turrets fore and aft of the bridge, crews sat in their anti-flash masks and green steel helmets deep inside the armour-plated screens and sweated with the weight of their flak-jackets cursing the Captain on his air-conditioned bridge.

The stub-nosed bow hardly moved. The horizon was steady and the sea, reflecting the day's last seconds of sunlight, was like a pond, mirror-still. Only the slightest swirl of current at the stern showed that the ship was under power and, except for the movement on the flight deck, the whole vessel could have been asleep and at ease in the twilight. But every man had been at action stations for the past fifteen minutes, and Captain Hanks was not on the bridge to watch the splendour of a mid-Eastern sunset. He was searching the sea for the first sign of the Soviet Seventh Fleet, the silhouettes of the Soviet carrier *Minsk* and its support ship the *Ivan Rogov*.

The *Okinawa* had not sailed down the southernmost coast of the Persian Gulf as instructed by US Naval Command in the Pentagon. Instead Captain Hanks had made his decision to take his warship at full power up to the Strait of Hormuz, the sea corridor through which all traffic entering and leaving the Gulf must pass by a deep water channel so narrow that a large ship sunk in it would delay passage and effectively block the movement of oil tankers and their vital cargo.

It was here, now, in the Strait of Hormuz, that Captain Hanks had positioned his carrier, broadside on, to face the oncoming Soviet fleet. He had mounted his own blockade across the only access the Arabian oil states had to their world markets, the only route the tankers could take. With the West's dependence on Arab oil, the Strait had long become the world's most vital sea corridor. Only Captain Hanks realized its strategic importance. Or so it seemed to him.

He had changed into a fresh uniform and stood, feet apart, his left hand holding binoculars, his right gently kneading the small black ball.

Lieutenant Ginsberg, Gunnery Officer, stood behind him and to one side, watching the ball turn; like the rest of the crew, he knew it was the mood indicator of the man. The ball turned slowly and regularly. Captain Hanks was as still inside as the sea he was scanning.

Lieutenant Vaduz, Communications Officer, knew it too, but he could not understand why. This was the time for Captain Hanks to be anxious. They had all listened to the President's speech. Some had been impressed by it. Many more, who remembered similar ultimatums in similar crises, called him a maverick and his speech bullshit. Men who despite their uniforms and their employment aboard a US warship, would not willingly go to war whatever the cause or call, not for oil, not for the President, not for America right or wrong. Lieutenant Vaduz saw the President's speech as a gambit, bluff, gusty fine platitudes in place of action because action of the kind necessary was not something American Presidents could ever indulge in again. Hadn't they tried it in Vietnam and failed? Hadn't they tried it in that fiasco in Cambodia when sixty-five marines died trying to rescue the merchant ship *Mayaguez*? Hadn't they tried it sending commandos to rescue American POWS in Son Tay prison, Hanoi, only to find it empty when they'd arrived? Hadn't they lost eight Americans and American pride in the Iranian desert? Hadn't every American foreign initiative, big and small, failed this generation? Wasn't that why the United States had been ridiculed in Cuba and humiliated in Iran?

And Lieutenant Vaduz knew that, even if America had lost its clout, even if it was a tottering, pitiful giant, Captain Hanks was not the man to put it right. Everyone could see the double deal. Strong words from the President out of Washington, and then a signal from the Pentagon to sail away from trouble. Captain Hanks had defied it, but how many of his men would in turn now defy him if he pressed confrontation with the Soviet fleet up front?

Lieutenant Vaduz watched his Captain's face in profile, watched for the jaw muscles to begin their flexing in and out, waited for the grating of his back teeth, and for the skin across his temples to tighten and glisten with sweat and the right hand to begin its violent convulsion with the ball. But there was none of it. The Captain pulled the binoculars to his eyes, using both hands, and Lieutenant Vaduz saw that he had placed the black rubber ball on the rack that held the fire extinguishers, abandoned.

'Four miles. And approaching.' The voice came up through the console speaker from Radar below.

Lieutenant Vaduz leant forward and pressed the reply switch.

'Thank you, Radar. We should have them visual any moment now.'

'I already have them visual, Mr Vaduz, 045 using the centre line as zero.' The Captain's voice was suddenly higher pitched than normal. Vaduz and Ginsberg followed the unfamiliar coordinates, using their binoculars to trace the line across the starboard corner of the carrier's flight deck. And then they too saw them, blurred shapes in the dusk but, to sea-eyes, unmistakable.

'The *Minsk* is second in line, sir,' said Lieutenant Ginsberg. 'The *Ivan Rogov* seems some distance back from her. A mile, maybe less.'

'Radar sir, three miles bearing 110 degrees, speed 14 knots and slowing.'

'110 and 14, slowing,' Lieutenant Vaduz repeated back.

'Now they've got us too,' said Ginsberg.

'They have had us for some time, Mr Ginsberg,' said Captain Hanks, in the same distant and high-pitched voice. 'For as long as I have had them. *Ivan Rogov* has distanced herself from the *Minsk*. She began turning away five minutes ago and eight—possibly nine—ships have followed. They've split. The *Minsk* and her battle group sailing to us, the others are moving port. There's some land that way, I believe?'

'The Malcolm Inlet, sir,' Lieutenant Ginsberg replied. 'Navigational for ten miles, but too shallow for anything large. There's nothing for them there.'

Captain Hanks nodded his head. 'I know their game. I know exactly their game. They've seen us broadside and now they want us to turn. They think I'm worried at having all my guns on one side.'

He adjusted the left-hand sight of his binoculars.

'We'll maintain our position and our tactic. Keep moving slowly fore and aft across the deep water channel. The bastards can't pass us and they know it.'

Lieutenant Ginsberg stepped forward. 'We have to let them pass, sir. These are territorial waters shared by Iran and Oman and we're breaking their laws. They have the right of innocent passage, sir.'

Captain Hanks adjusted the right sight-piece of his binoculars and said nothing.

'Sir,' said Lieutenant Vaduz, 'If we remain in this

position, it can be construed as a hostile act.'

'You can bet on it, boy,' replied Captain Hanks softly. 'You can safely bet it'll be exactly so construed. Innocent passage my ass!'

The door to the bridge opened and Lieutenant Commander Daniels, the *Okinawa*'s second-in-command, came in holding a single sheet of paper. The noise and bustle from the flight deck came in with him.

'Top priority—Washington—sir. From Admiral Holliwell himself.'

'Read it out,' said Captain Hanks, keeping the glasses to his eyes, as Radar interrupted:

'Two miles. Sonar Detection indicating they've reversed engines. Main vessels still on 110 degrees, other battle group three miles west on 127.'

'So,' said the Captain, 'they've stopped to ask the Kremlin what to do next.'

'Admiral Holliwell, sir,' said Commander Daniels, waving the signal at the Captain's back. 'He's ordered us to turn about.' He read from the signal. 'You are to avoid any confrontation. Utmost care—do not escalate situation—move away from Soviet fleet. Acknowledge receipt immediately.'

'Is that all?' asked Captain Hanks.

'That's all, sir.'

'What's the security prefix?'

'Beg pardon, sir?'

'You say it's from the Admiral? Pentagon? You say it's priority. Satellite communication. And uncoded?'

'Yessir.'

'Then there has to be a security prefix to match ours. You know that, Mr Daniels.'

'No, sir, not necessarily,' said Daniels.

'What d'you mean—not necessarily? Goddammit, is there a standard naval security procedure or isn't there? Are we going to have a debate on the bridge with Russian warships two miles off? Let me remind you this is suddenly an operational area and I'm confronting two of the cleverest warships of any navy of any sea and you tell me that I have to obey an uncoded order of this nature that has been sent over SATCOM for anyone to pick up? You're telling me the Admiral of the United States Navy sends such a thing with no security ident?' He pulled a handkerchief from his pocket and spat phlegm into it.

'Now you get back to Command, Mr Vaduz, and tell them of a signal we have received which purports to come from Admiral Holliwell—and you tell them, boy, that it is unorthodox and irregular and that I'm fucking suspicious. Now you just tell them that.'

'Captain,' said Daniels, 'we have already received two coded and security idented signals via SATCOM and we have, on your specific orders, failed to acknowledge either. Both signals have told us to move away from the Soviets, both have urged us to de-escalate the situation.'

Captain Hanks still held the binoculars to his eyes and Daniels stepped closer to him.

'Sir, it's plausible that Command are under the impression we cannot reply for technical or even security reasons, and Admiral Holliwell is anxious we move south. So he has broken routine security procedures to get through to us. And sir, I think it's also possible the Admiral has deliberately sent his signal this way so that the Soviets out there can pick it up and know we do not want confrontation. I really do think that's a possibility, sir.'

For half a minute, Captain Hanks said nothing. He held the binoculars to his eyes and scanned slowly from the main Soviet fleet ahead to the second convoy moving port. And then, to the dismay of his officers watching, he let the binoculars fall and hang the length of their short straps on his chest, and picked the black rubber ball up off the fire extinguisher rack. Lieutenant Vaduz saw his jaw muscles begin their angry contortions.

'Radar, sir, *Minsk* steady at two and a quarter miles.'

Captain Hanks turned to them raised his chin and spoke. 'Gentlemen, I appreciate the concern. I understand your explanations. I also remember less than two minutes ago telling Vaduz here to send a signal.'

In anxious reflex the young lieutenant backed painfully into the chart table again, saluted and left the bridge for the Satellite Communications Room.

'You talk of de-escalation,' the Captain continued after Vaduz had closed the bridge door. 'D'you not think that this is exactly what I am trying to do? De-escalate. Do you not think that allowing twenty-two Soviet warships into the Persian Gulf would lead to an immediate escalation of hostilities? Do you not see we are guarding the entrance to a little piece of sea that's suddenly vitally important to the United States? We know it, and so do those bastards out there, and why else d'you imagine it's coincidence? Were they not, those twenty-two ships, a hundred miles south of us, three days ago, on warm-water exercises? Then there's a coup and a new government and a shut-down of oil to the US and suddenly the *Minsk* leads her task force right in here.

'I'm a simple sailor with forty-two years' service and I know nothing of politics except that they double-deal us whether they're Democrats or Republicans. But I'll tell you one thing. The flags that are being waved on the streets of Riyadh today are of the same colour as those flying from those ships out there. I guarantee it. You heard the President. You heard what he said. I'll use his words again, because they are indelible on my mind. "Communist ambition," he said, "will attempt sooner or later to take it for itself. Because it is the Soviet's economic and military strategy to deny the United States Saudi oil." D'you remember him saying that? By God you should! What kind of world do we want to live in in five months, or five years from now?'

'Second convoy stopped, sir, bearing 124 degrees—one and a quarter miles.' The voice from radar control was quickly followed by a second urgent call from Lieutenant Vaduz.

'Sir. The *Minsk* is signalling, a one-liner. "CLEAR CHANNEL IMMEDIATELY." And we have a problem.'

'Problem? What problem? What problem Mr Vaduz?'

'I've lost SATCOM sir. All channels. I'm getting them but they can't get us. They're calling, but I can't answer.'

'Is the fault ours, Mr Vaduz?'

'Hard to say, sir, it's only just happened and we're on book check now. But the signal's leaving us strong so the fault could be at any of Wimex's relay computers.'

'Did you get my signal to Admiral Holliwell away?'

'Can't be sure, sir, but I think you must assume no.'
'No it is.'
'Sir, how shall I answer *Minsk*?'
'You just stand by, Mr Vaduz. You'll give them an answer when I have one for you to send.'
'Captain,' said Commander Daniels. 'With respect, sir, we are breaking all the laws of the sea and putting this ship in peril. We must answer the *Minsk*. This is the fourth signal in two days we've ignored.'
'You keeping count, Mr Daniels?'
'But sir, we just can't . . .'
'You can, d'you hear. So can you all. Goddammit, you are officers of the United States Navy and you will obey your Captain at sea!'
'But, sir, this is gross . . .'
'You'll do as you're fucking-well told and you will not question me in the presence of junior officers and ratings, d'you hear? Do you hear me? For God's sake, I *am* your Captain.'
His eyes were suddenly wide and bulging, his face had become quickly very white and his forehead glistened with sweat under the peak of his cap.
'We will not acknowledge the *Minsk*,' he shouted. 'We will not acknowledge any other signal without my permission because I do not believe they are being sent by our people.'
'Our people?' Daniels and Ginsberg said together.
'Our people—and God help your rotten deafness!' His voice had gone to a higher pitch still, there was spittle in the corners of his mouth and the squash ball was distorted in the fury of his fingers.
'Can't I make any of you understand? Don't you realize what they're doing? The other side?'
'I'm sorry, sir,' said Ginsberg, ignoring Daniel's gesture to move back. 'Are you saying you believe the signals ordering us to move south have been sent by the Soviets?'
Captain Hanks nodded and smiled. A trickle of sweat ran down the side of his right temple and into his eye, but he didn't seem to notice.
'Sometimes, Mr Ginsberg,' he said, his voice suddenly

quiet again, 'I am able to persuade myself you understand English.'

Lieutenant Ginsberg looked at his Captain, and there was shock in his young face.

'D'you suppose,' said Captain Hanks, 'that the President of the United States would stand up and say what he did, issue an ultimatum to the Communists and then order his only warship in the area to run south? Does that make sense to you? Didn't even the chicken-livered Carter, faced with the Iranians, send in his warships? Wasn't the *Coral Sea* and the *Nimitz* and the *Kitty Hawk* immediately ordered in? Carter was yellow with fright, but he did that. And this President's a hawk, a goddamned marvel and you suppose he would order us away? No sir, not in a million years. Wouldn't he instead be planning reinforcements? Don't you think that is exactly what is being prepared at this moment in the Pentagon? Is that so fucking preposterous?

'So we've had a breakdown in our satellite communications link, a faulty computer maybe, there's a lot of things to go wrong. Well, let me tell you it's the first time it's happened on this ship in all the years I have been in command. Just another coincidence? Balls! I'm telling you those motherfuckers out there have done it, jamming us, and I will not let those bastards through so they can put down their men and their planes for the fucking crippling commissars to deliver Saudi Arabia and its oil to the Kremlin. Let me tell you, when this is over, this ship will sail to Norfolk, Virginia to be scrapped—and so will I—but as God is my witness, the traditions of the United States Navy will not be buried with us. You want an answer for the *Minsk*? Very well, Mr Ginsberg, I'll give you one. You will fire two rounds dead centre of the *Minsk*, and the *Ivan Rogov*—dead centre, mind you, and well short, so there's no provocation. D'you hear? None!'

Lieutenant Ginsberg left the bridge, unsure suddenly of what was real and what wasn't, of what he thought he had heard and what perhaps he might have imagined. Was it possible that their cut-off from the Pentagon was simply a communications failure, another defective computer? Or could he believe in a Soviet conspiracy?

But Lieutenant Ginsberg was only twenty-two years old, ever-doubtful, and a stranger to crisis on sea or on land. However his conscience advised him, whatever his instinct warned him of, he climbed down the steel rungs to the flight deck and, as ordered, went across to Gunnery Control. It was the nearness of the waiting aircraft that began it: a memory of something long past, a film years ago, a late-night television movie about a B-52 bomber armed with an H-bomb on its way to blast a Russian city and all because something had gone wrong with the computers in the Pentagon. The bomber pilot had ignored all contra-measures, had switched off radioed orders from the President himself, ignored even the pleading, sobbing voice of his wife telling him to return to base, because he thought it all a Soviet trick.

Lieutenant Ginsberg got into his control booth, strapped on his harness and switched on the intercom relay connecting him directly with his gun and missile stations. He remembered the end of the film, but he couldn't remember the title. The pilot had dropped his bomb, on Kiev or Leningrad or some Soviet city and half a million people were annhiliated. Admitting the mistake, and to prevent retaliation and a nuclear war, the US President ordered the destruction of Philadelphia. Or was it Maine?

He began the preliminary standby calls—alerting station five to load and prepare to fire. He leaned forward to the master switch which provided the electrical power to the missile launchers—a switch that controlled the current to every item of fire-power on board. It could not be overridden, and the square of fine steel mesh covering it could be unlocked by only two men on board the *Okinawa*—the Captain and the Gunnery Officer. And he was Gunnery Officer.

By the mesh, painted in red, were the two words: FAIL SAFE, and Lieutenant Ginsberg remembered the title of the film. Then he cross-checked the computer printout giving him the range and exact position, and held the relay switch.

'Station five, prepare two rounds on co-ordinate 98—repeat 98—at one thousand yards. Acknowledge 98 at one thousand.'

WASHINGTON

'In the next war the survivors will envy the dead'

Across the United States the reality of what was happening and of what the President had threatened would happen if he did not get his oil was only now beginning to be appreciated. Only now did people wonder whether they really were about to enter the Age of Less.

Little by little items of news filtered into the White House contributing to a growing pile of macabre and impossible happenings that in the President's mind added up to global pandemonium.

Like the riots at Narita, Tokyo's new airport, when demonstrators set alight four JAL airliners in protest, according to news-agency reports, against wastage of fuel—destroying in the process eighteen of the demonstrators, fourteen airline staff, and twenty thousand gallons of Avgas.

Or the demonstrators in Turin, Northern Italy, who rampaged through a geriatric hospital, smashing isolation wards and the operating theatre and throwing refrigerated bottles of blood-plasma out on to the streets because of erroneous reports that old women had died through hypothermia because of the lack of fuel for the central heating system. The leaders of the rampage, members of an outraged local Communist party, later preferred to ignore the post mortem evidence and conclusions that the women had died of an uncommon virus and that the temperature of the wards had never fallen below the normal comfortable 62 degrees Fahrenheit.

Or like the convoy of five petrol tankers on their way from Le Havre to Paris, that were hijacked just after midnight on Autoroute de l'Ouest near Vauvray, each carrying two thousand gallons of fuel. The drivers were ordered at gunpoint to drive their tankers to a disused strip mine fifty miles away then drive one at a time into the shaft that ran four hundred yards deep in to the side of the workings. The five drivers were shot through the head as they sat in their cabs and the entrance to the mineshaft was blocked with boulders, leaving a supply of over ten thousand gallons of high octane fuel hidden and waiting to be collected and distributed as soon as the prices had risen high enough to make the operation properly profitable.

The French police found out about it by the sheerest fluke. One of the hijackers, a man who had shot dead two of the drivers, had returned home to Le Havre in the early hours to find his wife had given birth to a boy child three weeks prematurely. Overwhelmed with gratitude, the hijacker went to his church for prayers and thanksgiving. Kneeling there on the floor before the altar and the icon of the Holy Mary, he also thought it right and proper, as a good Catholic, to confess his overnight sins, which he did at some length and out loud. The dominie, sitting out of sight by the organ and quietly polishing brass, was astonished at what he overheard and quickly did his duty to the laws of God and France.

All these things and more found their way back to the President in short precise reports edited by the Press Secretary, Schlesinger, together with reports from State Governors and the FBI, causing the President to wonder if perhaps too much had been done too soon, if ultimatums too early delivered gave no room and no time for manoeuvre and whether he had pumped adrenalin into the system at a time when it perhaps needed a depressant. He had asked for calm and he had got hysteria. He had appealed for sacrifice and he had got greed. He had asked them to rally and instead they had run.

'There's been a shoot-out in Dallas, Mr President; three National Guardsmen dead and a helluva lot of casualties. The hospital is refusing to accept any more. Seems they went for another tanker convoy with shotguns.'

'Explosives have been thrown at the Egyptian Embassy here, sir, and at their Consulate in New York. Seems people don't know yet who are friendly Arabs and who aren't. Far as we know, only five dead. Happened fifteen minutes ago.'

'Our Ambassador in Tripoli has had to be helped out. Still twenty people inside the Embassy, sir, and Ghaddaffi's ignoring us.'

'Oil tankers have been lost—possibly hijacked, Mr President. Air Force have been searching at sea for slicks and flotsams, but they've come up with nothing yet. It's a big area, sir, could take days.'

'FBI reckon it's East Coast Mafia, Mr President. There's been a sudden petrol supply surplus in Iowa, Minnesota, Wisconsin and Maine. They say it's selling for five dollars a gallon and still they're queueing for it.'

'Truckers have packed their tankers against pumps in some of the big stations in Connecticut, sir, to prevent the sale of fuel. They're demanding it's for them. We've also had a report from the Houston, Galveston area of people dying from poisoning after syphoning petrol from car tanks.'

'The oil pipelines from Galveston have been blown up. It's the second attack in two days and we just don't have the personnel to guard every yard of that line, sir. Same old story. Sunbelt against Snowbelt.'

'And more campus riots, Mr President. North Western University in Chicago, Right versus Left. And there's been some blood at the University of Michigan, Arab students attacked. Strung two of them up from a lamp-post. By their necks.'

The President sat there and slowly stroked his nose with his forefinger. Then with his wide fingertips he covered his eyes and massaged them. The men stood around him waiting. There was no noise in the Situation Room except for the low hum of the air conditioning fans and the occasional flick of a faulty condenser in one of the strip lights. The chair scratched across the rubber-tiled floor and the President stood up and walked slowly to a wall-map of the United States. He turned and leaned back against it. Then he said very quietly—in a whisper almost, 'We couldn't have known it would go this way. No way could we have known.' He rested his head back against the map and looked up at the ceiling.

'D'you know the most sickening thing I've yet seen? Did you see it? On the news-casts tonight? A Vietnam Veterans' demo at the steps of the Lincoln Memorial. Christ! Less than half a mile away, guys in wheelchairs with plastic arms and legs—some for me, some against—men who only a few years ago had given all but their lives fighting together. And now fighting each other in wheelchairs, turning them over, pulling out power cables, slashing the tyres. My God!' He suddenly pushed himself away from the wall-map and faced them, his eyes wide in anger.

'I asked them to help me, and instead I see sprawling, legless Veterans fighting on the sidewalks of Washington. I addressed the nation, remember? When the chips are down, I said . . . what was that phrase? "The path we have chosen is full of hazards but it's the one most consistent with our character and courage." Shit! Character and courage, my ass! Killing National Guardsmen just so they fill up their lousy tanks . . . blowing up pipelines to let the bastards freeze . . . lynch rule on the campus, mob rule in the country. Jesus! I feel lousy with them . . . lousy d'you hear? I am ashamed, Godammed ashamed to be their President.'

His face was white and his jaw worked from side to side, and softly, very softly, he punched his left fist into the palm of his right hand. He looked at them each in turn, menacingly, like a drunk at a bar waiting for any response, any excuse, to hit them. But no one looked back. They looked at the floor, they looked at their finger-nails, at their shoes. No one looked at him. He went on in the same dangerous tone.

'While I was up at Camp David yesterday, looking through the great speeches of great American Presidents, I read a lot of JFK's, and I came across something I thought I'd forgotten, and my God, it hit me hard. "To recognize the possibilities of a nuclear war in the missile age without our citizens knowing what they should do or where they should go if the bombs begin to fall, would be a failure of Presidential responsibility." I was temped to use it last night, just to warn those people out there what we might be up against. But I thought it might create a little panic. D'you hear? I was worried it might cause a little panic. And God help me now, but I really do believe that if the bombs began to fall, they'd still be running after gasoline.'

The neon light flicked again and the President's hands were still. He sighed. His shoulders drooped. He turned on one foot, gently punched the wall-map of the United States, turned again and walked to his chair at the head of the long metal table. He sat down and beckoned the others to do the same. When the scraping of chairs had finished, he spoke again and quietly—the anger gone.

'We should have waited just a little longer, George,' he said. 'Just a couple more days.'

'No, sir,' said General Warner, Chairman of the Joint Chief of Staff. 'More likely we should have gone straight in from the start. But what's done's done.'

'I reckon,' said General Louis Wilson of the Marines, 'we should have gone in under cover of our evacuation planes and risked the casualties. We should have put our men on the ground from the start and used the same planes to bring the civilians out.'

'That right, Jarvis?' asked the President, turning to the General of the United Air Force.

'Could have been done, sir. Logistically feasible. No doubt about it.'

'Wasn't what I asked, General.'

'No, sir, it wasn't, but I'm not prepared to make a retrospective judgement on something we all agreed on two days ago. Except perhaps just to say that even if we had held back a little longer I doubt if things would have turned out any better. The pandemonium would have been delayed that much longer, but it would still have come.'

For a minute or more the President did not speak. Then, 'Gentlemen. There never was a moment of hysterical anger in this room. Nor an American President who disowned his people. It was something that could easily have happened, considering the strain and the disappointment, but not to this President. You understand? Not this one.'

He looked at each face in turn, holding the other man's eyes acknowledging, or so it seemed, receipt of his message. Then he sat up erect in his chair, suddenly brightly alert.

'General Jarvis. You say you have news?'

'Bad, I'm afraid, Mr President.'

'That's how it's going to be from now on.'

'I've had some reports from our radar tracking stations in Turkey—Ankora and Sinop, came in fifteen minutes ago. A squadron of Soviet Anatonovs, estimated over thirty aircraft, shuttling out of a base on the Caspian Sea, shifting two brigades, that's about ten thousand men and armour, to airstrips in the South Yemen.

'Radar followed them across Syria. They refuelled in Iraq, went down the centre of the Persian Gulf in a line from Abadan to Abu Dhabi, across Oman, then followed the coast of the Arabian peninsula to the airfields. Very blatant, Mr President. No attempt to hide their track. Almost as if they wanted us to know what they were about.'

'And what are they about, General?'

'Well, sir, we've another intelligence report that troopships have anchored off Aden, South Yemen, carrying another two brigades and a lot of mobile armour. We've good men there watching. They say Soviet merchant fleet freighters are unloading crated MiGs and Sam-6s. The Soviets already have fifteen thousand men stationed in

Aden as part of a defence treaty two years ago. It looks, Mr President, as if they're massing again. Maybe another Afghanistan?'

'With half an army still in Kabul?'

'Yes, sir, upwards of eighty thousand men.'

'Flying time, General Jarvis?'

'Kabul to the oilwells, sir, three and a half hours.'

'And from Aden?'

'Assuming they use their Antonovs, twelve hundred miles, three hours, sir.'

The President scribbled on the pad in front of him. 'By my reckoning,' he said, 'that's thirty-five thousand Soviet troops around three hours' flying time from the oilfields and, say, another eighty thousand to draw on, three and a half hours away. And we have one veteran assault ship with six hundred men and, what did you say Admiral . . . thirty aircraft aboard?'

'Thirty-eight, sir. And 609 men.'

'Your little additions, Admiral, aren't going to give us even odds.' He looked across to General Rogers. 'We've got our men ready?'

'Yes, sir. Five thousand on standby, three thousand of the 82nd in Adana Turkey, another two thousand of the 101st Airmobile at base, south of Naples.'

'And our planes are in a *go* situation,' added General Jarvis.

'Mr President, we're forgetting the *Minsk* and the *Ivan Rogov*,' said Admiral Holliwell. 'They are at this time just outside the Strait of Hormuz. Those ships, remember, have upwards of two thousand combat marines aboard and the helos to take them right into those oilfields.'

'And they are our problem, Mr President,' said General Wilson. 'They're the closest and the quickest, and there's no way I can see us beating them.'

For a minute the President said nothing. Then he leant back in his chair. 'Gentlemen,' he said, 'is it militarily possible for Moscow to have mounted these sea and air operations in direct response to my speech last night?' He looked to General Warner. Chief of Staff, for the answer, and General Warner in turn looked around the table at the shaking heads of the other generals and said, 'No, Mr President, it is not feasible. It would have taken them some days, a week maybe, unless of course their planes and men have been on alert standby.'

'So the slightest provocation, the slightest suspicion that we mean to go into those fields and they helo in off those ships, there before us and using our pretext as a peace-keeping force to beat us.'

The red light at the base of the white telephone flashed. He picked up the receiver and listened.

'Send them in,' he said. 'And some coffee. Lots of coffee.'

Richard Johns, Director of the CIA, came into the Situation Room and held the door for Tom Sorenson, the Foreign Affairs adviser.

'You look as if you've both come from a funeral,' the President said. 'What is it Tom?'

'Best you hear it from Johns, Mr President.'

'Go ahead. Things can't get worse.'

'Rahbar was put in by Moscow, Mr President,' Johns said, 'using Ghaddaffi, the Iraqis and OPEC to do it. Soviet-engineered, using OPEC to get rid of Fahd.'

Someone came in with a tray of coffee cups and a large thermos beaker, and placed it on top of the map chest by the wall. The President stood up and without a word went to the chest, unscrewed the thermos top and poured coffee into eight cups. He picked up a sugar lump, hesitated and dropped it back into the bowl again. Then he walked back to the table empty-handed and sat on the edge of it.

'How d'you get this, Richard?'

The President had never addressed his CIA director by his Christian name before, and everybody in the room understood.

'We had a man in Riyadh, sir. He came out, it seems, with the evacuation planes, debriefed in Cairo. Seems that a few hours ago before the coup, King Fahd called him in. It was partly our doing. We were getting edgy and we told Saudi State Security he was there just in case they wanted anything from us. The King gave him everything, said he was about to break with OPEC and that they'd been planning it for some months. But somehow Ghaddaffi found out, though the King didn't know.'

He paused, then went on, 'But we did. We had been told that Iraq's Defence Minister, Saadoun Karim, had been a KGB man since 1962 and during the past two and a half months he'd spent a lot of time in Baghdad, meeting Ghaddaffi, the Palestinians, the Yemenis, the Iranians and even Rahbar himself.'

'Is Rahbar with the Soviets?'

'No, Mr President. And our information is that he knows nothing about Karim's background. He thinks he's just another Moslem, just as devout and just as anxious that oil and Islam should be protected. He has no idea he is a Communist. Ghaddaffi doesn't know Karim's KGB connections. And Ghaddaffi's convinced the idea to depose Fahd was his alone.'

'No doubts?'

'No, sir. None. It's all suddenly coming together. Moscow set it up, Karim fed it to Ghaddaffi and then steered it through the meetings of the War Council in Baghdad. And we've finally established Karim's Soviet credentials. Proof came two days before the coup, though we had no idea then it had any connection. He sent a telex from the General Post Office in Baghdad to a carpet importer, in Budapest. We picked it up on relay and decoded. It said simply 'YAMANI GREEN LIGHT' Our man out of Riyadh says that Yamani was what Ghaddaffi was using as the code-name for the coup, used it to tell Moscow it was all systems go.'

'One moment, Johns,' said Admiral Holliwell. 'You said he sent his telex two days ago?'

'That's right. Seven thirty-five in the morning from Baghdad PTT.'

'The *Minsk* and *Ivan Rogov*,' said the Admiral, 'got their signals to move away from their warm-water exercises an hour later. We know their order to sail north to the Persian Gulf was acknowledged by them at 08h35 local time.'

'That figures,' said General Jarvis. 'The Soviet aircraft refuelled in Iraq en route to the Yemen.'

'Authorized by Karim,' said Johns. 'We know that too.'

'And who happens,' said Tom Sorenson, 'to be heir apparent to the Presidency of Iraq. In the New Year Saddam Hussein will retire. Karim replaces him.'

'A KGB man as President of Iraq. That's not possible.'

'Not only possible,' said Sorenson. 'It's inevitable!'

'A Soviet Iraq?'

'Yes, Mr President. A Soviet satellite exerting political and religious pressure on Saudi Arabia through Rahbar, with Iran still free-floating.'

'Is that the scenario, Tom? The Soviets inside the Gulf?'

'Yes, Mr President,' said Sorenson. 'They've outpaced us. You issued an ultimatum and they reckon they can ignore it because they're certain of Rahbar. They'll be in on those oilfields tonight. By tonight, sir.'

The President shifted his position on the edge of the table, and his hands fell on to his lap. He hunched his shoulders and in the unreal light of the underground room his skin looked grey and tight and shiny, like the smooth shine on an old man's forehead.

Speaking as if there was no one else in the room, the President said, very quietly, 'They're on the move again. Remember that line about probing and finding mush? So they're probing again. Yesterday we were worried about igniting, how did we say it, Islamic combustion? And all the time we've been missing it. I said there had to be Soviet involvement somewhere, but I never imagined Moscow openly going for the big number one. Not the Gulf. Not after what's happened since Iran and Afghanistan.' His voice was fading, so that only those close to him heard the last phrase. 'Right inside the Persian Gulf and I don't think there's a thing we can do about it.'

'Mr President.' Tom Sorenson spoke loudly, deliberately. 'Mr President. You said in this room yesterday that the oil was the stuff of our survival, you said they were our oilfields and you would use force to get them back. Your speech: "An attempt by outside forces to gain control of the Persian Gulf region will be regarded as an assault on the vital interests of the United States and will be repelled by any means necessary, including military force."'

The President stiffened. 'What are you advocating against the Soviets, nuclear confrontation? That speech was to show our muscle, not to be a declaration of war. You know the gamble, so does everyone in this room . . . Do we go to the final option or do we find a way to regain those oilfields short of it? The Soviets will soon be there and we don't have a force big enough outside the United States to move them. We do not have the capacity. You tell me it would take three weeks of preparation before landing units equipped to fight for any length of time could be on on the ground. So we fly a few B-52s from Guam over them to show we can project military power, and that'll be as frightening to them as saying boo to the Kremlin over the hot line.

'Do you want me to go on television a second time to spell it out and appeal for a war mandate against the Soviet Union because the Iranians and the Saudis and the Iraqis have screwed us up? Because that's how it'll look from the outside. Broken by the Arabs. *You* do the persuading then. Convince America and the rest of the world it was all part and parcel of a Soviet master plan. We're on our own . . . we're alone on this. Moscow has outpaced and outwitted us and God help me, we are about to lose the Gulf to them and somehow we are going to have to live with that reality and begin working on new strategies to get it back.'

'But Mr President . . .'

'No buts, General Warner. This is not Cuba, I am not JFK, and we are no longer in the game of bluff. We are too far from home on this one. We are the world's number one power and we cannot even extend that power to the Middle East unless we have three weeks' prior warning. Riots in San Salvador, an airlift to Nicaragua, a blockade of Cuba, and we're in business. But Soviet troops and warships move into the Gulf and we sit here and shake our heads and our fists. Short of an intercontinental missile launch, there's nothing else we can do about it.

'You tell me now the Soviets are offloading MiGs and Sam-6s in Aden. That Moscow shipped in there two hundred and eighty tanks as part of their so-called friendship treaty. That's five times the number of tanks assigned to a single US infantry division. Right, General Rogers?'

'Right, Mr President.'

'It's more than half as many as the entire US Marines Corps has, right, General Jarvis?'

'Right, Mr President?'

'Right! So I made a speech. It was delivered as a warning, but it was received as an ultimatum. Whatever the rights and wrongs, it's clear now that the Soviets were already underway and well advanced in their operation. You reckon they could have their troops on those wells tonight and if you're right . . . I can't see there's anything this President can do about it . . . nothing short of total war. Let me tell you what Khrushchev told Kennedy: "In the next war, the survivors will envy the dead." I will not be the one who gives mankind that epitaph.'

The faulty neon light gave a last loud click, and went out and one corner of the Situation Room was in shadow. The suddenness of it served to punctuate the end of the President's speech, but there was no reaction and, except for the regular low hum of the air conditioning, the only noise in the room was Admiral Holliwell's asthmatic breathing. The President looked at the cold cups of coffee and the seven men looked at him in silence.

Tom Sorenson dug his hands deep into his pockets. For the past two days he had listened to a President full of bluster and bluff, full of fine words and wisdom, seemingly turning the tide of American foreign relations and on the march again at home and abroad. Hadn't he promised to put Fahd back on the throne, even if it took a task force to do it? What was it he had shouted on that first day here in the Situation Room? 'I mean to get that oil before the Soviets go and get it themselves.' Fine words that fail the resolution. Presidential pugnacity, then throw in the

Presidential towel just as soon as the punches hurt. A hazardous path ahead, he'd warned the nation, but here he was leading out by the side door. Run and live to fight another day.

The door from the Operations and Radio Communications Room opened and the Situation Room was filled with yellow light and the noise of telex machines, radio talk, telephone bells and the general hubbub of work. A young officer saluted and handed Admiral Holliwell a slip of paper. There was a pause. Then the Admiral jumped from his chair and sat down again hard. 'Holy cow!' he shouted.

Holliwell handed the signal to the young officer who took it quickly to the President.

'It's from the *Okinawa*, sir. From Captain Hanks. He has not acknowledged my order to move south, away from the Soviet ships. Instead he's sailing into them, going to face them . . . says he will respond to intimidation in kind. He's firing shots across their bows.'

But already the President was ahead of him, reading the last line from Captain Hanks. 'As the President says, when the chips are down it's time for the true peacekeepers to stand up. The *Okinawa* will not be found wanting. He has my word on it.'

The President gulped down two cups of cold black coffee. 'Give me those flying times and distances again, General Jarvis.'

'Sir?'

'Flight times, General. I want to know exactly where the *Minsk* and *Ivan Rogov* are at this time and I want to know exactly how long it will take them to put their men down on those oilfields from their present position. I want to know exactly—and by exactly I mean to the minute—how long it will take for our men to get from standby to the dropping zones. Now, General. I want it now.'

General Jarvis collected a single sheet of paper from the others at the table; their estimates of timing were written on it, though none of them could even guess why the President should now suddenly demand the information so urgently.

'Mr President,' General Jarvis said, making the last calculation. 'From the Strait of Hormuz, where the Soviet Fleet is now positioned, to the oilfields is approximately four hundred flying miles. By helicopter that's two hours twenty minutes. By their vertical take-off Forger aircraft, forty-five. Moving our Rapid Deployment Force from Adana, Turkey, direct over the Mediterranean and through Syrian airspace is one thousand one hundred and five flying miles, and at C-130 maximum cruising speed, time to the dropping zone will be four hours and ten minutes.'

'That would mean,' said the President, 'the Soviets could have their men heloed into the oilfields an hour fifty minutes ahead of us, assuming the alert was given simultaneously?'

'That's right, sir.'

'There's no way, of course, to guarantee absolute secrecy for our C-130s on take-off or in flight?'

'No, sir. The odds may be with us, but there are no guarantees.'

'We could have a situation where our men were dropping on to an already Soviet-held position at the oilfields?'

'That's so, sir.'

'So we must find a way to delay the Russians.'

'Sir?'

'I said, we must find a way to delay . . . or divert the Soviet Fleet while we get our men there.'

'You think you have it, Mr President?'

'Tom, I have a proposition.'

'Yes, sir?'

'It will need the support of every single one of you. Especially you, Admiral Holliwell.'

'You have it, sir. You have it,' said the Admiral.

'You must hear it first,' replied the President, more pale now than anyone had ever seen him. Slowly he got up from the table and walked, hands still clasped in front of him, to the wall-map of Saudi Arabia and stood below the extinguished strip light, partly in shadow, his face hidden.

'The Soviets would beat us by nearly two hours,' he said.

'We would stand no chance if our take-off from Turkey was detected. So we need to prevent them thinking we mean to confront them in the air or on land by diverting them at sea.'

'On sea, sir,' interrupted Admiral Hilliwell, 'our nearest fleet is over three hundred miles south.

'But the *Okinawa*, Admiral, is facing them. Captain Hanks says he is broadside on and preparing to fire.' The President paused. 'I suggest,' he said quietly, 'we authorize him to do just that.'

Someone's hands hit the metal table-top. Johns and Sorenson moved closer to the President.

'Mr President?' said Admiral Holliwell. 'They'll blow him out of the sea. They'll destroy the *Okinawa* in minutes. No one will survive.'

The President went on as if he hadn't heard. 'I suggest we now send a message directly to the Commander of the Soviet Seventh Fleet warning him that the *Okinawa* is out of our control, that it is commanded by a captain who ignores our signals ordering him away from the area to avoid confrontation. Things must then take their course. A sea action, gentlemen, will divert their attention from the air. And we might just make it to those fields.'

Then Admiral Holliwell spoke, slowly, as if every word, every syllable, had first to be checked and cross-checked. The Generals clasped their hands together in front of them on the table-top.

'Mr President,' said Admiral Holliwell. 'You are asking me to endorse a sea action that will mean certain death to over six hundred officers and men of the United States Navy?'

'It is a request I could legitimately make in any wartime operation, Admiral.'

'But this is not war, sir. We are not at war.'

'Wrong, Admiral. Wrong. This is war. As real as you'll ever get it. Only the face of it has changed. I am asking, here in this war room, that you do what you would have done, without any hesitation, in the Midway, at Ford Island, at Iwo Jima, in Normandy, Haiphong and Da Nang. At every moment of sacrifice that has ever been made by Americans at a time of national crisis.'

'But we have not declared war on the Soviet Union.'

'The next war will not be declared, Admiral. It will just happen, and the losers will never know they've lost. Understand. I'm asking you all to realize what is at stake, and what our destiny will be if we lose tonight. I am asking you, Admiral Holliwell, to sacrifice good Americans for the salvation of America and its free-world allies. And believe me, if men die tonight they will take their wounds and scars to God's lap.'

No one could see the President's face. And had they not seen him walk into the shadow, minutes before, they might have doubted his identity. The voice so easily could have belonged to another.

'I'll not have further discussion, gentlemen,' he said. 'For my part I know there's no other way. By midnight tonight, we'll have pawned our heritage for lack of grit. But if that's how it is I cannot on my own do much about it. We do not have time for debate. The decision yes or no must be made now and it must be unanimous. Those who say no will say it now.' He waited, quite still in the shadow. Sorenson did not speak. Nor Johns. And the Generals sat at the table looking down at their hands.

The chair hit the floor with a bang and rolled on its side as Admiral Holliwell suddenly stood up. He swayed slightly and held the table for support. For ten seconds or more he stared at the shadow under the yellow lights. Then he coughed to clear his throat. There were flecks of spittle at the sides of his mouth.

'I will send the signal, sir,' he said hoarsely. 'I will need to send it to Captain Hanks now, instructing him to fire at the *Minsk* and *Ivan Rogov*. And I will signal the Soviets as you said.'

'But in your name, Admiral Holliwell.'

'In my name, Mr President.'

'It's looking fine'

The formation was thirty-three minutes, two hundred and forty miles from the dropping zone, flying south-east at an indicated airspeed of two hundred and seventy knots. A tail wind, varying slightly, gave them an actual speed over the ground of two hundred and eighty-five knots.

The flight engineer of the leading C-130, sitting between pilot and co-pilot behind the throttle and pitch levers, watched the mass of gauges in front of him. Eight in particular made him anxious. The turbine inlet temperatures and the torque indicators. They were his warnings of engine overstrain, and he knew as he watched the needles on all eight gauges moving towards the red markers that his pilot was taking the formation of aircraft into the dangerously uncertain. They were flying low and as the night's cold left the desert, ground temperature would rise and the engines would overheat. Then there was the risk of engine failure or, worse, fire.

He knew that the flight instructions to his pilot, Colonel James Pringle who was leading the Yellowbean formation had been very explicit. Eighty miles from the Lebanese coast out from Beirut, Pringle should take them down to three hundred feet above the Mediterranean and maintain that height at safe maximum speed until twenty miles from the dropping zone; the oilfields of Dhahran on the Saudi Arabian shores of the Persian Gulf.

They had taken off from Adana in Turkey on the Mediterranean's Aegean coast while it was still dark. Fifty C-130 Hercules aircraft, twenty-five of them full of men of the 82nd Marine Corps and twenty-five aircraft empty except for their flight crews and loadmasters. At thirty-two thousand feet over Cape St Andreas on the eastern edge of Cyprus, Yellowbean had made a rendezvous with another formation of fifty C-130s, callsigned Blackbean and flying from the United States parabase in Italy, south of Naples. Again, twenty-five of Blackbean's aircraft were empty, the other twenty-five packed with men of the 101st Airmobile.

On the co-ordinate above Cyprus, the fifty full aircraft combined and then descended from the rendezvous height in a spiral, as tight as a corkscrew, through international airspace, levelling out at three hundred feet above the sea to begin their low run across Lebanon, Syria and Iraq and well below radar detection levels. The remaining fifty empty aircraft assuming the Blackbean callsign then flew in a wide circle above Cyprus, for every country's radar surveillance systems to see. Then back to Adana where they refuelled for the final leg to Italy. It may have sounded melodramatic in later retelling, but it was a simple and well rehearsed ruse to persuade the Soviet radar tracking stations south of the Caspian Sea that a formation of fifty USAF aircraft had been employed on a routine, if pointless training exercise and had returned without incident to base.

The fifty Yellowbeans zigzagged across the three Arab countries, bypassing military airfields, domestic air routes, towns and main roads. It had added an extra eighty flying miles to the journey, but the flight path had been meticulously worked out by USAF flight command as the simplest way of avoiding detection. Colonel Pringle's own worry had not been radar, but the odds of chance detection. Everyone on the C-130 flight decks knew it only needed a single random private aircraft on charter from one town to another, or a single early morning Syrian or Iraqi Air Force training flight to spot them and radio an alert to their own air traffic control. Because of this possibility, Pringle had insisted that seven of the flanking planes be fitted with air to air missiles. But there had been no alerts and they had crossed the Iraqi border into Saudi Arabia thirty-eight minutes ago with all the missiles still safely secured.

It was now 05h25 local time, 03h25 Greenwich mean time, 22h25 Washington time, and Colonel Pringle's flight engineer tapped his shoulder and spoke into his flight intercom. The needles of the eight vital indicators of the four turbine engines had passed into the red danger area of their dials.

'We've been into VNE three minutes, sir. We gotta reduce speed or we'll have overheat.'

Colonel Pringle looked back over his shoulder to the navigator who was rechecking his calculations of speed, distance and drop time. Twice he ringed 06h00 on the pad on the table and he repeated it over the intercom. Colonel Pringle shook his head, kept his right hand on the bank of throttles on the centre console, and the engineer went back to his gauges and his worries.

Coming up ahead of them was the crossroads of Hafr al Batin; Colonel Pringle banked Yellowbean 720 to the left in a sharp detour and like a flock of huge black crows the Yellowbeans banked together after him. Five thousand combat paratroopers handpicked from the 82nd and the 101st were now less than thirty-five minutes from the oilfields.

Three thousand of the five thousand men had been flown to Turkey on the President's orders from Fort Bragg in West Virginia where the 82nd was based. It had been done in relays across the Atlantic to disguise any appearance of mobilization. Some were flown to Italy to join the two thousand men of the 101st. The rest were flown on a direct non-stop flight to Adana in Turkey. By midnight of Day Three, the five thousand who were to undertake Operation Snowball were ready, equipped and on standby.

'It's gonna be our Entebbe,' General Vernon C. Warner had told the President.

'Or our Waterloo,' the President had replied. But no one laughed. No joke had been intended.

Secrecy, General Warner had insisted, was the name of the game. Each man, he promised, had been handpicked on his combat experience, but no one, from the Joint Chiefs of Staff down, could guarantee how many loose tongues were among them. And only one was needed. So Operation Snowball had been kept secret from everyone except the most senior commanders. Colonel James Pringle knew only the dropping zone, when he and his navigator were briefed on the flight plan in the operations room in Adana just before take-off. The Marine Colonel commanding his small contingent of the Rapid Deployment Force had not been briefed on the target until his arrival in Adana, and even then he was only allowed to brief his separate unit commanders, who in turn told their men as they sat on the tarmac in the dark under the wings of their aircraft.

The plan of attack was uncomplicated and quickly explained. No military resistance was expected at the oilfields. There were only Aramco workers in the dormitory compounds and no one expected any show of force from the Aramco security guards once five thousand parachutes had been spotted in the sky. And surprise being essential—in case anyone attempted sabotage of the pumps, pipelines and rigs—the drop itself would have to be fast and from the lowest minimum height.

Colonel Pringle would fly his Yellowbean formation at three hundred feet above the desert until he was three miles from the fields. Then he would climb to the dropping height of eight hundred feet, called pop-up, and minutes later the first men would touch Saudi Arabian sand.

'Port Ten.'

'Ten of port wheel, sir.'

'Midships.'

'Wheel midships, sir.'
'Steady.'
'Steady as she is, sir . . . course 350.'

Captain Hanks stood back from the voicepiece, hesitated and walked to his favourite corner on the portside window of the bridge.

The Soviet fleet was a little under two thousand yards away, stationary black hulks made even more massive in the first grey light of morning. All night he had stood there waiting for them to move, all night his gunnery crews had been watching and waiting for his order to fire their second salvo. The first four-and-a-half-inch shells had been fired eleven hours earlier from Lieutenant Ginsberg's number five battery, landing a thousand yards short of the carrier *Minsk* while she was still two miles away. Captain Hanks had watched the Soviet fleet of twenty-two ships slow to a stop. And there they had stayed, eleven ships either side of the deep water channel, in the Straits of Hormuz.

During the night Captain Hanks had been invited by the Soviet Naval Commander to pass. The signal had read: YOU WILL AVOID FURTHER CONFRONTATION. I ALLOW YOU FREE PASSAGE CENTRE OF THE DEEP WATER CHANNEL. THIS IS INTERNATIONAL WATER AND I URGE YOU RESIST FURTHER PROVOCATION. PLEASE ACKNOWLEDGE AND ACT. The signal was signed Sergei Borgnev, Commander Soviet Seventh Fleet.

Captain Hanks had sent an immediate reply: THE 'OKINAWA' STAYS PUT UNTIL MY PRESIDENT TELLS ME TO MOVE.

But the President wouldn't. He knew that. This was his eyeball to eyeball, the only way left, if the United States was to keep its promise to every American boy who lay buried in some corner of a foreign field. The great Soviet war machine was now dithering. The *Minsk* had expected an easy passage but it had found seventeen thousand tons of good American steel in its way. At 02h00 Commander Sergei Borgnev had offered free water so that his warships and his combat marines and his helicopters and his vertical take-off escort fighters could move into the Gulf and take over every last barrel of oil there. But the President of the United States had said '*No*'. And then suddenly he'd received the signal from Admiral Holliwell authorizing him to fire a salvo to hit if necessary. Captain Edward Hanks was broadside on and there was nothing, absolutely nothing, the Soviets could do about it.

'They could blow us out of the water, Captain,' said Lieutenant Vaduz.

'No,' said the Captain, 'they'd break us in two and then they'd have no chance of passing. Sink the *Okinawa* in this channel and no motherfucker moves in or out. I know it, they know it and that's what'll save us.'

'But if they do, sir?'

'Then they do, Mr Vaduz.'

'You're contemplating suicide, sir?'

'I'm contemplating sweet fuck-all, boy.'

'It may be difficult, sir,' said Lieutenant Ginsberg, standing shoulder to shoulder with Vaduz.

'Difficult?'

'Admiral Holliwell's signal, sir, has got down to the lower decks.'

'Good! Now we all know the odds.'

'I'm not sure everyone does, sir . . . or will, sir.'

'Does sir or will sir. For Chrissake, Mr Ginsberg, talk English not Yiddish.'

Ginsberg stiffened. 'I'm saying sir, that there are men below deck who're saying they won't fight. They're saying it's suicide. They're saying, sir, that, you're . . .' He paused.

'Come on, Mr Ginsberg, be brave. If you're gonna be a tell-tale let's hear it. Out with your fucking rubbish.'

Lieutenant Ginsberg stepped forward, closer to the Captain.

'Some of the men, sir, are saying they have the right to refuse because . . .' Again he hesitated.

'Because! Because! Because!'

'Because they believe you're under strain.'

There was a moment's silence in the black corner. Then they saw the Captain's hand reach out for the squash ball from the ledge above the fire extinguishers. When he spoke again his voice was high and the words clipped, every consonant precisely made.

'Under strain, Mr Ginsberg, under strain? You mean they think I've gone mad?'

'They consider you're acting irresponsibly, sir.'

Captain Hanks squared his shoulders and the left hand behind his back began to distort the rubber ball. He looked out across the grey decks, across the grey sea to the grey Russian ships beyond.

'I'm acting irresponsibly on a signal I've received from the Pentagon, from Admiral Holliwell himself?'

'You ignored all the others, sir.'

'I didn't believe the others.'

'But you believe this one, sir.'

'Because I'm convinced it's his.'

'Because it tells you to fight when the others told you not to.'

'And that's irresponsible?'

'It's inconsistent, sir. And there are men below, a lot of them, who would prefer you to ignore this one too.'

Ginsberg and Vaduz waited for their Captain's response.

'Thank you, Ginsberg. What a show of democratic spirit. How egalitarian of you both to bring me the men's anxieties. But you're wasting your time, you're acting on behalf of cowards, motherfuckers, filthy dirty lousy un-American filth, who shame this ship, who shame its name, who shame its service. Today is the *Okinawa*'s finest hour. We have been given sudden responsibility, facing single-handed an enemy in a way and for a prize no other ship of the United States Navy has ever done. And perfectly placed to win. Look at them out there, a Soviet Armada that cannot move around us or under us, only through us—and they know they can't do that. Do you see how it's working? We cannot lose. And that's the way it is, gentlemen. So pass it on. We stay until they retreat. But if they advance I'll fire . . . God help me, I'll fire with or without those cowards below, even if I have to go and load the guns myself.'

'Would you want to see them, sir?'
'See them? See who, Mr Ginsberg?'
'The men, sir . . . address them. It might help.'
'I'll see them in hell first. Let it be known, so there's no misunderstanding later. They will respond to orders at sea. If they do not I'll have them shot. Section sixteen, US Uniform Code of Military Justice.'
'There are over six hundred officers and men aboard, sir.'
'I repeat, Misters Ginsberg and Vaduz. Article ten, section sixteen, United States Uniformed Code of Military Justice. The manuals are in my cabin. Now get to your stations. Vaduz, keep this ship sliding across the channel. We will not close below two thousand yards from the Soviets but we will not travel from them. That understood?'
'Yes, sir.'
'And you will tell Navigation and Radar to keep an eye on both flanks. They have shallow draught frigates who might move around us. Watch.'
'Yes, sir.'
'Mr Ginsberg.'
'Captain?'
'Return to Gunnery Control and remain there. Maintain standby alert on two stations and wait for my orders. You will fire when I order you to. And you will ignore all else. Understood?'
Lieutenant Ginsberg licked his dry lips.
'You understand?' the Captain shouted at him.
'Yessir, I understand.' Ginsberg tried to find the face hidden in the shadows. He could hear the Captain breathing, in the deep breaths that men sometimes use to control their own anxiety. Ginsberg saluted the shadow, turned on the ball of his foot and left the bridge for Gunnery Control.

Captain Hanks was alone again. In normal times it would have pleased him to stand this way on the bridge, looking across his command. It would have relaxed him and on those soft evenings with the warmth of evening sunlight, he might even have hummed to himself and have touched the scars on his lower back and remembered the Midway.

But not now. Not with the enemy a mile away and with the signal to engage in his pocket. Not with a ship half full of mutiny, an enemy beyond and within. But still he must wait. Since dusk the night before he had waited for the Russians to move, to initiate, to give him reason to fire. This was the chance. He knew it. If things went well, this morning he would die.

And how would they mourn? What posthumous awards? Such paths of glory. No longer doomed to solitary retirement in Pittsburgh and the slow death of loneliness. He would go the way all Captains dreamed, in command of a fighting, dying ship in the service of his nation, as all men of the sea . . .

'The men, Captain, would like a hearing.'

Captain Hanks spun round. There had to be a proper ending, no one would spoil it. No-one. 'Damn your men, Daniels, damn every motherfucker of them. This ship will fight, God help me it will fight.'

Commander Daniels closed the bridge door behind him. Softly, almost gently, he said, 'The men may not, sir. They don't see why. They don't know why. You must understand.'

Captain Hanks stayed in his dark corner. 'Is this some kind of new navy, Daniels, some exceptional sea-going democracy? Does it go to the vote? How will you vote?'

'I obey orders, sir, that's how it was in our day. But things have changed.'

'Changed, Daniels? Nothing changes at sea.'

'Most of these men haven't been under fire in their lives before, Captain. Few men in the entire US Navy under our age have. And it seems there's a lot of them below who reckon this is not the time nor the reason.'

'They want a hearing? I make a speech. I call for a vote and there's a show of hands as if I was some fucking trucker or longshoreman out on East Side. Is that the way it is now in the US Navy? Is that how we went to war in the Pacific, Daniels? Is it?'

'Captain . . . it's simply that they don't . . . they seem to work by a whole new set of rules . . . it's a new . . . understanding.'

'Fuck their new rules, Commander Daniels, just you stick to mine, which so happen to be the US Navy's. I have a signal here from Admiral Holliwell to one Captain Hanks, *USS Okinawa*, authorizing another salvo at the *Minsk* at precisely 06h00 local or sooner if provoked. You've read it? Right! I have waited all night for them to move. They have not. In just under fifteen minutes it will be 06h00 local and I fire. I know what's at stake. I seem to be alone on this ship but by Christ I do know. Suddenly in this little stretch of Arab water we represent everything . . . our country, our heritage, our freedom and every man who ever died at sea for it all. Our President is not prepared to forfeit any of it. Nor am I. I'm seeing it fresh as if I was a young man, like it was that Sunday morning in '41. The *USS Okinawa* will be defiant today and they'll print our names in gold for it.'

Commander Daniels waited. There was a sudden change in engine noise and vibration and the ship began to slow as the engines went into reverse. He saw how everything was grey, greyer than he could ever remember, the bridge, the decks below, the sky, even the air seemed grey and a still sea, grey all the way to the grey motionless hulks of the Soviet fleet a mile away.

He had come up to the bridge with an ultimatum, or something very close to it. The men had not presented it to him as such, they had not been so unwise. They had been sensibly cautious, but their message was clear enough. There were enough men aboard, they said, to sabotage any sea action, men who were not prepared to fight under such orders from such a Captain for such a reason and the Captain should know it and take whatever action he thought necessary before any alarm was sounded. They owed their Captain such a warning. In return he had a duty to the men.

'Captain,' he said. 'It's a difficult and unique position.'

'Go on.'

'Well, sir, I'm your second-in-command.'

'Correct.'

'And I think you are doing it all wrong.'

And only then did Captain Edward Hanks know what had to be done. It was like tearing out a cancer. There would be pain, there would be a wound, but once torn away there would be clean new flesh. And in that instant, like a divine signal of assent, the first rays of red morning sunlight touched the window of the bridge directly in front of Captain Hanks, spreading the glass crimson and he shielded his eyes with his right hand and saw the Soviet warships silhouetted. He turned slowly and faced Commander Daniels who saw a smile on his Captain's face.

'Thank you, Commander Daniels,' the Captain said quietly and evenly. 'Now you go tell the men to return to their stations and not to worry any more. I will do my duty by them the only way I know how!'

Commander Daniels saluted. 'Thank you, sir.'

Captain Hanks saluted back. 'You made the decision easy,' he said and he reached out and shook his second-in-command by the hand. 'You tell them that.'

He watched Daniels go down the ladder to the next deck and down the second to the flight deck. He watched him speak to the fifty or more men waiting there, saw them salute and quickly go their separate ways to their separate stations. Then Captain Hanks opened the side window of the bridge and threw out the black rubber squash ball, watched it bounce the one hundred feet on to the flight deck then shoot off and fall another hundred and twenty feet into the sea.

He straightened his cap and glanced at the clock above him.

'Coxwain, Bridge.'

'Aye, sir.'

'Reduce speed.'

'Reducing revolutions, sir.'

'Hold her steady centre of channel.'

'Aye, aye, sir.'

'Bridge to Radar.'

'Yessir.'

'Range?'

'Constant two thousand yards, minus twenty, sir.'

'Bearings?'

'*Minsk* 125 . . . *Ivan Rogov* 127, sir.'

'Two thousand minus twenty on 125 and 127. Correct?'

'Affirmative, sir.'

'Thank you, Radar.'

Captain Hanks looked again at the brass clock and checked it with his wristwatch. It was one minute before six o'clock. The sun was rising and the grey of the sky and the grey of the sea was turning salmon pink. Only the warships facing each other remained the same grey dullness, the colour of war at sea. He smoothed the short wiry tufts of hair over his ears and wiped his fingers across his lips and watched the thin red second hand sweeping upwards towards zero. How wonderfully final it was, how complete, how superbly rounded off. Forty-two years service and this was the way he had always dreamed it would be.

'Bridge to Gunnery. Mr Ginsberg, you on station?'

'Yessir.'

'This is your Captain.'

'Yessir.'

'Twelve rounds. Immediate fire, range two thousand minus twenty on 125 and 127.'

'Two thousand, sir, minus twenty?'

'That's the order, Mr Ginsberg. Go to it, boy. Your mama's with you.'

And Lieutenant Aubrey Ginsberg, twenty-two years old, hesitating for only an instant, flicked up the wire mesh above the Fail Safe switch and repeated, like automated secondary switchgear in a fast-moving machine, the fire order co-ordinates. 'Immediate fire range two thousand minus twenty on 125 and 127 . . . repeating two thousand minus twenty on 125 and 127, immediate fire stations five and seven rounds each.'

As the Yellowbeans approached their pop-up height, eight

hundred feet up and three miles from the drop, the fifty aircraft split into five flights of ten. Four would drop on each of the major wells, the fifth would drop on Ras Tanura, the tanker-loading berth on the long spit of land jutting out into the Gulf. The biggest of all the refineries was on Ras Tanura and it was essential that all the major wells be taken intact, and the Ras Tanura refinery kept operational.

Once the troops were despatched the aircraft were to disperse in separate directions southwards, the command C-130, Colonel Pringle's Yellowbean 720, overflying the fields watching the operations from a thousand feet, relaying reports back to US Command in Adana. Once a ground satellite link had been established, and it would take about an hour, Colonel Pringle would then take his aircraft up to twenty-nine thousand feet, fly due west over the island of Bahrain across the Gulf to Dubai, across friendly Oman and into international airspace above the Arabian Sea. Then he would turn south-west towards Mombasa on the Kenyan coast for refuelling and on to the British-American military base, Diego Garcia in the Indian ocean.

'Fire behind, sir,' said the flight engineer. 'Port side.'

Colonel Pringle turned quickly in his seat, tugging at his harness. Five aircraft back he could see one of the flankers two hundred yards to his left, its outside starboard engine in flames, smoke billowing so thick and so black that nothing of the rear fuselage could be seen.

The flight engineer unstrapped himself, left his flight deck seat and jumped down the stairs into the hold to see better. The aircraft had already lost height, was now less than two hundred feet above ground, still dipping. Suddenly it banked away, its starboard wing lifted to the sky and—for an instant—the underneath of the wing was clear of smoke, showing the large white figures '728' It was one of the five C-130s specially fitted with air-to-air missiles. Once the electrical firing circuits were damaged by the fire, the missiles would be released . . . missiles with a warhead and a guidance system dictated by its infra-red surveillance mechanism to lock on to the nearest heat source. Which would be the nearest C-130 to it. The flight engineer knew then what the pilot of 728 was doing. The risk was too high and he had banked from the formation, flying at right angles to point his missiles away from it. Through the tiny window, the engineer watched the aircraft sink lower and grow smaller, the black smoke trailing from the wing and then the flash and the orange mushroom as it hit the sand.

When the engineer got back to the flight deck, Colonel Pringle, the co-pilot and the navigator were drinking hot chocolate. He helped himself to some from the thermos container strapped to the back of the radio racks.

'Three minutes to LZ.' Colonel Pringle pulled the stick firmly back and Yellowbean 720 climbed to eight hundred feet and was steady again. At the back the dispatchers began checking the chute lines as the paratroopers each side of the aircraft stood in line, each checking the harness of the man in front of him. As they turned to face the rear of the aircraft, cold air filled the hold as the side doors opened. Then the air deflectors moved out either side of the aircraft's fuselage and shielded them from the blast. They hung on to the steel line above their heads as the aircraft decelerated to its dropping speed and they shuffled forward, tightening up their lines, towards the doors. The Master-Sergeant dispatcher pulled himself along the centre aisle by the canvas cargo webbing and stood dead centre of the two open doors, watching for the red light. He held up his hands and the hundred men looked at him as, in a deliberately exaggerated movement, he slapped his chest and stomach. The hundred men did their final harness checks on main and secondary chutes.

'Running in,' said the navigator and Colonel Pringle's right hand eased the throttles back a fraction until the air speed indicator read one hundred and twenty-seven knots.

'No activity below. You're clear,' he said in his intercom to the dispatcher who, as the hundred men watched him, pointed below and then gave a thumbs-up to them. He moved to the starboard side door and beckoned the first man forward and held his shoulder. Below was the desert, grey and cold, in the morning's first light.

The aircraft banked and they saw what they had come for sprawling beneath them, the vast silver-brown complex of pipelines and tanks and labour camps and beyond that the shine of the Persian Gulf.

Red light off, green on and the dispatcher slapped the man by him hard on the shoulder and they were away, jumping from both sides, spreading out like a stream of bright fluid streaking into the sky, the first brilliant rays of the dawn sun turning them red.

'Hullo, Snowball control, hullo, Snowball control this is Yellowbean, this is Yellowbean. We are dispatched at this time minus one. Repeating, we are dispatched at this time minus one. And it's looking fine. It's looking real fine.'

Captain Sergei Borgnev, Commander of the Soviet Seventh Fleet, stood on the bridge of the carrier *Minsk*, drank tea from a yellow plastic beaker, and watched the *Okinawa* split in two just aft of the control tower. The rear section sank immediately but the forward section, listing fifteen degrees to starboard, stayed afloat another four minutes—giving men time to jump though, as Commander Borgnev casually pointed out to those junior officers around him, few would survive from such a height. They would certain break their necks or backs, or both, as they hit the sea.

It had been quickly done. He had known exactly the *Okinawa*'s fire power, just as he assumed the American Captain had known of the destructive capacity of the Soviet Seventh Fleet, which was enormous. The *Minsk* and the *Ivan Rogov* sailing together with such a support flotilla constituted the most invincible fleet of any nation on any sea, anywhere in the world.

It had been an extraordinary act of bravery. But futile. Eleven missiles had ended it and the *Okinawa*'s initial salvo had caused only minor damage. If the American carrier's Gunnery Officer had used every shell in his armoury and every one had been a direct hit, as his twelve had been, the

Minsk and the *Ivan Rogov* would still be afloat and fighting. But it surprised Captain Borgnev that it should have been thought necessary, a US-Soviet sea action and an American vessel sunk by Soviet fire. But the signals had been clear enough. He had asked twice for reconfirmation and the same message quoting the same source had been returned immediately. The Admiral commanding the entire American Navy had signalled him via Odessa that the *Okinawa* was no longer under American control.

He poured more tea for himself from the vacuum flask into the yellow plastic beaker. The sea a mile and a half ahead was on fire from the oil that had poured from the *Okinawa*'s fractured fuel tanks. Black smoke, a mile wide, belched into the air five thousand feet up, and he watched his frigates manoeuvring close by the edge of the oil spraying foam under pressure to contain it. Others just behind them were picking up survivors: the living, the half-living, the dying and the dead. He nodded acknowledgement as an officer by his side updated the count. Eighty-two, from a ship that had carried over six hundred. And why? It made no sense.

He would wait another ten minutes until the centre channel had been cleared of burning oil and he would order his fleet forward, through the Straits of Hormuz and then turn due west at the end of the deep water channel into the Gulf for the final and most crucial phase of the operation. At coordinates 25 North—54 East, two thousand combat marines of the Soviet 12th Division would be airlifted by helicopter into the oilfields. They would be accompanied by Forger vertical take-off aircraft from both the *Minsk* and the *Ivan Rogov*. By 08h00 local time the men would be on the ground and in control, six hours behind the scheduled timing of the operation because of the *Okinawa*. But no matter, within two hours it would be done.

Commander Sergei Borgnev ordered his twenty-two warships forward and, gathering speed, ignored the bodies below them: men waving, men screaming, men covered in oil, men still on fire, men floating face down, men without faces, men without arms, all suddenly swept inwards by the surge, broken into little pieces by the power of the water and the scythe of the giant propellers.

But the forward frigates hadn't gone more than a thousand yards when the alarms were sounded, and they broke from their tight formation and scattered left and right within the confines of the deep water channel. Sonar on the forward tracking ships had detected massive underwater obstructions blocking the channel ahead. Quickly the sonar computerised the radio signals and translated them into picture outlines.

Commander Sergei Borgnev took the pictures and asked for more tea as he examined the sonar silhouettes of the two submerged but still floating hulks of the *Okinawa*.

Yellowbean 720 began its climb to twenty-nine thousand feet, twenty-two minutes after the first men of the Rapid Deployment Force had hit Saudi Arabian sand. The ground satellite station was now in direct contact with US Command in Adana in Turkey and Yellowbean's pilot, Colonel James Pringle, heard the first transmission safely sent and quickly acknowledged. 'THIS IS TWO. SNOWBALL FORCE RAPIDLY DEPLOYED AT THIS TIME. WE ARE ON THE GROUND AND SPREADING. REPEATING WE ARE SUCCESSFULLY DEPLOYED AT THIS TIME.' And Adana had come back via the Indian Ocean satellite: 'THAT'S HOW IT'S MEANT TO BE BULLY BOYS, THAT'S HOW IT'S MEANT TO BE. JUST KEEP IT MOVING OUT THERE.' Colonel Pringle wondered, as he had done at other moments of American drama, why it was that distant anonymous controllers always used the language of the movies.

The forty-eight other aircraft of the Yellowbean formation had scrambled forty-five minutes earlier, just as soon as they had dropped their paratroop sticks, and headed south for refuelling and rest on Diego Garcia.

From that base in the Indian Ocean they would fly nonstop return to Adana, and then reform to their separate squadrons in Europe. Colonel Pringle took the paper cup of hot chocolate and the barbecue chicken legs in foil from his flight engineer. The C-130 was climbing to cruising height on automatic and he turned in his seat and punched his co-pilot lightly on the shoulder. He knew, they all knew that things had gone so well they could still go wrong. That was the necessary caution of success. But soon they would be in international airspace and would casually exchange the time of day with the captains of Pan-Am and British Airways Boeings as they passed by. The original flight plan was to have taken Yellowbean 720 due south but Adana Control had warned of a flight of Soviet Antonovs on their way to Aden in the South Yemen from their base in the Caspian Sea. Colonel Pringle had been given an alternate that took him further east, towards the tip of Oman, within eighty miles of the Persian Gulf.

Over friendly Oman he would call Muscat Control and request permission to enter their airspace and clearance to thirty-three thousand feet for airway-routing south.

The morning was brilliant, and the desert five and a half miles below was so clear that Pringle could see the dunes and the ripples of sand which stretched for a thousand miles and regularly changed direction and shape overnight as the winds turned the desert around.

The engines changed tune as cruising height was reached. The flight engineer tapped Colonel Pringle on the shoulder.

'There's a helluva lot of smoke port side, Skipper.'

Colonel Pringle looked out through the left hand triangle of glass. Eighty miles away, maybe a little more, he could see the snake of water that he recognized from the map as the Strait of Hormuz. There were dots in it, a fleet though he couldn't count the number of ships.

'That's a lotta smoke,' he said back. 'Sea's on fire.'

Colonel Pringle pressed his mouthpiece closer to his lips, leaned forward and turned the radio frequency dials until he found Adana Control.

'Hullo Snowball control. Snowball control. This is Yellowbean 720 . . . Yellowbean 720 calling Snowball control.'

'Come in Yellowbean, this is Snowball. Go ahead.'

Colonel Pringle continued, 'We're approaching sector

yellow seven, repeat that's yellow seven and we're sighting a lotta smoke say eighty miles to the north east. Shall I take a look? Take some aerials? Over.'

There was a long pause, long enough for Colonel Pringle and his co-pilot to look at each other and wonder why.

'Yellowbean 720. This is Snowball . . . Yellowbean 720. This is Snowball. Acknowledge.'

'Yes Snowball, this is Yellowbean. Go ahead.'

'Yellowbean you will continue south on your present heading. Repeat you are ordered to maintain your present heading. Under no circumstances will you see smoke. Repeat you will not see smoke. Move south. Acknowledge.'

'I've got you Snowball. I repeat affirmative. Got you loud and clear and proceeding south. Yellowbean out.'

Colonel Pringle leaned forward again and turned his radio back to Muscat control local frequency. He looked again through the small window down towards the Persian Gulf and the dots of ships and the enormous column of black smoke rising from the narrow channel.

He looked across to his co-pilot and then to his flight engineer and navigator behind him.

'Well, first you see smoke and then you don't. I thought it was there but if Snowball says it isn't—well, boys, it isn't.

He pulled the stick sharply to the right and the seventy-five-ton aircraft peeled away through the thin white wisps of alto-stratus cloud, and higher into the blue.

'Shallow grave of snow'

The snow was falling thick now and Schneider knew her chances were good. Her one fear had been a clear night with a bright moon, a silent December night when the smallest sound would carry across the valley and the rippling of the stream over the stones down in the valley's centre would sound only yards away, a white moon that would reflect the flight of a barn owl along the length of Martindale and alert trackers to her direction.

She had prepared sacking to tie over the horses' hooves but as they had moved out from the cover and warmth of the enclosed tree-covered gulley the snow was already deep, and she had left the squares of sacking hanging on a bough. They would not be needed tonight.

The canister hung from the side of the pack-horse, tied length-ways along its left flank. To help it keep its balance, she had filled a sack full of stones to even out the weight. The two animals knew the area well and although Schneider had memorized the mountain route, she found the horses pulling at their halters, as if they knew their destination and their purpose and were anxious to be finished with it.

Twenty minutes ago they passed three hundred feet above Martindale church, then moved under the waterfall and were now climbing the steep slope of Hallin Fell following the sheep tracks, centuries-old paths now covered in snow but still just visible. The lead horse snorted as it stumbled over a dead sheep but the falling snow caught the sound and held it.

Schneider could feel the strong downdraught coming from the tip of the Knab flowing towards Lake Ullswater, half a mile away. It was this current of air she would use to send the radioactive contamination down to the man she had come to kill. She marvelled at the planning—it was not hers, she knew, but now at its conclusion she was the most vital part. The Arab who had come to the house in Bonngasse, Bonn, just two nights ago, had brought with him the plan with only the Dublin rendezvous to be completed. He had handed her travel documents, the itinerary, the Irish contact, the payment of two hundred thousand Deutschmarks and the promise that the second Arab in Dublin would provide the final part of the plan and the weapon of assassination.

Schneider had shot the little Arab through the head just as she had been told to do, just as she assumed the Irish in Dublin had got rid of the second Arab and just as she assumed someone would try and get rid of her once the contract had been completed. But she would go sideways. She would not rendezvous at the place called Newcastle on the north-east English coast, she would not catch the ferry to Norway across the North Sea—almost certaintly the planners intended to dump her into it. She would go south-west instead, go back to Dublin, to the young Irishman Kieran and stay in his rooms until it was safe to return to Bonn.

The wind stung her face and made her pull the balaclava helmet tighter over her head, leaving only a narrow slit for her eyes. Both horses were covered white and were beginning to stumble more now as the gusts of the blizzard wind caught them. But they knew each other well and the smaller mare behind tucked her head into the rump of the stronger, taller lead horse, and Schneider walked on the left of it, better protected, one hand clinging to the saddle.

Slabs of snow, hardened almost to ice, had formed across her chest and stomach and were beginning to hamper her movement and her breathing, but she felt strong, certain of success. Another thirty minutes, no longer, and she would be nearing the top of the mountain, and within an hour she would be back to this same position on her way out of Martindale, moving through the night towards Glenridding and south to safety.

She pressed hard against the flank of the horse and could feel its muscles straining against the slope, digging its hooves hard into the snow, all the time pushing forward and upwards. How easily it was working. Fahd was protected by a security cordon that would stop a fly. Radar surveillance, sonic beams, searchlights, dogs, anti-personnel mines, electronically detonated mortars, machine-gun posts and a private army on a twenty-four hour watch. But all the King's money and all the King's men would not stop the invisible death that would soon be carried by the wind into every seam of life below. And no-one would notice until they knew they were dying. It was the ultimate future weapon in the international terrorist armoury, and she would be the first to use it.

The lead horse stumbled again and Schneider kicked at another dead sheep, its stomach freshly torn open by a fox and filling with snow. She held on to the girth straps with both hands, but felt the slope easing and knew they were almost at the peak.

The British police chief and the army colonels in the Estate's farmhouse had been almost casual in their briefing. They had sat there in the large kitchen by the log fire, drinking mugs of tea and eating chocolate biscuits, and as Franklin had left the warm room and gone out into the blizzard he thought he had heard one of the policemen complain about the effect the weather would have on spring lambing.

Franklin closed his eyes for a moment against the blast of the snow and thought of Tamworth, New Hampshire and family winter holidays there tobogganning and skiing on the slopes of the White Mountains above Lake Winnipesaukee. The thought of Bill, strong and new out of Harvard with his Master's degree and the offer of a law partnership in Maine. Son Bill, bright and bronzed, the family's second ego and the best part of Franklin's marriage, slaloming to a gold medal in the winter sports and thirty immediate offers of marriage after the television interview that followed. Bill, who only a year later spent five days in a foxhole on the charred slopes of Khe San among the burnt and burst bodies of other young Marines, medivaced out to Da Nang, never to see or hear or think again. Bill, who had sat in bed for the past ten years at the Veteran's Sanatorium at St Albans, crying like a baby as the ward nurses rubbed cream into his bed-sores, but making no other sound. Growing older and fatter. A big blond empty balloon.

Snow had for ten years meant only sadness to Franklin and an ex-wife who had chosen him as the target for her sorrow. Snow always set off the memory in the same way. The same soft holidays on White Mountain and the same starched sheets on the same white bed where an only son sat staring with blue eyes seeing nothing ever again; no sun, no snow, no father, no hope.

But tonight snow meant something new and something appallingly different. Out there in the blizzard was an assassin who had come to kill not one man but a hundred years.

Everything had conspired to make Schneider's job easier, guaranteeing her success. The sudden blizzard had grounded the helicopters, had confused the army patrols, had hampered ground radio communiction, had slowed down the remaining civilian evacuation convoys out of the contamination area. And the radiographic metal detectors and the anti-contamination suits and helmets had not arrived because the helicoptor bringing them, risking everything against the weather, had crashed into the side of a mountain fifty miles south, killing the crew and destroying everything. And then it was suddenly too late, and Franklin and the other nine men could wait no longer.

A patrol in the lower valley had discovered the gulley where Schneider had waited. They had found strips of sacking and empty food tins and hoofmarks, and they had radioed that Schneider was on her way and closing in on the Howtown Estate.

The boffins at the Nuclear Research Establishment at Harwell had telephoned their conclusions on how Schneider would use the plutonium. It was a long shot, they said, but she would probably either roll the canister down the slopes of the mountain, expecting the buffeting to break open the lead covering, or she would explode it. The latter would almost certainly be her choice, because it was the most certain way. She would use a delay detonator, they said, to give her time to get out of the contaminated area. But not a long delay. She couldn't risk its being discovered by the army patrols. Those who had given her the canister almost certainly knew the area around Howtown and would advise Schneider to place the canister on a slope of a mountain facing the King's estate so that the down-draught off the mountain would carry the contamination downwards and fast. Such a method, they said, would also enable Schneider to get away before the warmer, lighter valley air distributed the radioactivity in all directions.

Ten men—Franklin plus two police local mountaineers and seven SAS Special Forces men who knew Ullswater and its mountains—were now spread evenly across the slopes moving up towards the peak. All of them realized that without their contamination suits and helmets they need only hear the explosion to know that the radioactivity had been released and even though they might walk back through the snow towards Howtown they would already be dying; they would be dead before they saw the lights of the estate.

Each man had to sweep a hundred yards each side of him and Franklin had taken the right flank on the slope nearest the lake. He had been climbing for nearly an hour now; not far above him was the mountain's peak, and somewhere along its ridge was Schneider, her horses, her lead canister and her explosives. Like the rest, Franklin had been armed with a pistol, a single-action rifle and one hand-grenade. They were told, quite matter-of-factly, that under no circumstances was the grenade to be used against Schneider. It was for their personal use, should they reach her too late. Aim only for Schneider, they had been told, aim only for her and not until you are one hundred per cent certain of hitting only her. The lead canister must not be pierced.

The wind was pushing him sideways and it took most of his strength to stay upright. It was hard to move forward and he knew he couldn't go for long if the blizzard continued. He stopped and dropped on one knee and breathed slowly and deeply. He was tiring faster than he'd expected. He'd never known such a wind. It blew you backwards and sideways at once and the snow was so thick he couldn't see ten yards anywhere. It was absurd. And it was suicide. If he didn't find her soon he would collapse and die buried. He had a radio, but no one would come looking for him now, even if he had the courage to call them. And if he found her she would almost certainly kill him first. She was fit. My God, he remembered how strong she was. And an expert shot. But most of all she would be coming down as he would be struggling up. Either way, he thought, he now had very little chance of ever going home.

Then he remembered yesterday and the blond Englishman who liked cold coffee and had told the tortured Kiernan he could have his trousers back. He remembered his words as he'd left Dublin. 'You Americans have style. Wonderful style.' It had made nonsense then. It made complete sense now. What was it he'd said to Cheaney in Cairo? 'I'm no regular, let a professional do it.' Cheaney must have laughed his balls off. They didn't need him on the mountain. Why should they send an old man up a mountain in a blizzard, fifty-year-old paunchy Franklin, who hadn't handled a gun in twenty years? Why send him if they didn't expect him to come back? They sent him *knowing* he wouldn't come back. He knew too much. It was King Fahd's briefing. The Agency hadn't expected that. No one had told the King's men that Franklin was off their books. A newspaperman with so much in his head. A risk.

So they didn't expect him to get Schneider. They hoped she would get him. Then the police and the Special Forces would get her and the canister. They reckoned he'd served a purpose. They'd strung him along, hoping he could be useful with the information he had and too scared to dump him in case he had more. And he hadn't.

He pushed himself up off his knee with his rifle and braced himself against the force of the blizzard. The snow gave a little beneath him. He tried to use the rifle again to steady himself but it sank too deep and his weight shifted suddenly away from the slope and the wind caught him and threw him down. He slid on his side, and then somersaulted. Using the rifle as an anchor, one hand on the butt, one on the barrel, he slowed down enough to curl his leg around an alder sapling just above a frozen stream. He stopped in the middle of a cart track.

Blood trickled into his left eye. He tried to wipe it away but stopped. What was it? Not the wind. A sound, but not a human sound. A sheep? Possibly. He pulled the hood of his anorak back from his ears and cupped his hands. The wind carried it through the snow—it wasn't a sheep. It was a horse. The whinny of a horse!

Schneider twisted the knife and quickly cut through the second hamstring, on the mare's right hind leg. It slumped forward, blood spurting now from both the severed tendons, and from the jugular vein. Schneider pushed hard against the animal so that it fell on to its right side, away from the canister. The second horse leaned down and began to nudge the other, digging its nose into the snow under its head as if trying to lift it. But the dying eyes were wide open and unblinking and snow gradually began to cover them.

Schneider went down on her knees and began to unpack the canvas bag hanging across the horse's belly. She pulled out a roll of wide adhesive tape, two slabs of plastic explosive and a small square metal time-delay detonator. Carefully she unwrapped the wax paper from the detonator and taped it to the explosive. She put both into her lap and stuck her fingers in her mouth to warm them before twisting the circuit wires together. Red to red, black to black. Then she wound up the detonator's simple clockwork timing mechanism, ready to strap it to the canister. She heard, but turned too late—and Franklin's first bullet went through her left shoulder, the force of it spinning her round.

'Put it down, Anna.' Franklin screamed it out above the wind and swirling snow. 'Put it down a yard in front of you and lie back.' He had crept to within twenty yards of her. She pulled off her goggles to see him better. Then she dropped the detonator into her lap and began pulling at her tunic buttons to get at her pistol. As Franklin saw the butt of it, he fired his second shot and the pistol spun away and buried itself. His second bullet had grazed the same shoulder, just above the first wound, and she fell backwards on to the belly of the dying mare, still clutching the detonator. Franklin stumbled through the snow shouting, 'Drop it, Anna, drop it . . . it's over, everybody's gone . . . evacuated. The King's gone . . . Anna, I'll kill you.'

She could hear his voice clearly and she hesitated. He understood why and pulled off his hood. 'It's Franklin . . . your one-night stand. Anna, believe me, it's over . . . we know about Kieran and the canister. You're beaten . . . you can only kill the valley now . . . you're too late.'

Her blood was spreading like a red rug across the snow to join the mare's. She began to speak, hesitated again and then heaved herself on to the mare's flanks and with her right hand began smashing the detonator against the lead canister, trying to break the timing spring inside. Franklin ran forward and threw himself on top of her, grabbing her round the neck, trying to pull her away. She twisted and kicked and then swung the detonator round and hit him first in the side of the face and then slammed it again into his head. He rolled away, just as the dying mare, in her final convulsion of life before death, shivered violently, lifted her head and shook herself as she had done on so many summer valley afternoons. Then she kicked feebly and rolled over on to her back and over again on to her left side, burying the canister beneath her deep in the snow.

The suddenness of the horse's movement threw Schneider up and forward to the edge of the track and the sheer drop a thousand feet to the valley road below. Still she had the detonator clasped to her.

Franklin reached for his rifle. 'Now it's really over, Anna. Throw it down . . . into the valley. No harm down there. Throw it down.'

She sat leaning into the wind. Her face was going grey and her hair looked quite yellow in the snow that covered her head. Blood from her shoulder wounds began forming a new red patch beneath her.

'Will you do a deal, Mr Franklin?' she shouted.

'A deal?'

'For old times' sake. You owe me a favour, I think?'

'What deal?'

'You have a grenade around your neck—'

'It stays there.'

'I give you the detonator. I get the grenade.'

'No!'

'It's my way out, as they say in the films.'

'In the films they would simply kill you.'

'Then will you simply kill me?'

'We're not made of the same meat, Anna.'

'Same meat?'

'I don't simply kill.'

'Then give me your grenade.'

'You're playing for time, Anna. You know when that thing's going off.'

'Just one final favour, Mr Franklin. For the one-night stand. You enjoyed it.'

'Anna, give it to me.'

'You liked it . . . didn't you, though? You liked what I did.'

'Now, Anna—'

'You liked Swiss-German sex? All those new ideas of mine?'

'Anna . . .'

'Come on, Matt, my pound of flesh . . . I won't be taken

back . . . Fair's fair, for an enthusiastic night of . . .'

'Anna, throw it down. You're playing with me. You know its timing. It can still blow the canister.'

Now she was laughing at him. 'Matt, Matt, Matt, you crazy lover . . . Next time get yourself a . . .'

'Schneider!'

'Why not again, Matt? For the last time, here in the snow with a bleeding woman. Doesn't that . . .'

He fired from ten yards and the bullet went through the bottom of her neck, an inch from her scar, hitting her with such velocity it threw her three yards back. Still upright, she sat in an obscene position with her legs wide apart, the detonator still clasped tight in her lap, her eyes wide open, as if she had just heard the most shocking story.

Another bullet sent her backwards over the edge, into the void and the thousand feet of snow.

But the body of Anna Schneider never reached the valley road. As Franklin dropped to his knees the explosion shook him and the ground and the blast of air did strange things to the snow. He would never be able to remember later whether it was four seconds, or six, but only he knew how close Anna Schneider had come to success.

The nearest soldier was over four hundred yards away when he heard the explosion. And the men drinking mugs of cocoa in the farmhouse heard it too. The soldier fired three shots in the air in three directions to indicate his position and he heard others fire back in answer. But he didn't kneel and pray as he had intended to do in the last moments of expected life. Instead, he moved blind through the snow towards the explosion and an hour later he found the horse and the lead canister strapped to the underside of it. And Matt Franklin heaping snow over the dead mare's face. But it would not be until the following morning, in the bright Cumbrian sunlight and blue skies and a still mountain that they would find the remains of Anna Schneider buried beneath the night's shallow grave of snow.

Christmas Eve

WASHINGTON

'The Good News Day'

The President was new again and for the first time since his mother's death he left the knitted black tie in his dresser drawer.

'I repeat what I said last night, Admiral. Had it been the Midway or a wartime Atlantic convoy we would have asked the same of them. Captain Hanks and his brave men did nothing more and nothing less than their country expected.' The President's voice was booming.

'But more than I had expected. Much, much more.'

Admiral Holliwell had aged ten years in the one night, just as his President had grown suddenly younger. He looked frail and his hands shook slightly as he spoke. He had forgotten to shave, or had not bothered, and the grey stubble and the grey eyes set deep in their grey sockets and the uncombed grey hair set him apart from normal business as he sat in the Oval Office watching his President.

Bright low December sunlight streamed in through the windows. The President had opened one and the early morning air was crisp and smelt of the new snow that had fallen overnight and now covered the White House lawns. A secretary had placed a bowl of white and yellow daffodils on a side table but the President, in keeping with his Good News Day mood, had picked them up and placed them dead centre on his desk.

'You must not fret unduly, Admiral,' he said, but not looking at Holliwell. 'They were your orders, I know, but they had my backing. The Generals knew that. And you cannot blame yourself for the casualties. They were high, much higher than I or anyone could have foreseen, but the sacrifice had to be made. Every man on that ship knew the odds and not a man turned away. You can bet on it.'

'But that's not true, Mr President,' said Admiral Holliwell in his frail grey voice. 'According to first reports there was talk of mutiny just before—'

'Admiral Holliwell,' cut in the President. 'These are obscene rumours. I don't have to tell you the enormous damage these lies could do if they are given any credibility. You will soon receive eighty-two survivors and you will hospitalize and convalesce them all. And you will keep them that way until we recover. I will dote on them, I will give them medals, I will promote them, I will make every momma, wife, sister and girlfriend, every American, so goddammed proud of them, there'll not be a man among them who'll step out of line. I'm going to have their families here together, a White House New Year's party for the families of every survivor. Hartmann's already making the arrangements. We're going to have it on television and we will make sure that every man off that ship who can watch TV is watching my party for his folks. You understand what we're after Admiral?'

'Yes, Mr President, I understand what you're after.'

Admiral Holliwell was not known as a drinker but that lunchtime he sat on his own in the private dining suite of the Pentagon and emptied an entire bottle of vintage Cockburn's Port. He was driven to his apartment in North Street, Georgetown and somehow he managed to climb the stairs. Somehow he managed to run a bath.

Whatever the reason—and few cared later—he ran only the hot tap and because of his age or his mood, the port or simply carelessness, he fell headfirst into the scalding water and was dead within ten seconds.

His naked and blistered body was found that afternoon by the Admiral's young aide who, responding to an instinct, made the decision to report the detail directly to Jack Hartmann, the White House Chief of Staff. It was inevitably to assure him rapid promotion.

The President decided the discovery was to be kept a secret, and so for another twenty-four hours, Admiral Holliwall was left floating.

The Admiral's death was the only blemish on what the President now referred to openly as his 'Good News Day'. Nothing—at least nothing else, it seemed—could go wrong.

The Good News Day had begun early with the signal from Snowball control, Adana, Turkey confirming that the Rapid Deployment Force was on the ground and active. Except for the aircraft that had crashed from engine failure on the way and the one hundred and eight men who had died, there had been no other US casualties. Only three Saudis had died in an exchange of small arms fire. All the wells had been taken without damage and pumping was continuing undisturbed, three tankers were ready for sailing from the Ras Tunara refinery and would clear the Gulf for their journey to the United States just as soon as the wreckage of the sunken *Okinawa* could be blown apart and the pieces towed well clear of the deep water channel.

A second signal was brought to the President shortly after nine o'clock Washington time, relayed via the Admiralty in London from British Naval Intelligence in Oman. It reported the movement of twenty-two warships of the Soviet Seventh Fleet—led by the *Minsk* and the *Ivan Rogov*—out of the Strait of Hormuz and into the Indian Ocean, bound, it was thought, for the port of Aden in South Yemen for anchorage, refuelling and resupply. According to the British report, the only flight activity off the carrier *Minsk* had been helicopters taking the *Okinawa*'s survivors to Muscat in Oman. There had not, the report had concluded, been any other air movements.

At just before ten o'clock, another message was brought into the Oval Office with the President's fifth pot of coffee. It was from the United States Ambassador to the United Nations. It read:

> International outrage at *Okinawa*'s sinking reflected immediately at UN with Security Council's call for emergency debate of entire Assembly scheduled this afternoon at four local time. Our resolution to declare the Persian Gulf an International Zone has multiple backers including Yugoslavia and Rumania plus Arabs and non-aligned. Sultan of Oman has offered full facilities at Muscat for US military.
>
> I will make a strong appeal for maintenance of US forces on the ground at oilfields until United Nations peacekeeping force arrives in expected ten to fourteen days. We are certain of success. This time it's ours.

The President beamed, and tossed the slip of paper across his desk to Peter Schlesinger, his Press Secretary and White House spokesman.

'Good News Day, Peter,' he said. Schlesinger read and beamed back.

'The world is indignant, Mr President, rightly indignant and we must press it to advantage quickly before the anger goes. Indignation is not a foreign policy nor a strategy but with strong plain American words we can use it well. Strong words. You've got to use them tonight, in your speech at the Cathedral.'

The President leaned forward. 'What words Peter?'

'This country is not prepared to sound retreat, it is ready to advance; it is willing to make its stand, it is willing to be on the march again. They're great words, Mr President, great words with a great meaning. They are the spirit of this day.'

The President smiled. 'That's the trouble with having other men write your speeches, Peter. You can never remember them.'

'Your speechwriter's coming?'

'He's working on the first draft now. But call him. Tell him what you want. You're right, Peter. That's the theme. Not just going to the brink, but vaulting it and taking the rest of the free world with us.'

Twenty minutes past one o'clock, as the President was finishing a light tray lunch of yoghurt, avocado pear stuffed with lobster, and strawberries with caramel cream, there was a telephone call from Richard Johns, Director of the CIA, from Cairo. The President swirled the antacid powder in the glass of water with a long thin ivory letter opener.

'Hi! Richard.'

'Good afternoon, Mr President.'

'You've got good news?'

'Yes, sir, very good.'

'That's take four then.'

'Say again, sir?'

'No matter,' said the President, laughing. 'What's new, Richard? Fahd alive and well?'

'Alive, Mr President, and feeling better by the minute. I flew with him from London and put it to him just as we planned.'

'He's with us of course?'

'All the way. Announced it at Cairo airport. We got the speech finished for him by the time we landed. And we've set up a press conference at the airport, just about to start now. So you'll have it on tapes any minute. It'll be announced simultaneously in Mecca, Medina and out on Riyadh Radio throughout the Middle East.'

'And Rahbar?'

'Already out. The Iraqis came for him just before midday our time. A signal from Baghdad was waiting for me here.'

'That's where I give you bad news, Richard.'

'I think I may already have it, sir.'

'Karim?'

'Yessir.'

'It's confirmed there?'

'They broke into their radio programmes a few minutes

ago to announce it. Karim in as Life President.'

'A Soviet Iraq?'

'In time, sir. For sure.'

'So they've won there. And maybe where it matters most.'

'Don't know about the most, Mr President. But certainly it matters.'

'But today's ours, Richard. Today's our win.'

'All the way, Mr President.'

'Come on home.'

'Be there tonight, sir.'

'Be sure to. I'm doing something at the Cathedral for the *Okinawa* boys—Sorenson and Schlesinger are working on it. They reckon it'll be better from the church.'

'I like it, sir.'

'And Richard.'

'Sir?'

'I'm proud of the way you worked it out.'

'Thank you, sir. See you at the carols.'

The President kicked off his left shoe and scratched his instep with the toe of his right. He stretched, yawned, slapped his hands together over his head and shouted, 'Jack.' Seconds later Jack Hartmann came through his door.

'Sorry to bawl you, Jack, but it doesn't seem right just now for whisperings into intercoms.'

'I fully agree,' said Hartmann. 'Absolutely, Mr President.'

'Jack, get Schlesinger and Sorenson back here. Tell them I want to start on the draft of the speech. And I want a for sure on the TV nets, if they're covering outside I want to know where they'll be and who's doing the commentating and you're gonna give me, remember, the names of the survivors' families who'll be there. I'll have a radio mike with me and I'm depending on you to give me the names as I move in on each one of them.'

'Yes, sir, we're working on them now. Everyone's on it, and I expect to have photographic idents on all we're expecting. The Cathedral people tell me that it'll be a candlelight service, but the TV crews are insisting on some lights in there.'

'Let them have lights, you tell everybody I want no balls-ups. How will it go?'

'You read the lesson, sir, and then lead into your address.'

'Great!'

'And just one hymn.'

'Sure.'

'"For Those in Peril on the Sea".'

'That's nice.'

'And your favourite carol.'

'I have a favourite carol?'

'"Oh Great and Mighty Wonder", Neale's St Germanus translation.'

'That's my favourite carol?'

'There will also be carol singers on the Cathedral steps as you leave, sir. After you've met with the families a little girl will come forward and give you a small wreath of holly and ivy.'

'Perfect.'

'Her name's Mary.'

'You think of everything.'

Hartmann turned on the ball of his right foot in the centre of the gold embossed crest on the blue carpet. The President waited for the door to close then took off his jacket and loosened his tie. Outside it was only two degrees above freezing but the sky was a brilliant blue.

He closed his eyes. Johns had done a good job. He had been told to put Fahd back on the throne but he had gone one better. Fahd was a pliable man with a proper understanding of *realpolitik*, returning with the promise of reform, and a new broom to sweep cleaner. Under American guidance he would pick up on the newly fired enthusiasm for Rahbar's Islamic reforms without destroying the Royal Family and the alliances.

What Fahd was now promising at his Cairo Press Conference was not only the survival of the Kingdom and the continuity of the House of Ibn Saud. He was promising something more, something new, something yet untried. Encouraged by Johns, he was to announce the formation of a *Majlis Ashura*, a consultative council made up of seventy or more commoners who would share legislative responsiblity under the Crown and whose first duty would be to draw up a set of constitutional guidelines to assist, not direct, but assist King Fahd steer a straighter fairer course of government. The *Majlis Ashura* would sit symbolically at the King's right hand. He had announced the date for its inception, and also the name of its first chairman, Saudi Arabia's most famous international commoner, Sheikh Ahmed Zaki Yamani, the King's ally, lawyer, negotiator, ambassador and oil minister extraordinaire.

The United States Middle Eastern Intelligence Service was convinced that King Fahd's Council of Commoners would galvanize and consolidate the dissident Saudi poor, the envious Saudi middle class and the outraged Saudi devotees of Islamic fundamentalism. It would quickly make them forget Rahbar and his Islamic People's Democratic Republic. At his press conference at the Hilton Hotel on the banks of the Nile, King Fahd was not only spelling out the New Grand Design, he was detailing the reforms that would bring Saudi Moslems back into the lap of God, back where they belonged within the severe and intolerant confines of Koranic law.

Hotel and other public swimming pools would be emptied forthwith to discourage mixed bathing. Dolls would be banned from the toyshops—dolls were idolatrous—frozen meat banned from public sale because it was considered unclean. The sale of dog food was banned—dogs were also considered unclean. Television, radio and cinema were henceforth to be forbidden as means of entertainment. In future they would only be used for religious and educational purposes. Purdah was to be reintroduced. No part of a woman's skin was hereafter to be shown in public. Public flogging, the cutting off of hands, arms and feet and public execution by beheading would continue by order of the magistrates or mullahs.

And the father of Saudi Arabia, who under the guidance of God and the prohphet Mohammed had wielded many desert peoples into one, would be revered anew. King Fahd announced in the final minutes of his press conference that Riyadh airport, where he would land later that day in triumphant return to his beloved country would be renamed after his father, the first desert King. In future it would be called Abdel Aziz bin Abdel Rahman al Saud.

The President read the tapes as they were brought to his desk. Fahd, he thought, was giving the Saudis their own solemn good news day and they were getting the reforms they deserved. So frozen meat went back to Texas, the dolls to Taiwan and too bad about the dogs. And if a man lusted after a woman in the water, let him take her to his bathroom. The United States had its oil. That's what mattered.

Four days in December, ninety-six hours to the brink and back again. But it was quietening down and the President seemed to remember somewhere, someone saying that it is commonly wise in the aftermath and post mortems of global crises for the world to stand back and re-assess itself. Thank God it was still alive to do so.

He did up his collar button and tightened the light blue silk tie. He pulled on his jacket and smoothed his hair, using his fingernails to comb back the tight grey crinkly curls around his ears. Shadows were spreading across the large room and the bright day's winter light was slowly turning.

Over three thousand Atlantic miles away, in the churchyard in the small grey village of Pooley Bridge in the Lake District in northern England, four men stood by an open grave and licked the snow from their lips as they silently mouthed the Lord's Prayer, staring at the elm coffin in the dark trench. Three of them, strangers to the dead girl, showed only professional remorse. The other, a foreigner, seemed genuinely depressed.

She had a name but the smallest man there, the vicar, wondered if it really belonged to her and he began to question, as he read the last rites, the professional ethics of burying someone whose given name you doubted. But on reflection he hardly thought it was worth the raising. Whoever was in there, he reasoned, would sooner or later have to own up.

The vicar wiped snow from his spectacles and a dribble of melted snow quivered on the end of his nose in the breeze. The gravedigger pounded the frozen earth with his shovel so that the others might have something to throw down. The undertaker from Windermere looked at the broken clock on the squat church tower as he always did during funerals here and saw the same hands, green with moss on rust, that had stopped at half-past four during his wife's burial exactly a generation ago.

The vicar turned to the stranger, the American, in the sad apologetic way he used at normal burials, forgetting this one had no substance of grief at all. The vicar thought he looked tired and ill and he noticed, as vicars do, that he walked with a limp and kept his gloved left hand to his stomach, as if hand or stomach or both were injured. He noticed too the cuts and bruising over his right cheek.

'Mr Franklin,' the vicar said, 'is there anything you'd like to add to my prayers before we cover the coffin?'

'No, sir. No thank you,' he replied. 'She knows where she's going.'

And with that he turned abruptly and walked away along the crunching footpath, past the black slate tombstones of good Cumbrian people, whose ghosts would for ever protest at the new company, on past the crosses and angels and a solitary gilt eagle to the waiting car. The gravedigger pickaxed his way into the frozen mound by the trench, and Franklin heard the first hard clods hit the long elm box as he closed the car door.

The undertaker drove his black hearse south along Lake Ullswater to his warm friendly funeral parlour in Windermere. Franklin was driven away in the opposite direction towards Penrith and the motorway that would take him south to London and the American Embassy.

And the vicar, relieved that the sordid business was over, went inside his dank and dark uncomfortable church which smelt of camphor and paraffin to register in his neat copperplate a fit and proper burial: Name: Anna Schneider. Age unknown. Born Bonn. No headstone required.

Suddenly America rallied. As the Good News Day infected Mr Everyman he was proud of himself. He saw the worst was over. He saw that the pumps would not run dry, that the wheels would not stop turning, the gears stop changing, or the pistons stop firing. The God-given right of American mobility had been restored and he was brave again.

So perhaps there had been a little panic. Perhaps some people got themselves hysterical, blood had been spilt and some political coats had changed colour, but these things happen.

America, in its effort to look forward, quickly forgot the past. National Guardsmen stopped riding shotgun on truckers' cabs, and truckers removed their forty-tonners from blocking the petrol stations, and petrol stations pulled the rolls of barbed wire away from their pumps, and the pumping relay stations from the refineries of the Southern States began pushing oil through the repaired pipelines to their friends in the North and car stickers in Texas no longer demanded that the bastards freeze, and the frozen carcasses from the abattoirs of the Mid-West were packed into the freezer wagons and railed to kitchens in Boston and San Francisco.

Department stores were suddenly packed as people grabbed Christmas presents they had almost forgotten to buy. Their cars barged around the snowslide streets of Washington, New York and Philadelphia, and in Los Angeles they stopped altogether in the last-minute rush of Yuletide generosity. There was suddenly so much to be pleased with, so much to be proud of in America, so many heroes to mourn, brave young American boys who had given their lives so that their nation should live on. Who in the USA did not lift their heads higher because of them? Who did not feel the sadness and the pride at the name *Okinawa* and who in America did not look to the one man who epitomized the spirit of the day, the essence of it all? The man, who by his own personal bravery, determination, constancy and true American grit, had sent the Russians packing! The man they were calling Mr America.

The President stepped out of the shiny black armour-plated Lincoln to a blaze of colour and a storm of sound. He held his hand in front of his face, momentarily blinded by the television lights, then waved to the crowd. It was as if Mardi Gras, St Patrick's Day, Thanksgiving, Hanukkah and the Fourth of July had been launched at the same hour together. Brass bands of the Salvation Army and the American Legion were playing separate tunes at a separate beat at both ends of the Cathedral steps so that it all sounded like wildly-syncopated stereo. The clergy of the Cathedral of St Peter and St Paul had pulled out a red carpet but as the President stepped on to it, it changed colour with confetti and streamers, rice and ticker-tape. He felt as if he was going to his second wedding then, remembering his wife behind him, turned and smiled the broad, public, unseeing, unblinking smile she knew was only for her.

Three yards either side of the Pilgrims' Steps had been roped off and security men, identically dressed in raincoats and brogues with welts the size of snowshoes, lined up either side, cordoning off the crowd that shouted its praise, screamed its adulation, chanted campaign slogans, held up his campaign posters and his portraits. It blew toy trumpets and banged toy drums, sang *God Bless America* and three-cheered Mr America as it flash-photographed and video-recorded his triumphal climb to the open Cathedral doors and the warm yellow glow inside.

'He has come to mourn his dead,' said a daring television reporter to the eye of his camera, 'in a style that would raise the roof of any campaign convention.' And people nodded agreement and laughed and were proud to say that Mr America did nothing by halves.

He reached the top of the Cathedral steps flushed with victory, a Caesar. He shook hands warmly and looked across the many Bishops' shoulders to the altar and the lines of candles inside, and saw the thousand faces looking over their shoulders from the pews. And the smile left his face. His eyes were suddenly dark and sad, and his head was high and his shoulders stiff and proud, a President saddened and outraged and coming to mourn unnecessary death. Those watching him, those who knew him well, saw at that moment again the proof that there was no one in American politics with such a sense of occasion, no one who could match his sense of drama or his impeccable timing.

Holding his wife's hand in a simple touching way that the cameramen could not miss, he walked slowly to his seat in the front row and stood, head bowed in prayer. Security men sat at both sides of and behind him and eleven more were distributed by the altar, discreetly hidden in the flickering candlelight shadows. Two more stood thirty feet up on the ledge below the stained glass windows, behind the heavy embroidered brocade, a radio transmitter-receiver in one hand and a machine-pistol in the other. The Bishop was into his thirteenth minute when an envelope was passed down the seated line of bodyguards, hand to hand, until it reached the President, a blue envelope with the flap stapled down. With his ears on the Bishop, he thumbed open the staple and pulled out a single sheet of blue paper, handwritten by Tom Sorenson.

> Good News Day. Forty-eight votes for, eleven against, with five abstentions including France who have their own deal. The United Nations condemns the Soviets, setting match to the fire, etc., and praises US restraint. We can keep our boys on the ground until UN arrives. Say a fortnight. And we've majority Gulf Arab support for UN sea patrol, pushed by Sultan of Oman on pressure from Brits: OPEC is alive. Repeat alive and we did it. Fundamental differences, etc., mutual agreement, guaranteed levels of production and so on. What a day! You're in the right place to say thank you, Mr President!
> Sorenson.

Carefully he folded the slip of paper and slid it back into the envelope and pushed it into his inside breast pocket. Then he closed his eyes to shut out the sight and sound of the Bishop's drone. OPEC alive! Three short telephone calls to three oil capitals, to three attentive Presidents; Caracas in Venezuela, Lagos in Nigeria and Tripoli in Libya. Simple words of warning and they agreed to toe the line. He opened his eyes and the Bishop was beckoning him to come to the brass-eagled pulpit, to the spotlights and the microphones that would amplify his words to the people at the furthest pews and to a thousand million people beyond them, beyond the loudspeakers on the Cathedral steps, beyond the television sets in Washington, beyond the East and West Coast shores and across the oceans to all those who might not understand his English but would not fail to grasp his message. Friends and foes.

He placed his hands on each end of the lectern that sat astride the brass eagle so that to the television cameras he seemed to be holding its great wide wings in flight. He looked all-powerful and there was silence.

'With your permission I shall not read the Scriptures. I shall instead tell you something of what I believe to be God's work, these past four December days. This nation was founded by men who carried the Bible, and today with His help, we have survived with that book still in our hands.

'I said to you at the onset of this crisis that it was not our power but our will that was being tested. I asked you whether we Americans, the strongest nation mankind will ever know, had the courage and the will to meet a direct challenge when the chips were down. I asked you whether you were prepared to pay any price, bear any burden, oppose any foe to assure the success of our liberty. And the officers and men of the USS *Okinawa* said yes. Those boys have paid the highest price for the defence of the country they loved!

'Now there was a risk we would be branded as aggressors by sending our boys to protect the very means of our survival. But I said then, and I say it again tonight, the